Praise for
CITADEL OF THE SKY

"Make room, GRRM: Chrysoula Tzavelas knows
how to bring on the pain.... This is a rare book that
I have every intention of re-reading before I read
its sequel, which, frankly, I would like to get my
grabby little hands on right now."

— C. E. Murphy,
author of *The Walker Papers*

And
INFINITY KEY

"Fast-paced.... In a genre that tends to emphasize
young women's romances with male supernatural
beings, this focus on female friendship and solidar-
ity is deeply refreshing."

— *Publisher's Weekly*

BY CHRYSOULA TZAVELAS

CHRYSOULA TZAVELAS

ETIQUETTE OF EXILES

and other stories

SENYAZA
BOOK 4

DREAMFARMER PRESS
DREAMFARMER.NET

Dreamfarmer Press
www.dreamfarmer.net

ETIQUETTE OF EXILES
ISBN: 978-1-943197-09-5

Cover art by Ravven Kitsune
www.ravven.com

ETIQUETTE OF EXILES

and other stories

For my readers. Yes, really. Nobody mattered more to this project than you.

INTRODUCTION

One day, this happened
and that happened,
and the faeries came back.

They came through doors in the wind
they would stay for an hour or a day or a week.
And then they would leave

Suddenly
Or
slowly….
Pulled away by invisible chains.

These are (mostly) stories about the first year after
they came back.

THE BOOKS in this volume map to the first three novels
in the Senyaza Series. There may be spoilers for early
books in later stories.

BOOK 1

She waited for him across from the opera house, wearing a cloak borrowed from a prostitute and the remains of her shoes tied around her feet. The falling snow made the illuminated building into something from a fairy tale. As a child, she'd liked fairy tales. Last summer, she'd thought she was in one. Even now, she hoped, although her feet stung with the cold. This was her last chance, and in a fairy tale she would certainly succeed in the end.

The baby shifted in her arms, and she whispered nonsense without looking down. It did no good to look down. She knew what she was here for, knew the baby was as hungry as she was. She knew the baby's perfect face too well. Looking down hurt. Without *him*, there was nothing she could do. And when *he* appeared from within the opera house, tall, immaculately groomed, laughing with his gentlemen friends, she stumbled across the street and caught his sleeve.

He looked down at her, the laughter in his eyes vanishing. But instead of recognition, there was only mild disgust. "Dear child, do not grab at me."

She wasn't the girl he'd once known, not after the baby and everything else that had followed. Her carefully planned words fled. "William, William, it's me, Julia. Don't you know me at all? After everything? I've waited and waited—"

Realization flickered in his eyes, but all he said was, "You have the wrong man." He glanced at his companions and repeated, "You certainly have the wrong man."

Julia held the baby out toward him. "I do not! Look at her! She has your face, William. She is your child, yes she is, and I was a good girl before you promised—"

He knocked her aside as he stepped away. "She's mad," he announced loudly. "Or worse. There's some who might have fallen for your game, little miss. I'm sure others have before. But not I. Not I."

She lunged after him and fell into the snow, twisting her body to protect the baby. He turned and strode abruptly away. When his companions followed him, a footman lifted Julia to her feet and gave her a shove down the street. "Away with you, before you get into trouble you can't walk away from, lass."

She trudged a few steps, her thoughts as numb as her feet. The women who had sheltered her had said that if she confronted him with the baby, she could at least get some money. They were *expecting* her to return with money, to pay for what they'd given her. If she didn't bring back money, she'd have to pay in other ways.

The baby squirmed in her arms, and she looked down at the little one's face. Dark hair, like his, and bright blue eyes and a cleft in her chin, just like his. That he could deny his lover she almost understood, but his own innocent child! At least her own father had waited until her innocence had been ruined before he'd sent her away.

She was so cold. Her cheeks felt numb and her hands were thick and clumsy. She couldn't go back home, or return to the kind women who'd advised her. And what was she to do with the child? She couldn't feed her, couldn't love her, couldn't even warm her as she cried.

She stumbled again, and fell again, then realized she was on a doorstep. It would have to do. She patted down the loose snow, making a nest. A snowflake caught in her eyelash and blurred her vision, and the light's reflection made the white nest glow like a halo. Sighing, she kissed her fingers and touched them to the snow, then laid her bundled baby within.

She didn't look back as she stumbled away. She thought, over and over like a prayer, that this way her baby could have any future, be anybody's child. But she kept seeing the halo and she knew the truth: that she was sending her baby back to God. Maybe, divorced from her, the child could find its way home. Maybe it wouldn't be dragged down with her.

Something caught her foot and she fell a third time into the snow. This time, she couldn't push herself to her feet again. What remained of her strength dissipated, pulled away by the street. There was nothing ahead of her and only ashes behind her.

At least the snowfall was pretty. She'd watch it for a while, her cheek on her hand, and then maybe she'd get up and go and return the cloak to the woman who had loaned it to her.

Or maybe she wouldn't. The spark that had carried her this far was lost. With the baby gone, she just couldn't *care* anymore.

A man's boots stopped in her field of vision. They were odd, she thought dreamily. Cleaner than any workman's boots, but sturdier than a gentleman's. What kind of boots did the devil wear? They'd be pointier than this man's, she decided, and fell into darkness.

WHEN SHE WOKE UP, she woke up to warmth. She was slumped over a table, her cheek resting on her folded hands. Had she fallen asleep during lessons again? Had it all been a bad dream: William, and her father's castigation, and the baby in the snow? Hope lifted her the rest of the way to consciousness and she raised her head to look around for her sisters.

As quickly as it had blossomed, hope died. She was in an unfamiliar room, lit only by a dying fire in a large hearth. In the dim light she wasn't even sure what kind of chamber it was. A kitchen, she decided after a moment. There were flagstones, and an iron pot on the hearth, and more hanging from the wall.

But that wasn't quite right and she didn't know why.

She looked down at the table, trying to remember how she'd arrived there. It was old and scarred, and the chair she was sitting in had a broken back and something prodding her through her skirt. Her fingers curled against the damaged table. She was so warm, far warmer than that little fire could account for. She remembered being cold. She remembered the snow, and putting down her baby, and falling.

Julia remembered the man stopping beside her.

He was leaning against the wall in the corner, watching her. She turned, she saw him clearly, and only then did she jump up in surprise.

"Sit down," he advised her. His voice was rough and rusty. "Don't be in such a hurry to get to work." The dying fire flared, but the light reflected from his eyes was as cold as starlight and the devil's laughter.

She sat down, all at once very frightened. He didn't speak further, only looked at her, and her fear grew. A childhood habit resurfaced and she started gnawing on her knuckles so she didn't cry out.

Then he said, "You should have died in the snow. You abandoned your child; what else did you have of value? You'd already abandoned morality, innocence, delicacy."

Julia wanted to respond, but her mind was blank and all that emerged was a whimper.

"Shh," he said. "You should have died, but lo, there is—" and Julia couldn't tell if he said 'mercy' or 'punishment'. The word garbled in her ears, which was odd because they were nothing alike. Were they?

He watched her confusion. "I have brought you here to keep house for me. You will be warm and fed. But you must obey my rules and you must never leave the house. There will be consequences if you do." He paused. "Or you can return to dying in the snow. I'll show you the way, if you wish."

A log collapsed and sparks glowed on the hearth. Julia shook her head instinctively and whispered, "I don't want to die."

He smiled, the expression cracking across his face until seemed too broad to be human. "Irrational, sinful, and yet so typical. Will you accept my protection, then?"

Julia thought of everything else that 'protection' implied, and remembered William moving against her in the straw of the stable. This man frightened her more than William ever could and yet a single man's 'protection' was the best she could hope for now. A small thing, to put off what waited beyond death for a while longer.

She bowed her head and said, "Yes."

"How charming." He cracked his knuckles. "First, clean this room. Don't go exploring the rest of the house; everything you need is here. I imagine soon enough I'll have your next chore. You may sleep, if it takes you that long, by the hearth." His inhuman smile grew even larger. "My little Cinderella. But no prince will be coming for you, will he?"

Julia thought of her baby and couldn't answer. She lowered her eyes and rose from her chair again. Her back twinged, but her fingers and toes were warm. That would take the place of any prince. "Do you want me to begin now, sir?" She brought her hands to the loosely gathered top of her dress.

When there was no answer, she looked up. Although she'd heard no door open or close, her new master was gone.

She sat for a long time in the near darkness. Even with her frightening master gone, her mind was numb. Though she was warm, the spark that she'd lost in the snow had not returned. In the end, it was only the empty gnawing of her stomach that drove her to look around.

The fire was mere coals. She found a cord of wood in a wardrobe in the corner, beside a bucket of water underneath a shelf stocked with cleaning supplies. He was right; there was everything, fresh and unused.

The coals resisted being coaxed into a full blaze, but she was a country girl from a household with only two servants, and she knew some tricks. She worked at her task without thinking, building the fire larger and larger. Her father would have scolded her for waste, but she didn't care. When it was as big as the hearth could hold, she went looking for food.

At first she found only the remnants of food, in a kitchen so filthy it had probably never been cleaned. A sideboard displayed plate crusted with the remains of forgotten meals. The rag carpet crunched underfoot. The walls were coated in scum and grease. There was a tiny scullery but no pantry and she didn't dare go through either of the big heavy doors that occupied opposite walls. One of them led outside; there were windows blackened by filth beside it.

Finally, in a small cupboard near the outside door, she found food: a rusted tin of tea, a stale loaf of bread, some hard cheese, and some withered apples. She ate an apple slowly, watching the fire. When she was done, she tossed the stem into the flames, took the bucket of water and the soap, and got to work, because it was either that or remembering.

The windows were disgusting. She could draw lines in the

gummed on filth with her fingernails, and hard scrubbing with both brush and rag only lightened the grime. She caught a glimpse of the snow pressing against the windows and turned away to build up the fire again and to heat water. Once it was nearly scalding, she turned her attention to the grimy floors, scrubbing on her hands and knees. It was exhausting work, and by the time she managed to get one of the flagstones bright again, her water was cold and her arms ached.

She heated it again, staring into the fire until she fell asleep.

When she woke sometime later, the cauldron had boiled dry, and both the floor and the window were as filthy as they'd been when she started.

There was something wrong with the water, Julia eventually decided. It didn't clean things properly. She scrubbed and scrubbed until her hands were swollen and her back ached. The floor or the table or the plate appeared clean until she looked away for a moment. But the cleanliness was a trick of the light and she always had more to do.

Her protector spilled out a sack onto the table. He left hard bread and dry cheese and old figs behind, and took milk and honey with him to the house beyond. As he did, he glanced around. "Your mother would be ashamed of you."

Instantly Julia knew it was true. Her mother *was* ashamed of her, for her sin. And if her mother could see the kitchen Julia lived in now, her tears would be bitter indeed. What redemption could there be for a girl who couldn't even clean a kitchen?

She sloshed grey wash water down the scullery drain and wondered where it went. She felt a kinship with it. They'd both been used up to no purpose, and thrown away.

A memory stirred, and she remembered holding something helpless. But she pushed the thought away.

Later he came in stinking of blood. His clothes and hands were covered in it. He began to strip out of his stained garments right in front of her: jacket, shirt and trousers. She watched in shocked anticipation, but all he said, "You haven't done a thing with the kitchen, but perhaps you can manage to launder these," before walking away.

"The water's no good," she called after him, after the door had closed. She didn't dare say it where he could see her, not to her nameless master with the blood-stained clothes.

She tried. And much to her surprise, the bloodstains lifted right away, even off his white shirt. It was impossible.

"There's a trick to it," he told her when he reclaimed them.

"I just washed them as I wash my own clothes," she whispered.

He gave her a look like she was stupid. "It's not in the washing. It's in the doing of the things that would otherwise stain." He looked her up and down. "You obviously haven't learned it." He patted his jacket, then reached inside to a pocket and pulled out an undistinguished lump, which he frowned at before tossing it into the fire. "Next time, have the sense to check the pockets." The smile he favored her with was as frightening as his first one. "You can keep whatever you find."

The fire burned green as it consumed what he'd fed it.

After that, she made a habit of checking his pockets. One day, she found teeth in his jacket: back teeth, front teeth, big teeth and small teeth. She put them in a green glass bottle on top of the dust-shrouded mantle. They gleamed as she vainly scrubbed the floor, and she remembered when she'd lost her last baby tooth. She'd been twelve, like her second youngest sister was now.

Another day, she found a woman's golden braid, cleanly cut and tied with a ribbon. She touched her own hair, grown out but still with ragged ends. Her father had cut her own hair when he'd learned of her pregnancy, stony-faced as she wept. He'd swept the curls into the fire and they stunk as they burned.

She put the braid on the mantel, beside the bottle of teeth, and turned her attention to the walls. They were grey with grease and soot and badly needed scrubbing. Her fingernails made streaks in the grime that filled in with her filthy water. William had flattered her hair, when he first strolled with her outside the rectory. She'd always thought it was plain brown, but he told her that it was copper when it caught the sun, and he'd caught a curl around his finger, then asked her to dance with him with only the birds as their orchestra.

She wrote his name, and hers, in the scum on the wall: WILLIAM JULIA. Then she sloshed the entire bucket of wash water over the wall. She'd never named her baby. She'd hoped that if she saved that privilege for him, he'd take care of them, just like he promised he would.

When she woke up again, her benefactor was watching her. He smiled like a gargoyle and said, "You're making it dirtier. That's not how this is supposed to go. But at least you can clean my clothes." He dumped a bag of laundry onto the flagstones, then pulled off his jacket again. "I've brought you a brush for the clothes. The mud can be so sticky." Still grinning, he picked up the jar of milk from the table and walked into the rest of the house.

She left the clothing on the floor and went to clean the windows. They were icy under her fingers, with frost glinting when she managed to scratch enough of the muck away. She scrubbed the whole window, top to bottom, then emptied the bucket onto the floor and smashed it into the glass.

The vibration numbed her hands and wrists and the bucket dropped onto her foot and rolled away. The window remained unbroken, although the blow had scratched a tiny bit of tarnish off the metal setting for the pane. She turned to the door beside the window, the outdoor one her protector entered from in his stained clothes. It wasn't locked. He never locked it. She could just walk away, walk back out into the snow and curl up and wait.

Instead she went to his clothes and started looking for the remnant she knew she'd find. Tucked into the inner pocket of his jacket, she found a pair of golden wedding rings. One of them shone, and the other was scratched and dented and stained. She threw them both into the fire without a second thought. She didn't want to think about weddings. She'd thought about weddings enough for a lifetime. Her entire girlhood had been filled with, "When you marry…." and "When you have a household of your own." But she'd never marry, and she'd never have a household, because she'd been stupid enough to believe a man.

She ate dry bread. She slept. She woke. The fire was blazing bright, and on the mantle the two rings glinted, the woman's ring burned clean by the flames. She knelt in front of the fire and felt its searing heat. It couldn't burn her clean. Even her death wouldn't clean her. Nothing would. She'd left her only path to salvation in the snow.

Other things accumulated on the mantle as her protector went about his strange business. A pair of women's dancing slippers. A boning knife. A sack stitched of thin, mismatched strips of pale leather, with a pebble and some dried petals inside. Sometimes she picked up remnants and her fingers tingled: a box, a locket, a girl's ring. Once, she cried for an hour over a half-knitted baby sock, then tucked it away safely, but when she woke up, it was gone.

That day, she reached into his jacket and pulled out a small jar with a thick black fluid inside. She loosened the cork and recoiled from the odor of death that instantly filled the room. The vial dropped from her hand and a droplet of the fluid squeezed out from under the loosened cork. She backed away from it before it crawled inside her.

Then her benefactor came back into the room. He scooped

up the vial and the droplet clinging to the rim. "Ah," he said. "I forgot about this. It almost escaped, I see."

Julia nodded, her hand clamped over her mouth and nose. She could still smell the stench over the scent of her well-soaped hand.

He tilted his head, looking at her a half-smile. "Unbearable, is it?"

She nodded again, and glanced at the door. He clicked his tongue. "Tsk. All it takes is a bad smell for you to consider breaking my simple rules? You *are* a naughty girl." He looked at her a moment longer, then strode toward her.

She backed away and he said, "Don't be idiotish, or I'll leave you with the remnant." He caught her wrist and pulled her to him, then pried her hand away from her face. Before she could react, he lowered his head to hers and inhaled sharply, stealing her breath away utterly. She couldn't smell anything. She couldn't *breathe.* Then he exhaled, and burnt sweetness surrounded her and carried away her consciousness.

She heard him whispering amidst her nightmares. "Leaving that was an accident, my cinder-girl. But a thought occurs: you chose to open the vial. Perhaps you wanted what it contained, deep inside? Shall I leave it on the mantle for you to find again? You can drink it, then, and it will take you beyond the reach of Hell itself. Shall I leave it, then?"

"No, no," she cried. "I was only doing as I was asked. I was only curious. I didn't know that it contained such death! You didn't tell me!"

"Ah," he said. "You prefer this Hell, then." And a cold wind blew over her, snow stinging her face, and she woke up next to a fireplace that was guttering with the draft from the chimney and a dark and open door.

She stumbled over and slammed the door closed, the flagstones like ice under her feet. The wind howled outside. She went to build up the fire again and realized that under the wind's howl, someone was singing beyond the other door. It was her protector, and he was singing a lullaby. She pressed her ear to the door and heard little sounds under the song. Little sounds she recognized.

With a sharp spike of pain and fear, Julia remembered the milk and knew, *knew* her benefactor hadn't just brought her home. He'd also brought home her baby.

She sat by the fire, rocking back and forth and hugging her chest. He had her baby. She'd seen him bringing milk in, and she'd never wondered why. She'd tried so hard not to wonder what had happened after she'd placed the child in the nest of snow, and she'd never thought past that. She couldn't. She'd abandoned her baby. She'd abandoned everything.

He had her baby and he'd been crooning a lullaby. The soft lilt of the tune circled in her mind, inescapable.

Hours later, he emerged from the door and crossed the kitchen to the exit. He glanced at her only once. As he looked away again, he smiled, as if amused by the way she huddled against the hearth.

She'd been trying to gather up her courage all that time. Now, as he was about to walk away, she took what scraps she had to hand. "Sir?"

He paused. "Yes?"

"Can I see her? My baby? I heard you singing."

He gave her that laughing smile again, his eyes like cold starlight. "No. You don't deserve your baby. You abandoned her in the snow. She's mine now. I've named her Ciara."

Julia lowered her eyes. He was right.

And yet, was it her fault? What else could she have done, with William's betrayal? She had surely given up after he rejected her for the final time, but he was the baby's father and the child was the result of his lies. Didn't what happened to the child also lay at his feet?

But that didn't bring her baby back.

She crept to the inner door after her protector returned through it, hoping to hear her baby's gurgle. When she didn't, she turned away and went to the fire. It didn't warm her anymore, even when she held her hands so close that they hurt.

She'd always followed the rules, until William. She'd lived surrounded by the rules, until William had seduced her away from them. And once she'd broken the rules, she'd lost everything.

Julia looked at the door. The rules, she decided, did not apply where William was concerned.

She waited until her protector went out. He was always gone for hours when he left via the kitchen door. This time after he left, she went out too.

It was snowing beyond, and she wasn't bundled against the cold. Yet just as the fire hadn't warmed her, so the cold didn't deepen her chill. She tied paper 'round her feet and a scrap of ribbon in her hair and she went walking until she found William's lodgings. She'd known the address once, before she'd fallen in the snow and a monster had saved her baby. She didn't know the number anymore, but she still knew the way.

She didn't knock. She knew what would happen if she knocked. She wouldn't get a toe past the threshold, if indeed they even answered it for her rather than sending somebody out to drive her off. No. She didn't knock. She waited. When he came out, polished and shining, swinging a cane and tipping his hat to a passing acquaintance, she didn't approach him.

Instead, she followed him, drifting along in his wake. She followed him to his club, and then to a party, where she waited outside until he went home again. Then she went home again too, to her protector's house.

He wasn't waiting to punish her when she returned. She went to the door her baby was behind and listened to the gentle sounds of the stirring child. She couldn't tell if he was also beyond. She didn't dare open the door and find out. Instead, she turned to the stones of the hearth and scrubbed them until she couldn't keep her eyes open anymore.

The next day, and the next, she left the kitchen and went into the night to follow her lover. Nobody ever noticed her. She trod right by fine carriages and ladies in ermine wraps and they never saw her. She was nothing, she was nobody. She'd broken the rules and she'd stopped existing.

But she did exist. She knew she existed. She couldn't clean the stains from her kitchen, but she could see her breath in the fog she blew onto the windows of his study. She had broken the rules and fallen but he was the one who had lied. He was a stain, too.

The third time she followed him, he went to a house late in the evening and stood outside for a moment. When he went within, it was only for a few moments, not enough time to even remove his gloves. He paused outside and looked around, as if he could feel her stare from where she lingered by the servants' stairs. Then he shivered, drew his scarf around his neck, and strode down the street.

She didn't go after him right away. Something called to her from the house he'd visited so briefly. She waited.

After the clouds had blown across the stars, she heard a cry from high in the house. It was a sound of betrayal and of denial. She knew that cry; she'd uttered it often enough. The realization of a broken life always sounded the same.

For another day, she followed him. She watched as he went to three parties, bright and enthusiastic and just as lovely as the day she had met him. He thought nothing of the business he'd concluded the night before, but as he left his final party and wandered toward his club, he stopped and turned in the snow.

Julia wondered if he would see her, address her. Once the thought would have made her heart leap with joy, but now it only thudded in her chest like the drumbeat of a dirge.

His eyes flickered over her and he recoiled, then turned away and hastened to his club in a rapid shambling walk, as if he'd wanted to run but he'd forgotten how. It made her laugh in spite of herself.

At her master's house, she dropped off asleep by the hearth, still upright. She woke when her master returned, as he was dropping a pile of laundry on the table. "I can almost see some change," he told her. "Maybe you're finally getting the hang of keeping clean."

She ate something, scrubbed the plate until she saw a glint of the metal underneath the tarnish. Her protector didn't know what he was talking about; she was still no better than she had been at cleaning this mess. So she turned to the laundry, which practically cleaned itself. She went through the garments absently and found a scrap of paper in an inside pocket, wrapped around a thin blade. Her fingers tingled when she touched it: the shock of a shared scream. The paper was a torn scrap, stained with blood and bearing the words, "Why god does he go on like this? How can—"

Out of nowhere—she was sure he hadn't been in the room— her protector said, "There's no point in trying to clean *that*." He plucked the paper out of her hand. "There's hardly anything left to be going on with." When he opened his fingers, it fluttered over to the fire. The flames grew and brightened as they consumed the fragment, as if it was a much larger piece of fuel.

The knife, he ignored. Instead he went to the table and took a seat, stretching out his legs in a simulacrum of rest. "Would you like to hear about Ciara? She's an adorable child. So good for those who care for her. So loving." He flashed his wide smile. "She always looks to me when I enter the room, follows me with her eyes. She knows who cares for her."

Julia looked down at the knife in her hand, then slowly turned away to put it on the mantel full of trophies.

"I can't decide if she looks like her father, or takes after her mother," her protector went on.

"I thought she looked like him once," Julia said, and felt like her heart was breaking. She wanted to hold her baby again. But this man, this strange monster in the shape of a man, with his bloody trophies had claimed her and he, even he, a monster was a better father than her true father. A better parent than her mother. "Perhaps she'll take after you now."

"Perhaps," said the man, and smiled again. Then, pleasantly, he asked, "How is the gentleman in question lately?"

Hatred spiked through her, sudden and furious. "He is what he's always been. Gay to dissolution, all flash and poison. I was just a paper doll to him, I and all the others."

In the blink of an eye, her protector moved from his seat by the table to backing her against the side of the fireplace. "Have you been leaving the house, my little cinder-girl? Breaking my rules?" He touched her cheek with the back of his fingers. It was gentle, intimate in a way William had never been intimate, and it scared Julia to her core.

"I— I—" She couldn't answer. She could barely *think*.

His hand moved to her tangled hair. "Don't lie," he said softly. "I know all your lies."

"I hate him," she whispered. It was the truth. "I hate him so much."

Her protector's hands moved to her shoulders, down her arms. His fingers skimmed over her hands, then brushed her hips. He knelt, bringing his hands down her legs lightly. Then he placed his palms over her feet. "Such cold feet. You've walked through snow on these feet, cinder-girl." He pressed harder and pain exploded in her feet, as if there were needles between his fingers.

She moaned and swayed back against the warm hearth. The fire were still bright and high and she thought she might fall into it. He was going to kill her for breaking his rules. She'd had a chance to live and she'd throw it away. Her mother and sister flashed through her mind and away; her father flickered away even faster. William sparkled at her through cut glass. And then, finally, she saw the face of her daughter, the little soul she had abandoned and a monster had saved.

Living wasn't the answer, she realized.

Not *just* living.

"What would you be without rules, little Julia?" murmured her protector in her ear. "You would be nothing. Not even a cinder-girl. Don't the rules keep you safe? Don't we protect you?" His arms caged her against the hearth and his forehead rested against hers.

She found her voice. "Are you going to kill me?"

He lifted his head so she could see his wide smile. "I'm not *your* murderer, cinder-girl. "

The pain in her feet ebbed. "You're a liar, just like he is. You're all liars and killers. Go away and lie to each other, if you're not going to kill me." She ducked under his imprisoning arms and stepped past the fire. A spark landed on her skirt and she absently beat it out.

William was worthless. All the men of his type were worthless. Maybe all men were worthless.

Everything was worthless.

The door closed behind her protector, as if he'd gotten bored.

Everything was worthless. She knew that, she admitted it to herself, and yet she still *wanted* things. Worthless things, except for maybe one.

Everything was worthless, and that included her. William had made her worthless, and she had let him.

She looked at all the tokens on the mantle. Unbidden, her hand drifted over the mementos: the dance shoe, the ring, the locket, the coil of hair. The candy box. One after another, she picked them up and tucked them in a basket, taking the knife last of all. Then she picked up her protector's stainless shirt and walked, once again, out into the snow.

It was just before the dinner hour when she walked into the kitchen at William's lodgings. The staff looked at her, but not one of them moved to stop her. They couldn't, not when she was wearing her protector's shirt over her smock. He was stainless and so was she.

She climbed the stairs until she reached the floor William occupied, then went through the rooms until she found him in the saloon. He had two friends with him, young men as bright and shining as him. She was glad. It was better that way.

"Hello, William," she said softly, but her voice carried.

He whirled around, then dropped his drink. The crystal shattered on the floor. "Who... who are you?"

She smiled at him, just as she'd smiled all those months ago. "I've come with gifts, William. Mementos, of the gifts you've given others." As she put the basket on the polished table, one of William's friends stirred, as if he wanted to interfere. She hummed a snatch of song that she'd heard somewhere, a lullaby, and he stilled again, staring at her with fascinated, horrified eyes.

"What do you have there?" asked William apprehensively. "Where's the footman?"

"They're near," Julia told him. "Very near. Here, William. Do you remember this?" She pulled out the dancing slipper and put it in his hand. "She wept over it, like a child. She's not weeping now, though."

"I don't know what you're talking about," began William.

"And this. Do you remember this?" She showed William the ring. "She turned it over and over on her finger and waited for you."

"I only told her it was pretty," he said sharply. "And that she might find an even prettier one someday. It was hardly a promise."

Julia smiled at him warmly and put the ring on his smallest finger. Then she pulled out the candy box. "A gift for a girl still in the schoolroom. There's blood smeared inside the lid, you see?"

"Oh, ugh, how disgusting," said William, and tried to pull away. Tried, and failed.

Julia unclasped the locket and put it around his neck. "You made promises, William. So many promises. You think that because you didn't say the words, it wasn't a promise. But it was. A promise in skin." She put the lock of hair to his mouth, pushed it between his lips. "We gave you everything you wanted and all you gave us was our own destruction."

He gagged on the hair, then managed, "Julia? You're mad. What did you do with the child?"

Julia shook her head. "No, William. That you can't have, not where you're going." Instead she put the knife into his hand and closed his fingers around it. He stared down at it, at the crimson edge, as if mesmerized.

She smiled again at William's two friends, then walked out of the room, past the gathered lodging house staff. They parted like the sea for her, then closed up behind her, and that was right. Then there was a shocked shout from one of William's friends and that was right, too.

She went back to her dark kitchen. Her protector sat in the kitchen chair, his feet on the table. "I see you took my shirt," he drawled.

Julia looked at him blankly as she dropped the shirt on the floor. "I want my baby."

Raising his eyebrows, he said, "Do you deserve such a wonderful baby, so sweet and innocent? So unstained?"

She stared at him for a long moment, waiting to see if he had anything else to say. When he didn't, she walked past him and through the other door.

The room beyond was as dark and filthy as the kitchen, no place to keep a child. But there was a cot in the corner where something wrapped in blankets moved and cooed, and glowed like a beacon.

It was easy, so easy to walk across the room. Had it always been that easy? Had she really spent hours staring at the door between her and her child?

She went and picked up the bundle, looked into the child's eyes. They were the color of joy, and the darkness fled away. She was in a house, an ordinary house, with walls scrubbed white and a window that let in the early spring sunshine, and she was holding her daughter.

OTHER REASONS

Corbin could feel Ice's heartbeat alongside his own through the lifebinding he'd done. It was the only reassurance he had that the man over his shoulders was still alive. The wounds on Ice's chest and legs had been roughly bandaged, but it didn't matter. As long as Corbin's strength held out, so would Ice's flickering life. And as soon as the connection was broken, unless they were in a really well-equipped ER, the leader of the kaiju-hunters would die.

He'd tied Mack's life to Simon's. Grendel was still on his feet, but only barely. Every time he stumbled, Simon sneered and prodded him with a sparking finger. The big man would roar and spin around, strength and alertness flooding his frame as he glared at the smaller kaiju hunter. "I can still take you apart, Simon."

"Try it, asshole. You're barely on your feet," Simon said.

Grendel made a fist, then squeezed his eyes shut. "How did we get so trashed?"

"The angel's bastard agent had some tricky friends. Made things a little complicated."

"But we won, right?"

"Hey, we're still alive. We must have." Simon rolled his eyes in Corbin's direction.

Grendel's fading gaze swept his companions: Ice over Corbin's shoulders, Mack over Simon's. "Yeah." He turned and trudged forward, in the direction they'd been going before he almost fell.

Corbin caught his arm and readjusted his path, then exchanged glances with Simon. "Anyone you can walk away from, eh?"

"Hey, I'm a pragmatic fellow. I don't think they wanted to leave us alive. We are; therefore we won."

They continued on the ruined road winding through the mist-shrouded Castdown Way. It hadn't been mist-shrouded when they traveled the Way before, but simply one of the many, vast streets of the long-empty Far City of the Backworld. It didn't seem empty now. There were whispers from nowhere and the buildings looming in the mist seemed closer, as if the city had come to life and was trying to swallow them. That was only one of many things that had gone horribly wrong on the mission.

Ten endless minutes later Grendel's energy faded, and the whole scene repeated itself.

"This feels a lot like torturing a dying dog, mate," said Simon, once Grendel, his gaze fixed on some inner vision, was moving again.

"You think you can carry both of them? I can't."

Simon shook his head. "Not enough leverage. But you could skip on ahead and bring back some extra hands."

A raven flapped through the mist to land at Corbin's feet. Two more joined it, pecking at the cobbles. They were nervous. Corbin didn't blame them. He shook his head. "I don't think there'd be anything to come back for. Absolven's associates haven't wandered off. They're playing with us."

"And you think sticking with us is going to stop that?" Simon's inquiry was friendly, but pointed. Corbin was the tagalong kid, the junior auxiliary member of the LA branch of Senyaza's Special Investigations. But the truth was, he'd convinced them to go on this miserable adventure and he was damn well going to get them out alive or die in the attempt. He shook his head bitterly. But to do that he couldn't even send Simon on ahead. Without Simon, without the ability to keep both Grendel and Mack moving, they'd be nothing but prey for whatever Absolven had left behind to finish them off.

He held out a fist to one of the ravens and it flapped up to perch there. Caressing the feathered head with a knuckle, he let the information hovering at the top of the bird's mind flow into his own. He swore. "There's an intersection ahead. It's not on the map."

"There's a bloody surprise," said Simon, and caught Grendel's arm. "Take a breather, big guy." Grendel growled but stilled, as if obedience was only possible under protest. That was usually the case.

Corbin crouched down and laid Ice in the clean gutter of the cobbled street. Then he spread his fingers wide and the three ravens awaiting his instructions scattered into the air. "They'll scout the forks. One of the roads will be the one we arrived on. Has to be." A brief break was far preferable to getting truly lost in the Far City. The books Corbin had read were full of anecdotes of explorers who had vanished in the Far City, as completely as if they'd been eaten.

"Unless we've gotten totally turned around in the mist. Are you so sure we haven't?"

Corbin hesitated. "Pretty sure." The memory charm he'd equipped before setting out helped with things like that. "But the birds are absolutely certain. They always know where I am."

Simon shrugged. "If you say so. Look, if we're going to camp and wait for the intel, maybe, just maybe, we should head into one of the buildings?"

"See, I may have an idea about how to get out of here, but I have no idea if there's such things as carnivorous buildings and that worries me. You're old. Do you know?" He already knew the answer; Simon didn't make a habit of retaining any memories weak enough to be washed away by Scotch and that included obscure knowledge about the depths of the Backworld.

Simon squinted at the mist. "Good point. Maybe we can make a little barricade of the others." He leaned Mack against Ice, then surveyed them. "Itty, bitty barricade."

Corbin checked the lifebinding charms on himself and Simon. Then he checked the injuries on Mack and Ice and then he checked the charms again. Grendel sat down suddenly, so heavily the pavement seemed to tremble, and Corbin wondered if he ought to add another lifebind between the big kaiju-hunter and himself, just in case.

"What do you reckon is doing the whispering?" asked Simon, sitting on the curb beside Grendel and pulling out a crumpled pack of cigarettes.

"I've been trying not to listen." Grendel's injuries were doing better than the other two's. Every time Simon provoked Grendel into threatening him or swinging at him, the wounds inflicted by Absolven and his terrible blade healed a tiny increment faster than before. But it had to be done carefully, without over-stretching Grendel's resources so much that he passed out. Unconscious, he was just a big slab of flesh.

"I mean, do you think it's the man-eating buildings? Saying, 'Come to us, tasty morsels?'" He cocked his head. "I think they're giggling, myself. Mocking us. Annoying little prats."

Now Corbin couldn't help but listen.

Look at them poor boys get them get them let them run closer to the edge they're so sweet so earnest is this what is left this what we're afraid of? Only two left the two weakest don't break all the toys.... As Corbin listened, the whispers grew louder, clearer. He stared into the mist, trying to understand who was talking.

Then Simon leaned over and flicked his forehead with a

sparking finger. The man had moved right in front of him, and he hadn't even noticed. "Stay alert. Maybe leave the listening to ghost voices to me. I've got experience ignoring stuff like that."

The whispers became giggles. Corbin shook his head. "Right. I wonder where Absolven dug up these little bastards." He turned his attention to the scouting ravens. He couldn't pull knowledge from them unless they were very close, but he could sense how far they were. One of them was already on the way back. He stood up, and as he did, he realized the mist was moving rather more than the still air suggested. A shape loomed out of the corner of his eye, and he ducked sideways, almost stumbling as he avoided....

Mist. Mist and laughter.

He growled in annoyance. Simon swiveled his head to follow Corbin even as his gaze darted around. He put a hand on the triangular knife at his belt. "Something's about. Get down."

"They're playing with—" Corbin half-said, before something exploded out of the mist. A troop of silhouettes, each foggy shape edged with silver sharpness, swarming in low and close to the ground. Corbin crouched down, pulling his own stealth charm around him like a coat. Simon's knife was already drawn and sparking; an arc of incandescent light sprang from the blade to two of the moving figures before a third one caught him low and left crimson behind.

Corbin moved closer to Simon and unrolled a broad, silver ribbon from within his sleeve and set it to dancing around them. It sparkled and twisted, attracting the attention of the attackers. Their silvered edges sliced at it, mostly catching only its sparkles. He wasn't a warrior like the kaiju-hunters. His weapons were information and distraction. In a straight-up fight, it was all he could do to keep himself out of trouble. But that attitude wasn't going to help at all right now.

He flicked the ribbon into a different pattern. One of the

attackers laughed and jumped toward Grendel, who was still sitting slumped next to the pile of Mack and Ice. The attacker landed behind him, fully visible for a brief moment. He was slim, smaller than Corbin, dressed in rags with wild hair, a mad grin, and blades on the edge of his hands and his sleek black boots. He grabbed Grendel's head and leaned forward to whisper in his ear. Or at least, that seemed to be his intention. As soon as his fingers slid into Grendel's blood-stiffened hair, the big man's head came up, his eyes half-opening.

Then with a roar, he surged to his feet, reaching over his shoulder to pull the attacker off him, flinging him into the air. He turned a half-aware gaze on the crew of similar figures veiled in mist playing tag with Simon's lightning and Corbin's ribbon, and his eyes widened. Then a feral grin curved his mouth and he strode forward, tugging the scratched and pitted sword out of the scabbard on his back.

The giggling that still emerged from the mist quieted for a moment, and the attackers seemed to pause at the menace that radiated off Grendel. But it didn't last. Corbin smiled grimly as he moved behind the melee to haul Ice over his shoulder again. "We need to go," he shouted at Simon. The ravens hadn't made it back yet, but he thought heading in the direction of the one already returning couldn't be too terrible an idea.

Better than staying here, anyhow.

Simon sent an arc of electricity through the figure in front of him then backed up, joining Corbin. He picked up Mack like a sack of potatoes. "Grendel, come on!"

But Grendel was busy. There were six of the clouded figures, although both the mist and the flickering arcs of light left behind by Simon made it hard to be sure. When one fell, it faded into yet more mist, and then there were six again. Corbin wondered how many there actually were. But Grendel clearly didn't care.

The battle was waking him up, healing his injuries, bringing him back to life. Running away was the last thing on his mind. Which was unfortunate, because he could still be overwhelmed by sheer numbers. And if Absolver showed up again, wielding the Ragged Blade, Grendel could even be killed while the blade shut down his native response to strife.

"Do you think he can take them out?" Corbin asked Simon.

Simon shook his head, blood from a slice along his hairline dripping into his eye. "If it was really only six little guys, maybe. But what are we facing? How many are there? Bloody hell, I hate the Backworld. Full of tricks and lies." He dropped Mack again and waded back into the fight.

Something plucked at Corbin's hair. Corbin looked up sharply, hoping to see one of his ravens. Instead, Ice stood behind him, his skin corpse-pale, his eyes utterly white. Blood leaked from his mouth and fingers tipped with red plucked blindly at Corbin's face. And over Corbin's shoulder was a leaking burlap bag, moving and struggling like bones come to life.

Shocked, Corbin let the bag of bones slide from his shoulder and stumbled backward from the zombie's hands. "What—?" Then the whispers from the mist became laughter, and the zombie shaped like his friend faded away. Ice lay in a heap where Corbin had dropped him. Looking around wildly, Corbin realized that the mist had separated him from the others. He'd only been a few yards away, but he couldn't remember the direction or hear the sounds of their battle.

He knelt down and checked Ice, then Mack. Then, after only a moment's thought, he severed Mack's connection to Simon and instead tied the flickering life force to his own. He took a deep breath, feeling the drag against his skin and heart. Then his intrinsic magic, inherited from his celestial forebear, picked up, sustaining his body against the demands he was making of it. He was used to the little ways it helped: making him stronger and faster than pure humans. This was different. It pulled on him, as if trying to reshape him into something else.

Normally he far preferred mortal magic, and he'd never, ever advise somebody to tie mortal magic that was actually sustaining a life to a part-celestial nature. But in this case—

He looked up and let his intrinsic magic reshape him.

A pool of darkness swirled deep inside. Memories from beyond Corbin's own experience flashed within him, experiences he couldn't put words, or even images to, pulled from a pit of raw sensation. One of them crawled up into his mind. Half his vision went black, and agony swept over him. He squeezed his eyes shut and opened them again. The mist was gone, replaced by long shadows streaked with crimson. Grendel and Simon were a few yards away; Simon knelt at Grendel's feet with his head down, supporting himself on a fist, his other hand still gripping his knife. Grendel stood protectively above him, swinging at—

Arcs of light and mist, curved into the shape of men. Each one was connected by a thread to a trio of tall and shining figures standing in the distant shadow of one of the empty buildings. Each time Grendel struck one down, the arc of light split open, bleeding mist, and the entity on the other end of the thread pulled it in and reshaped it.

Corbin lifted his arm and the first of his ravens landed on it. It had found a dead end, not the way home. It didn't matter, though. It was very hard, with the darkness streaking his vision, to understand what mattered. But the shining figures were a problem.

He threw the raven into the air again. It knew his mind as he knew its, and it dived toward one of the flickering threads that was all that remained of one of Grendel's assailants. Without hesitation, the bird captured the flickering thread and flapped into the air.

The reaction from the trio of figures was near instantaneous: the one holding the thread shouted, while the other two recoiled, yanking their threads back like collaring an aggressive dog. The first figure's shout rippled along the thread until it reached the end that the raven still held and exploded in light. But the raven wasn't going to let a shiny bit of string escape that easily. Maintaining its grip, it climbed until it landed on the head of a gargoyle adorning a building a block down. Then it carefully began to investigate the twitching thread.

The figure who yet held the other end turned, following the raven with its gaze. When the raven landed, the glow around the shining figure brightened and Corbin could feel the gathering of power like the world had taken a deep breath. At his silent command, the raven released the thread just before the end exploded with living sharpness. The bird flew into the air, cawing laughter as the thread flew back to its owner.

The trio of figures turned to look at Corbin, and then all at once they faded away.

Corbin returned his attention to his companions. Grendel was kneeling beside Simon, who had slumped over.

"Aw, he's fine, the weakling," announced Grendel. "Bit of a bump, bit of blood loss. He won't even have any decent scars." He stood up, hefting Simon under one arm, then paused, staring at Corbin. "You okay, kid? You don't look right. What did you do to them, anyhow?"

"I saw them," said Corbin. His voice sounded… odd.

Grendel narrowed his eyes. "Yeah. This is that thing again, isn't it? Used to happen to your dad sometimes too, I heard."

Corbin shuddered and raised his hands to his face, then his eyes. They felt… as odd as his voice had sounded. One felt hard, the other empty.

He yanked his hands away. Memories rose up again from the

dark pool, this time as images. A pair of glowing, rotating rings. A head tilted quizzically, warm eyes waiting for an answer. A wasteland. A field of ice and a bridge and lightning—

He was on his knees, staring at Grendel's boot. The dark pool had receded, back to the depths where it had come from. "Come on, get up. See, it's gone away. You feel better." Anxiety overshadowed the big man's cajolery, and the toe of one of his boots nudged Corbin.

"Yeah." His voice was normal again. The mist had returned, or had never left, and he shuddered. "Yeah, I'm fine." He stood up and frowned at Simon, under Grendel's arm. "I guess I ought to thank the bastards for helping you feel better, but I'm not sure how we're going to manage Mack now."

"Eh, I got it." Grendel stomped over and scooped up Mack under his other arm. Corbin blinked. He never really thought about just how big Grendel was. Mack, taller than Simon, had his boots dragging on the pavement, but otherwise Grendel seemed perfectly at his ease carrying both of them. "You have to figure out where we're going, though. Your friends came back while you were off communing with your ancestors or whatever." He nodded at where all three ravens perched.

Slowly, Corbin held out his fists to the birds. He felt stretched, as if something far too large to contain had been expelled from him. But as the birds settled on his arms, they brought normalcy with them. Normalcy and information. "I know which way to go." He bent slowly and hauled Ice over his shoulders again. Then he turned and trudged after the three ravens.

The shining figures bothered him. He'd seen them, interacted with them as they actually were, and that had caused them to flee. Even the whispers had faded away. It was like a game where he didn't know the rules, but he'd accidentally made the right move anyhow. He'd convinced his friends to come on this outing because *he'd* been convinced that something important was going on. The Ragged Blade was certainly dangerous, and Absolven had claimed it for his celestial allies—but where did the shining figures fit in? As far as Corbin knew, angels didn't play games, and they didn't run away when their tricks were revealed. And yet, who else would be helping Absolven?

He stumbled over a crack in the pavement, and Grendel said, "Watch out, you. Pay attention." There was a brooding note to his voice, and Corbin looked at him.

"Are you relapsing again?"

"Nah, I'll be fine for a while yet. But I can't help thinking about what happened back at the wizard's safehouse. It's ridiculous. How could we be overwhelmed by one traitor nephilim and some tricks? I mean, me! I've tracked and killed the Blood Deepness across four of his rebirths. Alone. It doesn't make sense."

"They lose their cunning when they're reborn," Corbin pointed out. "I'm thinking Absolven's friends haven't been reborn in a very long time." He stared down at the crack he'd stumbled over. Most of the roads in the Far City were both unused and in perfect repair. This one looked like an old street back in LA. As he walked along the crack, it lengthened. "I'd really like to know their connection to this city, myself."

The crack suddenly split apart and Corbin tumbled down into a vast ravine.

Or at least an image of Corbin did. He stared down at the ravine he apparently hovered over, both astonished and utterly unsurprised.

"Corbin—" said Grendel, starting forward, eyes bulging as he stared down at the ravine.

"No!" said Corbin, and one of his ravens fluttered into Grendel's face. Grendel stumbled backward, and the other two ravens landed on Ice's back, over Corbin's shoulders. Corbin edged his way off the illusionary ravine, until he was standing beside Grendel. Grendel stared at the ravens, then at Corbin, looking decidedly displeased.

"I think we're almost home," said Corbin, trying for lightness. "You can see me, right?"

"I can. But how do I know it's actually you?"

"Trust the ravens," Corbin suggested.

"But how do I know they're actually—"

"Grendel! Take it easy, man. You're giving into them."

"This is why I prefer to work alone," Grendel grumbled, shifting his burdens under his arms. "So, is this the crossover point?"

Corbin backed away from the ravine. It'd be so convenient if it faded away. What good was it now, except for making him nervous? Then again, that was probably plenty.

He closed his eyes and activated the crossover charm. The magic reached out tendrils into the space around him, probing for a soft spot in the curtain. While it was active, he could sense the previous openings of the curtain nearby. But it was like they'd been stitched closed… and a wall had been shoved onto the other side, making hard the spots that should be soft. Corbin wondered if this too was illusion. He didn't want to reach into the dark space again. He wasn't sure if he'd come back himself if he did so a second time, so quickly.

The two ravens perched on his burden leapt into the air as something moved past them. Grendel made a frustrated sound as Corbin realized they were being attacked again. He felt the jarring thud as Mack was dropped on the ground, and for a moment the whole world spun around him. He let Ice slide from his shoulders, blinking rapidly as he tried to reassert himself against the seductive pull of the darkness. As he pulled himself back from the ledge, Grendel tripped him and he stumbled and fell to the ground.

"Stay down and out of the way, kid." Then Grendel was

moving again, before Corbin had worked out what was attacking them this time. He looked around wildly, and at first he saw nothing but Grendel charging for a shadow. He clenched his fists in frustration. Had Grendel been tricked by another illusion?

But the ravens had seen something, too. The ravens knew. He took a deep breath and listened to them.

Absolven, who they'd battled and lost at the hiding spot for the Ragged Blade, had returned to finish them off. In the mind's eye of the ravens, he saw the bestial shadow of the ancient nephilim pass overhead before the man who cast the shadow landed lightly behind Grendel. The Ragged Blade darted out, but Grendel, warned by the motion of the ravens, ducked and spun out a booted foot.

Now Absolven lurked in the shadows of a building, just as the trio of shining figures had before. He even seemed wrapped in the same kind of darkness, and Corbin would have quite liked to know more about the magic spawning it. It was certainly a lot more effective than his own stealth charm. But there was no time, because Grendel had his scent and no shadows were going to help him escape Grendel's wrath.

The only problem was that he, and his allies, had already beaten Grendel once before. Grendel and Ice and Mack and Simon, leaving Corbin to pick up the pieces. But Grendel wasn't thinking of that. Grendel wasn't thinking. That was apparently Corbin's job.

It was the Ragged Blade that was the problem. It was what they'd come to protect, what they'd failed to protect: a human-crafted artifact of unique and disturbing power. If they could just get it away from him, Grendel would have a shot at driving him off or even defeating him, and they could reclaim the honor of their mission and perform a great service to all their people.

Corbin stared until his eyes burned as Grendel and Absolven

fought. But he couldn't come up with a way to get the weapon out of Absolven's hands and into Grendel's. He pressed his palms against his eyes in frustration and remembered the feel of his eyes under the influence of the dark pool. If he let himself sink down again....

But he'd drown. Who knew if whatever came out of the pool would care about the Ragged Blade or his friends or his people? And how would he take himself back again? It was too dangerous, here and now, in an environment he had no control over. He couldn't give up that last bit of control over himself.

He couldn't. He wouldn't be himself anymore.

Grendel grunted, soft and horrifying. Corbin yanked his hands away from his eyes to see the big man fall to his knees, his blood staining the whole of the Ragged Blade crimson. He turned his head toward Corbin, staring at him, then curled himself into a ball around his injury before finally going limp.

Absolven stood over him, ready to finish him off, but his clear blue gaze was on Corbin. Corbin shouted and flung out his distraction charm even as one of the ravens plummeted down to scratch at Absolven's face. He fended the bird off with a swipe of his weapon, shearing feathers off the raven's tail as it fluttered out of the way. The distraction charm fluttered and snapped in a long line between Corbin and Absolven, and Absolven sliced at it experimentally before nodding and stepping forward toward Corbin. Grendel lay forgotten on the ground.

"You're just a boy," said Absolven. "I'd let you go, if I could. But he tells me you will be as dangerous as all the others, that you are a traitor twice over."

"He's lying," snapped Corbin. "I've hardly had time to betray anybody. Unlike you." Sweat ran into his eyes. But if he was going to die, he was going to die as himself, and fighting. He tensed his muscles, ready to move.

Simon groaned where he'd been dropped, and Corbin flinched. Suddenly it wasn't about redeeming the honor of their mission or dying in the attempt. It was about survival. He couldn't die fighting, or they all would. He couldn't die and he couldn't run. But with a flash of clarity, very different from the vivid vision of the dark pool, he knew what to do.

The raven with the injured tail feathers fluttered precariously to a rooftop, while the other two circled above, crying. One dived, a feint that still drew Absolven's attention. Corbin took a deep breath and threw himself into the minds of all three birds. The rushing of air over and under the birds' wings rustled, and little whistles emerged from their open beaks. Then, all at once, the sounds came together as whispers.

"Absolven," the air whispered. "Where are you? I need the Blade, Absolven. Bring it to me."

Corbin made the distraction ribbon vanish and pulled his own poor stealth over him at the same moment. Absolven blinked and looked up into the air. "Teacher? I haven't ended them yet."

"It doesn't matter anymore. I need the Blade, Absolven. I need it now. Come to me."

"At once!" Absolven sheathed the Blade and looked around, his gaze passing right over Corbin with only a hint of confusion. He glanced up at the ravens circling, then around at the fallen bodies of the rest of the kaiju-hunters. Then, with a shrug, he turned and let the mist swallow him.

Corbin lay on the pavement, clinging to it as he let himself breathe again. One threat down. Now he just had to figure out how to get out of here.

A quiet laugh came from somewhere nearby. He rolled over and saw the three shining figures standing above him. "Did you hear?" said one.

"It doesn't matter," said another.

"Convincing," said the third.

"Very," said the first.

"He's right, too. Oh, this will be fun." None of the three looked down at him, and Corbin tried and failed to make out their faces beyond the misty glow.

"Shall we go?"

"Yes, let's. We have more work to do, after all."

"We'll let the ravens carry off the bodies. Hungry little beasts."

"Perhaps if we lower the barrier, they'll even bring their friends."

"Faster that way."

"Oh yes."

They laughed again, and one of them snapped his fingers. The wall behind the curtain between worlds vanished, and one after another the three figures faded away.

Corbin didn't wait. He invoked the opening charm as he rolled to his feet. A neat hole opened in the world, and Corbin started dragging his friends through, certain that at some point he was going to be interrupted and attacked. His ravens flew through after him, one of them landing on the emergency switch that would summon medical assistance directly from Senyaza.

Once all four of the injured men had been transported, Corbin turned to look at the passage to the Backworld. From this side, it looked like a shimmer of frosted glass. For a long, tense moment Corbin waited, unwilling to believe they'd escaped.

Then one of the voices said, "Silly child. We'll be seeing *you* later," and a slender hand reached through the shimmer, and pulled it closed.

You are born in lightning and fury and shame, but you are calm at your first awakening. You open your eyes in the place that was prepared and your first thought is, "How beautiful," and then, more surprisingly, "It won't last."

You rise from the slab where you were stored and pace the confines of your box. It is a cube, unadorned except for the gold veining the creamy marble walls in fractured patterns. Only you know what beautiful shape you saw within the lines.

You remember to touch the stone walls here and there to open a door, drawing the knowledge from a river below your thoughts, but you do not remember your name. It is well. Your name will come to you in time.

Beyond the door is a boulder. It is an illusion, but you do not know this, because it is as new as you are. You cannot stay in the chamber you awoke in, though. Already you display a personality: restless, assertive. You push into the illusion and pass through, and thus learn an important lesson: dreams cannot stop you.

You stand upon the road in the shadow world and decide what to do next. There is a road, and it leads somewhere else and that is enough for now. You follow the golden stone road as it passes through strange territory: vast sunlit fields of waving azure grass and white wildflowers, with spotted pink mushrooms rising taller than yourself above the grass. You know that the land is strange even though you do not know your own name. That namelessness is strange too, but you do not question. It has not yet occurred to you to question. Your head is full of knowledge, after all. What is there that you do not know?

A figure emerges from the grass onto the road ahead and you slow. "How beautiful," you think, and, "It must not be trusted." Why? You cannot say. He is as tall as you, with wild hair a mixture of the azure of the grass and the pink of the mushrooms, and he is smiling as he holds a hand out to you. The smile distorts his face so that his beauty is warped and alien.

"Hold," says he. "I know you. I've been waiting for you." He laughs, but you cannot see what is funny. You wait, in case he explains himself.

He paces toward you, a cruel cast to his twisted smile. "Look at you. Exiled. Weak. *Powerless.* And yet you're strolling along the road as if you haven't a care in the world. You ought to be running."

"I don't think so," you say mildly. It is the first time you have spoken to another.

Your enemy—it is clear to you now that this is your enemy—sneers. "You don't think so? Has being abandoned by Heaven scrambled what little wit you had?"

"I might run later," you continue. You think, and what you want to say unfolds like a chrysanthemum. "But not because a creature like you thinks I should. Go back to your dozing dreams, mushroom faerie. The real world will hurt you too much." You mean the words as kind advice to a lost creature, one you have recognized from the vast, impersonal stores of information underlying your mind, but he reels as if you struck him.

Then he lunges forward, his hands curved like claws. You step out of the way and do what comes naturally: you pull the Ragged Blade from the space where it is hidden. It shouldn't be possible;

the Blade should be gone in the same flash of lightning that brought you to life. And yet you have it, the jagged edge glinting like a shark's smile.

Your enemy is surprised too, when he wheels around and sees the Ragged Blade. "Oh," he says.

"Oh," you agree.

"You have that, do you?"

"Apparently." You inspect the Blade. It feels like an extension of your arm, like your twin in metal and acid heart-magic. You can feel the twisted throb of the edge.

"You're not *supposed* to have that," complains the mushroom faerie. "He said you'd have nothing now."

Curiosity tugs at you. You wonder: did you exist before you were born? "Who said that?"

The mushroom faerie backs away. "I shan't say. You'll find out eventually, won't you?" Then he jumps off the road and back into the meadow. You know, from the endless stores below your mind, that following him would be painful and unproductive, so you let him go.

The Ragged Blade returns to its hiding place when you flick your hand, but leaves a mark: an unclean nick just below your thumb. You lick it clean and notice there are no other scars on your hand or anywhere else on your body. That too is curious, and there are no answers bubbling to the surface from the river of knowledge.

You continue down the road and nobody appears to slow you, though the terrain changes from the mushroom meadows to a bluebell forest to a black-baked wasteland. But at the end of the road there is another boulder and this time you do not hesitate before walking through.

On the other side, it is night. The road continues on, but it is black and much wider. It winds down a wooded mountain, and it turns out that it is not a road for walking. It takes a moment for the river of knowledge to change its course, but soon enough you recognize the trucks and passenger cars for what they are and stay out of their way until one pulls over and offers you a ride.

You accept, although you cannot tell him where you are going. "Aw, that's okay," says the driver. "Sometimes I don't know where I'm going either, without the GPS. I'll take you down the mountain and you can get your phone charged up and sorted out. What's your name?"

It's a simple question, and you do not know the answer.

And then you do. "Cat," you say. You know you've been called Cat before, and that is all you know about yourself. Cat. It's your name.

The truck driver is amiable, chatting without prying and just as pleased to see the back of you when you reach a shopping center. You wander through the plaza, through throngs of people who look at you and look away. Your clothes mark you as different, pale, loose flowing trousers and a similar tunic, but they do not seem to mind the difference.

This is where you wanted to be, you are sure, but why? The question makes you uncomfortable and you discover that you dislike not having the answers. There is a store full of books; it invites you in and you spend time among the volumes. There is much in the river of knowledge below your mind, but here there is more.

A woman touches your arm: small and dark-skinned with shining hair and red fire at her back. You realize she's not a woman at all, but distant kin to the mushroom faerie and a trespasser in this mortal store. She smiles. "You've been in here for hours. Let me buy you some coffee and maybe that book you've been reading."

She is a trespasser but so are you, you realize. Trespassers together, you go to a coffee shop and when she gives you your coffee, she also gives you an envelope with paperwork and plastic in it. "You'll need that eventually, but tell me how you're doing. I don't think anybody expected to see you so soon."

"I'm not who you think I am," you tell her.

She smiles. "Who do I think you are?"

"Somebody with a past," you say, and her smile broadens.

"Call me Tia. There's a document in there that you can write your name on—whatever name you choose—and that will make it official. Well, official enough."

Your fingertips dance over the envelope. "Why are you giving this to me?"

"Because the world isn't very friendly to people without pasts, and I'm a helper. There's money, too. It won't take care of you for long, but I'm sure other opportunities will come along eventually."

"You will want something in return," you observe as you open the packet and look through the paperwork. "I have nothing to offer, though." She cannot need the river of knowledge in your head, and the Ragged Blade is not yours to be offered.

Her smile becomes quiet and smug, "You have a future."

You raise your eyebrows. "Don't get too caught up in cleverness, now. You'll cut yourself."

Her smile fades. "I think you'll be interesting. But not if you're murdered over a blanket or imprisoned for stealing bread. That will be boring for all of us. The envelope is an investment in your future. Is that dull enough for you?"

"Poor Tia. Did your newest toy bite you?" says a voice of bronze beside you, and Tia stiffens as if she too is facing the lightning. A third trespasser stands at the table, dark-haired, with a tie, and his white sleeves rolled up. The wind blows off his back, but the other patrons of the coffeeshop do not seem to feel it.

Tia slowly raises her gaze to the newcomer, then casually sips her coffee. "What brings you here?"

"Curiosity. And a problematic sense of responsibility." The newcomer studies you, and you stare back. There is something almost familiar about this one.

Slowly Tia says, "I'm fairly sure you're not responsible for him."

"He's nameless. Doesn't that make him my responsibility?"

"I have a name," you interject, impatient with being talked over.

The newcomer meets your gaze. "Perhaps you will, someday. I can already see that this time it fits you much better than last time. Which was, alas, my fault." His gaze goes far away and, just for a moment, an image bobs up to the surface of the river of knowledge: a very young woman. You do not know her name, or even really know her face, but you know she existed, and you know he is lying about something.

"I would be very interested in hearing about what you're seeing," says Tia carefully.

"I'm sure you would, but I don't hear any reason why I should tell you." He keeps looking at you as if you're an experiment he's about to take notes on.

You pick up the packet and stand. "I don't think you two need me here for this negotiation, so I'll be on my way." And you leave. Neither of them try to stop you as they continue their discussion. You're not sure either of them even really notice.

The first place you find to sleep is very cheap, because you don't know how long the money will need to last. But you hear rats in the walls as you lie in the dark. Their claws skitter against the walls, stilling for only a moment when a neighbor pounds a fist against the wall. The sound makes you uncomfortable: images of blood and traps and rage rise to the surface of the river of knowledge.

You are too uncomfortable to sleep, so you do the practical thing and leave in the middle of the night without any plan to return.

The next place you find is more expensive and more insulated from the natural world. You hear nothing but the air conditioning when you rest at night, which does not take away the memory of the rats in the walls.

"It's sad, but if they go where they don't belong, they need to die. There's no other way to keep them away," you remember me saying. You roll over. You don't want to listen. But now, in the silence, you can hear my whispers. You exist for a reason, and you must remember it and find her. You must become what I failed to be.

The next morning you look at the people in the public places. Your eye is drawn, naturally, to the young women. They are all beautiful, in the ways young women have always been beautiful, and you do not find the exercise tedious. After a while, though, you consider that it is not productive, and simultaneously you realize you are searching for something familiar in the faces that pass by.

Is it the pale-skinned girl or the dark-skinned girl? They both have dark hair and that, at least, is right. The sunny-haired women become background noise. But neither dark-skinned nor light-skinned is familiar. Young. Dark-haired. Find her, and make everything better again.

You wonder how you can have habits when you don't have memories. Your attention turns inward even as you let your eyes rest on the passing crowds, and you study the river of knowledge. Something bubbles there: not information, but a pattern. Lines make letters, letters make words, and you will not listen to me, but you learn to read what even I cannot.

"It seems," you say aloud, "that whatever was previously here has left a sticky residue behind. Perhaps we ought to scrub it out."

You stand up and leave the public place, returning to the room you've claimed as a temporary home. You stay only for a moment, and then you go out and find a library.

She's out there, whether or not you listen. You won't be able to forget that. The yearning is part of you.

But you read books instead. You learn things. Sometimes it is something we already knew, but there is always the fiction section. The river of knowledge doesn't retain the fiction. Lies and rats in the walls. A girl with dark hair walks by. Is it her? Pale skin? Dark skin?

But you do not look up. You will not listen. You read a strange story about the adventures of a girl who shares a body with her brother, and you only look up when the brother vanishes for good. "I like this one," you say.

Why won't you listen to me? I know the only story that matters. Listen! Just listen. You'll like it.

But you push down on what I send to the surface. It makes no sense. Neither of us can rest while you resist like this.

It is night and you stand in front of a mirror, looking at yourself. Your eyes narrow and you frown. It is only your reflection, my child. I'm not in the mirror. Let me draw you under again and show you what you need to know.

"No," you say. "No. You've run away and left me behind. I am not you, whoever you are." You are hard, harder than I ever was. If you were sent to kill the rats, you would not grieve for them.

What have I done?

I try to explain, but you turn on music and pour the noise into your ears. It is an assault on what lingers. You will not listen. I wanted to be nothing, and you are answering my wish. I would regret—

The knock on your door is loud enough to cut through your music and my weeping. You open it. Two women stand there.

Dark haired, both, one with light skin and one with dark. Before the dark-skinned one, smaller than her companion, can do more than greet you, you turn away and close the door. Good. It wasn't her.

You pause and open the door again. The smaller woman raises her eyebrows. "Hi there. Cat? I'm Ascensción Flores Galvinez and this is my companion, Jen. Tia pointed us in your direction." The taller woman meets your eyes. She isn't young at all, not like the woman we must find.

But you ignore me and step out into the hall to join them, as you think, "How beautiful," and then, "It will last."

BOOK 2

CHILDREN'S GAME

CHAPTER 1

This afternoon, let's go on an adventure," said the babysitter, as she buckled Kari and Lissa into the car.

"Are we going to Disneyland?" Kari asked. She really wanted to go to Disneyland someday.

"Are we going to the moon?" That was Lissa. She thought the moon was okay, but she loved to tease her twin sister.

The babysitter, whose name was Marley, smiled. "We wouldn't be back in time for dinner if we went to either of those places. But I found a new playground. Let's go explore!"

The new playground was in the middle of a park with a ball field and some buildings. There was a row of little houses along one edge. Some old men played chess on tables in front of the houses.

Marley said, "We won't bother them." She frowned. "It's funny. There were lots of kids when I scouted the place, but today it's almost empty."

Lissa and Kari didn't mind. If there were lots of kids at the playground, you had to wait in line and take turns more. They spent some time looking at the toys before deciding what to do first. There was a castle with a hanging bridge, four towers, and three slides. And a merry-go-round with a net. And a giant jungle gym shaped like a star. And a pirate ship. And a music center. And tunnels. And a balancing log. And a see-saw, too. But she and Kari had to stay away from see-saws.

Kari shouted, "I'm going to have fun," and ran over to the castle. She climbed up a rope ladder to one of the tall towers. It had a blue roof like an upside down ice cream cone, which was exactly right. "Lissa! Come be a princess." Then she looked over the playground, pretending it was her kingdom. Maybe she could find a prince to rescue.

Lissa climbed up beside her. "We have to find a dragon to talk to."

"You always want to talk," said Kari. "I want to fight through dire peril to rescue Han Solo. Smash! Pow!"

"Fine. Who are you going to fight?" Lissa asked. Kari looked at the playground again. There were a few other kids, but two of them were babies and the rest of them were big kids. Big kids always seemed to forget how to play. Kari hoped that would never happen to her. She wished she could fight off whatever made them so boring, but Marley always said *No, leave them alone.*

Then Kari spotted somebody their own age. "He looks like he needs rescuing. Let's go see!" She hopped down a step and went down the spiral slide. It was so smooth and slippery that she slid right off and landed on her bottom. Then Lissa crashed into her back. "Oof!"

"Sorry!" said Lissa. They helped each other up and went over to where a little boy sat on a small hill.

"Do you want to play?" asked Kari, as soon as they got close enough. He was a little bit bigger than they were, with light hair, blue eyes, and a big nose.

"No," he said. "Go away."

Kari bit her lip, but Lissa walked closer. "She's Kari. I'm Lissa. What's your name?"

The boy sniffed and wiped his nose. "Eli."

Kari realized he was sad, not mean. She sat down beside him. "Why are you crying? Did you fall and hurt yourself?"

Lissa sat down on Eli's other side. "Did a big kid push you?"

"Nobody pushed me." He sighed. "I used to have a friend. But he got sick and he doesn't remember me anymore."

Kari frowned. "A kid?"

Eli shook his head. "A grandpa." He pointed at the row of little houses and the old men playing chess. A lady stood beside one old man in a wheelchair. He looked like he was about to fall asleep.

"He told me stories," Eli said sadly. "And he carved sticks. See?" He pulled out a wooden owl from his pocket.

"It's not done," objected Kari. There was still a lot of stick left. The top of the owl's head and feet were barely carved. It was more like a wand than an owl.

"No, it's supposed to look like that," Lissa said. "It has a voice."

Kari stuck her tongue out. "I can't hear anything."

"She's right," Eli said. "It's finished. He did it a long time ago."

Shading her eyes, Kari studied the distant old man. "Is he asleep all the time now? We know somebody who was asleep for days and days, but she finally woke up. All better now!"

"He's awake a lot. He just doesn't remember me anymore. His brain broke." Eli looked down at the owl. "Sometimes he gets mad. My mom said he's had to fight a lot of demons in his life."

Kari's eyes opened wide. "Demons?"

Lissa poked at the ground with her finger. "We were supposed to help the sleeping lady, but we couldn't."

"Demons, Liss," Kari repeated, urgently. "If he's a monster hunter, we should help him."

Lissa looked up. "Yeah. We should."

"You can't help him," Eli said. "Even the doctors can't help him."

"Our uncle says that we'll be able to do anything we want someday," Kari explained. "But we couldn't help our friend Penny. So I want to try."

Eli looked puzzled. "How?"

"We'll go on an adventure. We can find what he lost. Give me that stick."

Interested, the boy handed over his stick. Kari looked at it a moment with her magic eyes. She didn't know how to talk about what she saw, but she knew it was enough. "Help me, Lissa."

Lissa held Kari's hand. Kari used the stick to draw a big circle in the air, then pushed the stick into the center and turned it like a key. The light flickered and the invisible door opened. "Okay, now we step through. Come on, Eli!"

CHAPTER 2

Eli jumped to his feet and stepped through the circle. Lissa followed and Kari went last, letting the invisible door close behind them before returning the stick to Eli.

On the other side of the door, the park looked almost the same. Almost. There was all the playground equipment and the grown-ups doing their grown-up things. But the grown-ups were made of scribbles of crayon, all except Eli's grandpa. *He* was completely gone.

"Come on!" Kari said and set off toward the playground. The equipment was bigger than it had been before. As they got closer, it seemed a lot bigger. They stood in front of a full-size castle with broken walls and a closed drawbridge.

"Hello!" called Lissa. "Can we come in?" A head looked over the broken wall, then vanished.

The drawbridge rattled down slowly. A lady in armor waited on the other side. She had a lance and a sad face.

"Mom!" Eli said. "I want to see my grandpa, please."

The knight shook her head. "You can't, Eli. He's locked inside a room in the castle and nobody has the key."

"We'll find the key!" Kari said boldly.

"If only you could," the knight said, and touched her hand to her forehead. "If you did, I would show you the room and you could speak with him again. But nobody can. It's impossible."

"We'll do it." Lissa's voice was firm.

The knight shrugged and went back inside the castle. Kari turned to Eli and her sister. "She could have given us a hint."

"We'll have to ask *her* instead," Lissa said. She looked up at the sky.

"Her?" Eli asked, looking confused.

"A good spirit who watches us sometimes," Lissa explained.

"She's our fairy godmother." Kari bounced on her feet. She kept hoping the good spirit would give her a fancy costume one day, but it hadn't happened yet.

Lissa shook her head. "Not a fairy. Something else." She raised her voice and sweetly called, "Good spirit, good spirit, can you hear us?"

Kari turned around and around, listening hard. Usually the good spirit talked to them at night, but sometimes they heard her when they needed advice during the day. But when another lady appeared in front of them, Kari was so surprised, she fell down. "Ouch!"

"Are you the good spirit?" asked Lissa.

The lady had a wreath of flowers in her dark hair and she wore a long blue princess dress. She smiled. "Today I'm your oracle, it seems."

As soon as the lady spoke, Kari bounced to her feet. She'd

never *seen* the good spirit before, but she recognized her voice. "Yay! I knew you'd help us. Do you know where we can find the key to unlock Eli's grandpa?"

The lady in blue spread her arms and closed her eyes. "The key has been broken into four crystal orbs and hidden in earth, wind, water, and fire! But if you are brave and wise and a good friend, then you can find it and achieve your goal." She opened one eye, peeking at them. "How does that sound?"

Lissa giggled. "Silly."

Eli said, "Scary! But if it will help my grandpa, I can do it!"

Kari threw her shoulders back. "Thank you very much!" The good spirit smiled, curtseyed, and faded away. Kari said, "Okay! Now that we have a prophecy, let's go, everybody!" She raced away from the castle to the exact middle of the playground, then had to stop and wait for the other two to catch up.

"Where are you going, Kari?" Lissa asked, exasperated.

"Earth, wind, water, fire!" repeated Kari. "Look at that desert! I'm sure one of the crystal orbs is in there!"

CHAPTER 3

The golden desert glittered in the distance. When Kari shaded her eyes she could just see a strange fortress on top of a steep dune.

Eli said uncertainly, "How would a key to my grandpa get all the way out there?"

"I don't know," Kari said. "Maybe it was stolen by harpies. It doesn't matter! We have to save him!" She set forward into the sandy wasteland and promptly tripped over a rock. "Ow!"

Lissa sighed and held out her hand. "You keep falling down. Hold my hand and I'll help."

"The oracle did say we had to be good friends," Eli added. He held out his hand, too.

Kari pouted. "I can do it on my own. Heroes need to be tough!"

Eli and Lissa looked at each other, then shrugged. Kari nodded and stomped ahead. At first it was hard to walk through the sand because her feet kept sinking. Her shoes filled up and she had to stop twice to empty them. The second time, Lissa said, "The ground changes ahead."

Kari had been so focused on the weird fortress on top of the hill that she hadn't noticed. But up ahead the ground was hard and dusty, with scattered, tough-looking plants. She frowned. "I thought deserts were sandy."

"Not all of them," said Eli. "I've heard stories." He walked past Kari, and she scrambled to catch up, making sure to avoid the spiky bushes.

"Look," called Lissa. She pointed at a helmet under one of the trees. "How sad."

Kari ventured over to it. It was round and smooth, except for a hole on one side. She picked it up and held out it out to Lissa.

Lissa shook her head. "I don't want to know."

"There's more over there," said Eli. He went off to one side and up a mound. Some small bits of metal clattered down the hill. "Look, something's buried."

Kari climbed up after him. The mound had thorny plants growing all over it, which scratched her bare legs. Eli stood beside a big tube sticking out of the mound, poking it. There was another helmet at his feet. On the far side of the mound were even more lost things: rifles and tires and backpacks, all in ugly shades of beige and tan.

Lissa said, "Do you think we should pick this stuff up and take it to the fortress? Maybe the grandpa lost it."

"Maybe it would help us find the key," said Kari doubtfully.

Eli chewed on a fingernail. "I don't know. It doesn't look like it was lost. It looks like it was left behind. Thrown away."

"Hidden," suggested Lissa, thumping on the big tube.

"I don't know how we'd carry it anyhow," finished Eli. "There's a lot."

"Oh, that's easy. We use this." Lissa patted the tube. "We just have to dig a little down to the hatch and once we get inside, it's easy."

Kari made a face. Lissa could say that because Kari would be doing all the work. "Fine, you two dig, and I'll pick stuff up from that field."

She carried over the ancient rifles and the straps and the boots and the backpacks and piled them beside Eli and Lissa, then sat and waited. They dug a hole with shovels, which were the first thing Kari had found. But once they clanged on the hatch, it was Kari's turn.

She leaned into the hole after they climbed out and touched the hatch. As soon as she did, it sprang open. Kari slid down into the cabin and into a seat. There was another seat further in so she squeezed through a narrow opening to the belly of the tank. As she did, she called, "Come on down, there's plenty of room."

The lower seat had what she was looking for: the various mechanical bits that would wake the metal beast up. She ran her hands over the board with all the dials. The others slid down after her, with all their loot. Once they were in, Kari gave the dashboard a shove.

It did its best to wake up, but it was still covered by a lot of earth. That was definitely a problem, no matter how much Lissa wanted to describe it as 'easy'.

The tube, which was actually a giant cannon, rattled and swiveled back and forth, loosening more dirt. But it wasn't enough. The treads of the tank turned and metal squealed and Kari got more and more frustrated.

"Can I just burn it all up?" she demanded.

"No!" Lissa shook her head violently. "We mustn't."

Eli held up the carved owl stick. "I know what to do!" He stood on the back of Lissa's seat and stuck his head out of the hatch, waving the wand. "We're going to rescue you, Grandpa! Come and help us!"

The owl on the wand flapped its wings once, twice, three times. Each flap made the wings grow bigger and bigger. Soon the flapping wings made a whirlwind around the little hill. Then Eli ducked back down. "Try driving now!"

Kari hit the dashboard with her palm, and the tank shifted gears. The hill shuddered around them, and the tank shifted gears again. Something groaned, and Kari clasped her hands together. "Hold on!"

There was a jolt and a jar. The whole tank wriggled. Then the hill came apart around them, and the tank rolled out into the sunshine.

"Yes!" crowed Kari. "Onward, to the fortress, Tankie!"

"It's not called Tankie," Lissa objected.

"It is for now!" Kari stared through the narrow window above the dashboard. The strange fortress on the high hill got closer and closer. After a moment the tank tilted back as it started climbing the hill. The weird fortress was round, with three triangle towers and a crooked door. Shadows moved on the towers

Kari grinned over her shoulder at the others, then flipped a switch on the dash. When she spoke, her voice echoed loudly over the desert. "We've come for the orb of Earth. Hand it over!"

"You cannot take it!" The voice from the tower was scratchy, like a monster who wasn't very good at talking.

Lissa popped her head up through the hatch. "I'm going to count to three, and then you're going to be sad! One!"

The shadows grew thicker around the front tower.

"Two!"

"I think they're planning something!" Eli said urgently.

"Three!"

A dark bubble grew around the top of the fortress. Lissa ducked down, slamming the hatch, and pushed the big FIRE button for the cannon. "Cover your ears!"

CHAPTER 4

There was a huge boom, and dust and black smoke obscured the viewports. When it finally settled, the whole fortress had collapsed into a pile of sand.

Kari laughed and patted Tankie's dashboard. "Good job! Now let's find that orb!" But Tankie didn't move. Lissa popped out of the hatch and said, "It's no good. There's goo all over the treads. Gumming everything up."

Eli climbed out after her. "But I think I see the orb!" He ran over to the ruins of the fortress and picked up a big, orange ball. "This has to be it!"

Kari patted the console of the tank for a while, trying to get it going again. Lissa leaned down and said, "Come on, Kari! It did what it was supposed to. And I bet if we can fix Eli's Grandpa, that will fix the tank too!"

Kari sighed. "Okay." She climbed out of the tank. Eli was cradling the orb, which had shrunk down to the size of a marble. "I guess we should work on getting the next one. Air, probably."

Lissa looked up into the sky. "That might be kind of... tough. Let's get out of this desert, first."

Kari started walking. And walking. And walking. "I hate getting out of the desert. It's so much slower than getting in. And we don't even know where to go."

Lissa said, "Eli, can your owl friend help us out again?"

Eli frowned and waved the owl wand. "Oh, owl of my grandpa. Where do we go next?"

Once again the owl's wings grew and flapped. Eli had to hold on with both hands as it dragged him along the ground.

"Let it go!" Lissa jumped up and down.

"I don't want to lose it!"

"Don't worry," Kari said. "We'll follow it."

Eli's grip loosened, and the owl yanked itself out of his hand and flew ahead, low to the ground. It was fast, but Kari was too. She set off after it, knowing that if she could keep the owl in sight, the others could catch up.

It led her out of the desert and onto a big field with dry, yellow-green grass. It flew and flew and she ran and ran, until suddenly the owl swooped upward and Kari realized there was something in their way. It was a sparkling blue wall, slanted. She skidded to a stop just before running into it.

A minute later, when Eli and Lissa ran up, Kari was still staring at the wall. "What is it, Lissa?"

The owl fluttered down and landed on Eli's hand again, hooting softly. He petted it. "It looks like ice."

Lissa put her hand on the smooth slope. "It's not cold." She looked up. "It's a mountain. I think we have to climb."

"The orb of wind must be at the top!" decided Kari. She threw herself at the shiny blue slope and started climbing it on her hands and knees. But she only made it up a few feet before she slid back down again.

"Come on, Lissa, push me!"

Lissa patted the side of the mountain and looked up at the high peak. "I don't think that's going to work."

"Hey, over here!" said Eli, walking along the base of the mountain. "There's steps."

Kari slid down a second time and went to go see. At first she couldn't even see what Eli was talking about. Then she saw the curves in the mountainside. "Those aren't really steps. Maybe scoops."

Eli shrugged, put the owl wand in his pocket, and started climbing. In only a minute, he was much higher than Kari had managed on her own. She called, "Hey, wait up! Come on, Lissa." She hesitated, then said, "You go first and I'll catch you if you fall."

Lissa said scornfully, "I'm not going to fall. You just hate being in the middle."

Kari shrugged and waited. Lissa stuck her tongue out and started climbing as well, and only then did Kari go up after.

They climbed for a long time. It seemed like days and days. Once Eli slipped, and Kari and Lissa both caught him, which was very heroic. Once Kari slipped too, but she caught herself. But Lissa didn't slip at all, just like she said.

After Kari slipped a second time, one of the adults looming at the edge of the world came over. It was Marley, her face resolving from the crayon scribbles that covered all the other adult faces.

"How are you guys doing?" she asked.

"We're playing," said Lissa, quickly, before Kari could tell her what they were really doing. "Everything's fine. We're having fun with Eli."

Marley looked at them as if she was suspicious of something. Kari gave her a big, bright smile. Marley frowned. "Well, be careful. It's not fun if somebody gets hurt."

"We know that, Marley," said Lissa in exasperation. "Go away please, so we can keep playing."

Marley hesitated, looked at Eli like she could see everything, then shook her head and went back to the edge of the world.

After that, they worked fast to get to the peak. Eli pulled himself onto the flattened top first and lay there panting as the sisters joined him. "Was that your mom?"

"Not yet," said Lissa, which just confused Eli.

"She's our babysitter. But we hope she'll be our mom someday," Kari explained. "Anyhow, where's the wind orb?" But there was nothing up there except a tube. "Oh no, another cannon?"

Lissa patted the tube. "I don't think so. I hear something...." She pressed her ear to the tube. "Voices. Like somebody's talking. Singing? I can't tell."

Kari stood up on the mountain peak and looked out over the rest of the world. "Well, if the orb isn't here, maybe we can get an idea of where else it could be. A good view."

"Maybe the voice will tell us where the orb is?" Eli suggested. "Let me listen."

Instead, Lissa looked down into the tube. "Oh. That's why I can't hear clearly. Something's blocking the tube."

"The orb!" said Kari, brightening. "Can you reach?" She tried to push Lissa aside.

Lissa pushed her back. "No. It's really far down."

"Maybe the owl can help again," suggested Eli. He fished the wand out of his pocket and waved it around. But Lissa caught his hand.

"Wait. If we loosen it, it will roll down the tube and get lost. Somebody has to go to the other end to pick it up."

"I see where to go!" Kari had spotted another tube just like this one, sticking out of the ground at the mountain's far side. "I'll do it!" Quick as a wink, she sat down and pushed herself over the edge of the mountain. "Woohoo!" she shouted as she slid all the way to the bottom.

It was over too soon. She hit the ground and rolled, which wasn't quite as much fun as sliding. Then Kari scrambled to her feet, ran to the tube she'd seen from above, and waved at the tiny figures far atop the mountain. "I'm ready!"

The tiny Eli waved his wand, and the owl's wings grew and grew once again. Even from the bottom of the mountain, Kari could feel the wind. At first nothing happened. Then there was a rattling sound and the whole tube shook until POP, a blue orb jumped out and into Kari's hands. As soon as she caught it, a flurry of voices surrounded her: a woman singing, a man chanting something, an old lady saying a lullaby, and a little boy that sounded like Eli saying, "One more, Grandpa!"

Eli and Lissa came sliding down the mountain, and Kari handed the boy the blue orb. "It was stuck with a whole bunch of voices. But they're free now, and we have the second orb!"

Eli looked at the orb for a minute, looking sad and serious. Then, just like the earth orb, it shrank down to a marble, and he put it in his pocket.

Lissa looked over at where Marley stood guarding the edge of the world. "We'd better hurry," she said uneasily. "I think we're running out of time."

CHAPTER 5

They ran across the big field until they found a dry stream bed. Eli said, "If we're looking for water, let's start here."

"We can follow it," Kari agreed. "It'll go somewhere eventually."

She was right. At first it was dry as summer, then the ground got damp, then muddy, and then they were splashing through puddles. After that, the puddles joined together until there was a stream flowing around their ankles.

"We have to keep going," Lissa said. "There's a *lot* of water at the end of the creek."

It rose to the middle of their shins. "We might have to swim," said Kari. Swimming was fun, but she was a little worried about

Eli. Sometimes kids drowned. That wouldn't happen to her and Kari, because Marley was their babysitter and they knew how to swim, but their uncle was pretty strict about them luring other kids into deep water.

She looked around. "Wait, no, we don't!" On the side of the creek was an old tire. "We can float!" All three of them gathered around the tire and pushed it hard, until it flipped end over end and into the rapidly flowing water.

"This is great!" said Eli, as they threw themselves aboard. "White water rafting! Let's make it spin!"

They didn't have to do much work. The stream broadened and got deeper, but it also got a whole lot faster, with big rocks that jutted up so that the water crashed and swirled everywhere. Spinning happened naturally. They got soaked, too. Around and around they went, leaning together to steer the tire around the rocks. Once Lissa almost fell off, but Eli grabbed her and pulled her back.

Then the river came up against a rock so big it couldn't go around. Instead it got bigger and quieter and wider, spilling out into a lake.

"Is this the place?" Eli asked. He fished his wand out of his pocket.

Lissa looked around as the tire drifted into the center of the water. "This isn't a good lake. It's sick."

Even Kari could see that. The water was murky and the shore of the lake was brown and stinky, not sandy or green. "The water's supposed to be flowing."

"Can we move the rock?" Eli waved his wand. The owl's wings flapped twice and then settled into place again.

"It's a really big rock," said Kari. It was more like a wall than a rock: big and grey and smooth, curving out like a full belly.

"Let's paddle to shore," said Lissa. "We can't do anything here."

They used their hands at first, until Kari slipped into the water and kicked, propelling the tire and the other two ahead of her like she was the motor on a motorboat. When she could reach the bottom, it was strange under her feet. Definitely not a healthy lake.

The others got out as the tire bumped the earth, and Lissa ran around the side of the lake until she reached some smaller stacked stones that formed the edge. They were as big around as Lissa's head, but they looked like gravel compared to the giant rock making the lake.

"Aha!" said Lissa. She pointed beyond the stacked stones. "I don't think we can move the big rock, but we can help the water go around."

Kari looked to where Lissa was pointing. There were a bunch of fallen logs all tumbled every which way, like an entire forest had been knocked over in a wind storm. "I don't see it."

Lissa clambered over to the closest fallen log and pushed it. It swiveled at the center, like the spinner in a game, thumping against the top of the stacked stones. It was hollow inside and the noise echoed weirdly.

"We just need to make a new path for the water to the other side of the big rock. Then we can move one of those little stones and the whole creek can flow again." She looked proud of herself.

Kari looked at the tangle of logs. Even if they all swiveled, it was still a giant mess.

"What if we just take the little stone out and let it go here?" asked Eli.

"It'll just make another pool," said Lissa. "It has to connect up with the rest of the river. I can do it. You two go explore and find the other side."

Kari said, "I can do that!" She ran into the mess of fallen logs, jumping and climbing her way through, until she heard Eli calling for her.

He wasn't as fast as she was. Really, he might as well have stayed behind with Lissa, except that Lissa was thinking hard and didn't want to be distracted. So, although she didn't want to, Kari waited until Eli was closer, then gave him instructions on the best way through the tangle.

"I think the other side of the river is over here," he said when he caught up. He pointed off to his right. "See, the rock turns into a big cliff. But getting there will be a big pain."

"We'll figure it out," Kari promised him, grinning. He was slow, but he did notice things, which Kari thought was awesome. "Then we can help Lissa show the logs the way."

Together they picked their way through the jumble of logs. It was slower with Eli, but some parts of it were easier, too, because they could help each other. It wasn't the same as doing things with her sister, but it occurred to Kari that maybe even normal boys could be more than just princes to be rescued.

Finally they reached the edge of the field of logs. Beyond was a rocky canyon. "Is this it?" Kari wondered.

"There's a little bit of water at the bottom." Eli squinted. "Maybe coming from under the big rock."

"Okay," said Kari. She turned to look back at what Lissa had accomplished.

She hadn't gotten very far, but what she'd done was easy to see. Where she'd been, the mess of logs had been cleaned up: either spun so they formed a single path, or carefully aligned out of the way. It was sort of like when their Uncle cleaned their bedroom, except Uncle Zach was a lot faster.

"I'll go back and show her the way," said Kari. "You climb up on something and stay here so we don't get lost."

"Should I send the owl?" Eli twisted his wand.

"Nah, keep it. We can do this!" Kari bounded back across the field to Lissa. "This way, Lissa."

"Oh, you're back. Hush, I'm thinking."

"Don't you wish Uncle Zach was here?"

Lissa glanced at her. "Silly. He wouldn't let us do this. Where's Eli?"

"Back at the riverbed. See? You have to steer toward him."

"Oh. Right," said Lissa. "Here, you go push those four logs so they're out of the way."

The twins worked together, Kari chattering and Lissa thinking, and slowly made their way over to Eli. As Lissa pushed the final log into place, Eli climbed down from it and said, "It's a road!"

"Yep," said Lissa happily. "Let's run back along it, and then we can free the river!"

They all climbed up. The logs had spun so easily that it should have wobbled when they walked, but it didn't, probably because of magic. It did make a great thumping sound as they ran back to the lake though.

"Everybody off!" said Lissa and shoved at the rock. It was a lot smaller than the giant stone dam but it was still really heavy. "Kari, help me."

Kari came over and leaned on the rock, too. It didn't move, even when Lissa whispered to it and Kari treated it like a stuck door.

"I guess it takes all three of us," said Eli, and squeezed in between them. He grabbed hold of the rock and said, "One, two, three, pull!"

CHAPTER 6

They all pulled together. The rock came out with a pop, they fell to the side, and the lake gushed into the path Lissa had made. All three of them were soaked by the spray.

"It looks like a water slide," said Kari wistfully, standing up again. "Do you think we could...?"

"Look!" said Lissa. The lake was draining like a bathtub, and something had been hidden under the water. At first it looked like a tree but then—

"Oh wow!" said Eli. "It's a sunken pirate ship!" He slid down the wet rocks to the shrinking edge of the lake. "No wonder the owl didn't lead us anywhere."

As soon as the deck of the ship appeared above the water, Eli set out wading across the remains of the lake. Kari and Lissa went after him.

"Should we let him go first?" Kari asked.

"He knows where he's going, and it's his grandpa," pointed out Lissa.

"I guess," said Kari.

Meanwhile, Eli jumped up and caught a ladder dangling from the deck. He went up. "We have to find the treasure chest. There's always a treasure chest."

"Are there any skeletons?" asked Lissa hopefully.

"No skeletons!" said Kari, in her best Marley voice. She didn't like skeletons the way Lissa did.

"I don't see any," Eli said. Lissa sighed, and the twins followed him up.

The ship was old and wet but not slimy or covered with seaweed. "Because the lake was sick, so nothing grew," explained Lissa. "Where's the chest?"

"Down here!" Eli called. His voice echoed from the darkness under the top deck. "But it's locked. And the wand isn't opening it."

Lissa smiled at Kari and Kari grinned back before running down the stairs. "I can do *this* part." The chest was big and old and bound with metal straps and a giant lock. Kari gave it a stern look, then touched the lock.

It sprang apart, and she flung the lid open. "There you go!"

A watery blue ball floated out of chest and into Eli's hand. "Yay!"

"Everybody, we have to get out of here!" Lissa shouted from above. "Hurry!"

The other two kids scrambled up the ladder as the ship started shaking around them.

"Without the lake the ship is falling apart!" gasped Lissa. "We need to run!"

The planks cracked apart beneath them. They hurried over to the ladder and scrambled down and back across the lake bed to their tire boat. Eli and Lissa started shoving the tire into the new path of the river while Kari watched the ship sadly. "I hoped we could sail it."

"We still have this. And you did want to go on a water slide," Eli said as the tire splashed down. "Quick, get on!"

Once everybody was on board, the tire started spinning its way down the river path. It wasn't as fast as a slide and it was a whole lot bumpier, but it was still kind of fun. Once they slid into the river, the journey got faster and faster until they were shooting along. Then, without warning, they shot out into the air as the river went over a little waterfall. Before they quite realized they were flying, they thumped into the water again. And this time they weren't on a little lake. This was the sea.

"Where do we go now?" Lissa twisted her hands together. "We have one more orb and not a lot of time."

"The owl will show us," said Eli confidently. He waved the wand and the wings burst from the end, bigger and stronger than ever. They flapped hard, propelling the tire forward, faster than they could paddle or Kari could kick.

"Is that a cloud?" Kari asked, shielding her eyes from the afternoon sun. "We're headed straight for it."

"It looks like smoke," said Lissa, biting her lip.

"It's a volcano," said Eli. "That's where we're going next."

Kari brightened. "Oh, okay." Eli gave her a funny look, but she ignored him. She wasn't supposed to play with fire but if they had to, she was looking forward to it.

The volcano was a black mountain on a black island with spots of green around the edges: big bushes and brightly colored flowers. Once the tire crunched against the shore, they could see that the ground was as hard and shiny as glass.

"But where do we go now?" said Eli nervously. "I don't want to get burned."

Lissa cocked her head, listening. "It's not in the fire," she said. "It's in the ashes."

Kari looked around. "Right! This way!" She led them over to the slope of the volcano. "Sometimes they burn through the side. See? Here's a little box." She reached into a square hole the size of a TV. "We just have to dig through the ashes."

"Kari Thorne, what in the world are you doing?" Marley's voice cracked like thunder from only a few feet away. Too close. Too real.

CHAPTER 7

Kari froze, afraid to look around, afraid to ruin it. She took a deep breath and fumbled in the ashes.

"Oh no," muttered Lissa. "Marley, listen—"

"How did the two of you manage to get so filthy, and while I was watching? And now you're playing in the barbecue?" Marley shook her head, her eyes flashing. "And getting your new friend involved?" Her voice gentled as she addressed Eli. "Kari and Lissa have to go home now. Do you want me to take you to your mom?"

Eli shook his head frantically, clutching his owl wand. Kari plunged both hands into the ash box and fumbled around desperately. She could have told Eli the wand wouldn't work on Marley, but she didn't want Marley to know what they were doing because then it would be ruined.

"Marley, we can't go yet," said Lissa. "We're not done playing. We have to finish."

Marley frowned, then looked at Kari again. "Come on, Kari. I'm going to have to give you a bath before dinner as it is."

"I can't find it," Kari whispered, on the edge of tears.

Lissa whispered back, "You talk to her," and bumped Kari aside with her hip. As soon as Kari pulled her hands from the box and moved between Lissa and Marley, Lissa started digging in the box herself.

"Lissa?" Marley looked confused. "What's going on?"

Kari took a deep breath and wiped her eyes. A little smile flickered across Marley's face and Kari tried to smile back. "We're playing a game, and we're almost done, Marley. We just need to do a couple more things and then we'll take Eli back to his mom. Please?" She opened herself up, trying to show Marley there was nothing to worry about. "Honest, we'll be done soon."

Marley softened. She glanced at her phone. Then she muttered, "All right, but I'm going to take a picture of you for next time I ask for a raise."

Kari didn't quite understand, but she obediently gave Marley a big smile for the camera on her phone.

When Marley was done taking the picture, she said, "You have ten minutes. Then no arguing."

Lissa caught Kari's eye and nodded. So Kari nodded at Marley. Then Eli said, "Thank you, Miss. They're being good friends."

Sometimes, Marley was like an ice cream cone on a hot day. When Eli thanked her, she melted. "I'm happy to hear that. Have fun, okay?" Then, slowly, looking at her phone and shaking her head, she went back to the edge of the world.

Lissa pulled her hands out of the ashes, whispering, "I found it." In her hand was a small, black rock.

Eli poked it. When nothing happened he asked, "Are you sure?"

"Yes. But you have to clean it somehow." Lissa gave Eli an expectant look. He banged it on the pavement, but nothing happened. Then he shrugged helplessly.

Kari said, "Let's take it to the castle and see if it will open the gate as it is."

They went back to the great castle in the center of the world, where the knight had first sent them on their mission. Once again, she emerged from the gate. "I'm sorry, children…."

"We found the orbs!" interrupted Kari. "Show her, Eli!"

Eli held out his hands, with the marbles piled in them. The black rock was hidden on the bottom. "See?"

The knight hesitated, then said, "Follow me." She led them under the big wooden gate, down a hall, and up some stairs to a high tower sealed by a big door. In the door were four depressions just the right size for marbles.

Kari nodded at Eli. He took a deep breath and stepped forward, putting the orbs in place.

Three of them fit perfectly, sticking in the depressions like they'd been glued in. But the black rock just fell onto the floor.

CHAPTER 8

Slowly, Eli picked the black stone up. "I don't know what to do."

Kari realized something. "It's all burned out. You have to light it again."

Lissa nodded. "Set it on fire."

"Give it some of *your* fire," corrected Kari.

Eli looked between the two of them, tears swimming in his eyes. Then he held the black chunk to his chest, hugging it like it was a doll. "Please, Grandpa. You don't know me anymore, you called me a brat and you threw your book at me. But I still love you. I want to see you again. I want you to see me."

His tears spilled over, leaving burning tracks in his dirty face, dripping onto the rock. When the tears touched the stone, it lit up, like somebody had struck a match in a dark room. The black crust around the rock fell away, leaving a brilliant, glowing orb.

Wiping his nose with the back of his hand, Eli put the final marble in place. The knight reached over their heads, and pushed the door open.

Inside, on a jewel-encrusted throne, an ancient king was sleeping. When they piled into the room, he jerked awake. He smiled when he saw Eli. "My boy. It's been a while. Come here and give me a hug."

Eli ran over and squeezed the old man. "Grandpa, we've saved you!"

The old man looked over at Kari and Lissa. "Oh, kids. Thank you for this chance. This dream. It can't last, but...." He stroked Eli's hair. "At least it makes parting easier. A proper farewell."

"Grandpa?" said Eli, lifting his head. "No!"

"Eli, this happens," said the old man gently. "I'll always be with you in your heart. You have to remember me like this, not the other way."

Irritated, Kari said, "Stop saying goodbye. We did save you. We did all the work to rescue a prince, and now you're saved."

The old man smiled sadly, looking at the two of them with clear, blue eyes. "Little ladies, I don't know what you are, but you've done a good thing, letting me be myself again for a few moments. Remember that."

"Stop it!" said Kari again.

"He *is* dying," said Lissa, subdued. "I can hear it." She glanced up at the stones of the tower and took Kari's hands. "But he doesn't have to."

The old man's eyes widened. "I'm ready to go, children. It's all right."

"No, it's not!" said Eli. "Stay!"

"Yeah," said Kari. "We saved you, so you stay with Eli."

She and Lissa squeezed each other's hands tightly. Then Kari reached out for Eli's hand, and Lissa reached back for the orbs on the door. Light rose around them, dazzling and wonderful and binding.

When it faded, they were standing on top of the big play structure in the middle of the playground. Marley was calling Kari and Lissa. Eli was holding his owl wand.

Lissa looked around. "You'd better go to your mom now." She pointed. Eli's mom was standing over his grandpa's wheelchair, her head down. The grandpa looked like he was sleeping still. The sisters knew better.

Eli blinked at them warily, then looked around at a world once again normal. But the wand in his hand flapped its wings, and he looked down at it. "You did something…? I can hear him. In the wand."

"Give your mom lots of hugs," urged Kari. "She'll be sad. You have to hug them all you can."

Eli's fingers tightened on the wand. "Thanks." He slid down the slide and ran toward his mom, holding the wand above him. The wings flapped once more, then folded away.

Lissa and Kari went down the slide too. "That was nice," said Kari.

"He'll have his grandpa forever now. Not just a remembory," Lissa said.

"We had fun, Marley!" Kari added, as they got to their babysitter.

"Time for dinner!" said Marley. "But baths first. Let's go home."

BRANWYN AND THE STONE

The black gemstone in the clamp on her worktable worried Branwyn, although she'd never admit it, even to her friends. It was none of their business.

The previous owner would have sensed her concern, though. That was part of what worried her. He would have laughed and used it against her.

It looked like the sort of black diamond that was so large it had to be artificial. And it was. At least, it wasn't just a diamond. There was a nearly microscopic assemblage of bars and discs within the stone, and it had a will of its own. It was, in fact, a fragment of a celestial Machine, stolen from Heaven so that a monster could use it as a weapon.

She'd worked with Machine fragments before, even worked one into a weapon. Machine fragments always liked her, and they were always eager to find a way to be of use. This one was different, though.

Once again, Branwyn touched the stone with one finger. It whispered to her in the language of promises. Part of her understood: the part of her that had stood at a crossroads and said *not this, not now* and would have died to hold that line.

All things considered, she'd rather not die over this stone. But she couldn't easily translate the language of promises into anything as complicated and verbal as English, nor translate her will into something the stone would understand. Unlike all the other fragments she'd worked with, which had been kept as decoration or artifacts, this one *had* a purpose already. And it was not her friend, no, not that, although it was as glad to interact with her as any of the previous fragments had been.

She kept one finger on the stone and put her other hand on the long hammer she'd made. There was a socket that fit the stone perfectly, but she wanted to do more than *set* the stone. She wanted to merge the two: granting the stone's awareness and hyper-real strength to the whole hammer. That was a hard task, a new task, and she was still feeling her way along how possible it really was.

The energy of the stone ran through her and met the smooth lines of the hammer in the forge of her soul. In that metaphysical workplace, she could do amazing things with the help of a fragment like the stone.

At the very least, she could wake up the hammer, as she'd woken up other mundane objects before. The stone would be happy to help by lending the divine spark required. But it wanted a say in what the hammer would become. It wanted the hammer to be like itself: a weapon, not just a tool.

Branwyn broke the connection between the stone and the hammer, scowling, and touched the stone with both hands. Maybe this time—

No.

The promise that the monster's rage had embedded deep within the stone rose to the surface, sweeping over her once again. She'd been angry in her life, oh yes, sometimes so angry that there was nothing else left of her. It exhilarated her, purified her, gave her unshakeable focus.

This rage wasn't like that.

It was the tainted, hurting rage of a soul betrayed and determined to lash out. It was ugly and twisted and jagged, a rage that tore ravines into her heart. And it was beyond old, so ancient that it had been transmuted from tar to diamond. The pain had become comfortable, the rage normal, and the savage pleasure of violent victory the only source of joy.

The stone promised her that she too would be a weapon. It promised her she would enjoy it. Were there not many in the world who needed to be punished? Those who hurt the weak and twisted the innocent? Those who used their strength for nothing other than destruction? The heartlessly greedy? The thoughtlessly cruel? Those who thought they were monarchs of the world, who had forgotten their original role as servants?

The promises changed, becoming stranger, and then all at once, Branwyn was swept into one of her own memories: her little brother Howl, nine years old at the time, being pushed and taunted on a playground by kids both older and younger than him. She'd climbed the fence and flung herself into the crowd: stomping, kicking, pulling hair, and shoving. One of the biggest boys had tried to catch her and hold her until she'd calmed down, and she'd bitten him so hard he'd needed stitches.

That had been the first time she'd been taken into police custody.

And it hadn't mattered. Howl had to go school with some of those kids, and they only became more subtle in their cruelty. He hid it from her and the rest of the family, but she knew and there was nothing she could do about it.

You didn't punish them enough, whispered the stone, in a voice too familiar, and she knew she was too deep in, if she could understand its sentiments as words. *We have to find their weakness, and squeeze it until they become different people to escape the pain. Smarter people. Better people. People who know not to make you angry.*

Gasping, Branwyn pushed the stone in its swivel clamp out

of her reach, rolling her chair away from the worktable. Sweat beaded her forehead and she could taste blood, just like she had when she'd bitten that boy.

It would be so easy to make it a weapon. Hammers were tools, yes, but they were weapons, too. She looked at how big she'd made her hammer: the long handle, the spiked head. It wasn't a delicate instrument. If she dared call it a tool, she ought to recognize that it was a tool of war.

She hefted the hammer, felt its weight, felt the steel of it. The fog of the black diamond's perspective faded. Big hammers were tools too: tools for building railroads, tools for building fences. Tools for, yes, occasionally guarding them. A tool could do many tasks; that was the *point* of a tool. Her hammer wasn't for punishing the guilty.

Branwyn went to the electric kettle on the other side of the room, where she started brewing herself a mug of tea. She stared at the diamond the entire time, and by the time she was halfway through the hot drink she felt fortified enough to wade back into the battle.

The monster had touched the black diamond, carried it close. And it was a peculiar feature of Machine fragments that when creatures of celestial origin touched them, the Machine absorbed the essence of the celestial. Branwyn had heard that when a Machine sword killed a celestial, they didn't reincarnate because the sword had absorbed everything that *could* reincarnate. Machine weapons ate celestial souls.

The monster had been hale right up until Branwyn had taken the black diamond from him, but it was clear *something* of his nature had been absorbed by the black diamond. Maybe the two of them were weapons together.

Possibly the right thing to do was to chuck the diamond into the ocean.

But that would be *losing*. Branwyn didn't like to lose. So she finished her tea and strode back over and placed both hands firmly on the stone.

This time she was prepared for the wave that tried to knock her off balance. "Railroads," she said firmly. "Fences. Protection. Tools. You can be useful, not just dangerous."

There's no point in being useful, it whispered. *There's only punishment. Vengeance.*

"The future needs tools, not weapons," argued Branwyn. "Weapons go looking for fights."

So do you, purred the black diamond.

Branwyn scowled. It was too much like its previous owner. She wanted to pick it up and bash it into the table until it stopped being so annoying.

Instead she took a deep breath and said, "I only look for fights that need to be fought. I'd rather build something that works than destroy something."

Things need to be destroyed, though.

And on the heels of the stone's words came her own voice in the back of her head, *I don't look for fights. I'd be happy to not fight if they'd just let me win....*

Flushing, Branwyn pulled her hands away, but the stone caught her thought anyhow, and the web of energy from the stone stayed tangled around her. *You need a weapon. They stop fighting if you have a powerful enough weapon.*

"A tool," said Branwyn and her voice sounded weak and reedy, even to herself. "Change the world. Build the world. We'll bring energy from rocks and life from fire."

You'll fight. You'll destroy. You'll win. You won't be able to stop yourself.

Branwyn unscrewed the clamp holding the black diamond and let it drop into her hand. She took up the hammer and brought the stone close to the socket, concentrating on the soul forge again. With effort, she could mold not just the substance but the very *nature* of Machine fragments. This one was resistant rather than amenable, but that would only make the task harder, not impossible.

"I don't have to use you as a weapon." She stared hard at the magical structure of the hammer and the fragment. "I can make you what I want you to be, whether or not you agree."

She thought she heard the monster laugh, and froze. He shouldn't be anywhere near her, not now, not after what had happened after she'd finished her last project. They'd told her he'd probably be gone for *months*.

A knock came, for the second time. The realization it was the *second* knock jerked Branwyn out of her reverie and brought her back to the mundane world. The door to her studio opened, and Branwyn's grandmother Tara said crisply, "Time for lunch, Branwyn."

Tara had never been a tall woman and age had made her smaller. She had short, immaculately styled silver hair, and wore nice slacks and a classy teal blouse that made her eyes glow. She was, most recently, a writer, and while she normally lived with Branwyn's mother and siblings, she'd been away from home on a sabbatical for weeks. Her extended trip wasn't over, but she'd been passing through Pasadena on her way to a conference and made time to check in on the family she normally ruled as undisputed matriarch.

Branwyn exhaled in a rush, put the stone and the hammer down, and rose to her feet. "Grandma. I'm sorry, I was in the middle of something."

"Yes, dear, I know. You always are when you miss a knock," said Tara, her eyes glinting as she looked over Branwyn's worktable. "My, what a large hammer that is. Planning to knock some sense into people?"

Branwyn flushed and grabbed her backpack. "Let's go."

It was a lovely day. They went to a food truck specializing in tacos that parked nearby on Wednesdays. As they waited in line, Tara said pleasantly, "Holly tells me you've gotten yourself *involved* in something again, dear. Something unusual, even for you."

Moodily, Branwyn said, "It's mostly good. I'm pretty sure I saved Penny's life. And stopped something bad from happening in the process. Besides," she added with a touch of irritation, "I'm hardly the only one in the family. Have you heard Jaimie's new song?"

"Mmm. And seen the video. Videos. But I had breakfast with Jaimie and Holly *hours* ago. Now I am with you. So. You are getting into trouble. What is your goal?" Tara was a veteran of many civil rights campaigns, and it showed in the way she'd always cut straight to the *purpose* of any fracas Branwyn waded into. She'd never allowed Branwyn to simply go along with the flow, oh no. She could join the crowd, sing the chant, write the letters, but she always, always had to have a concrete goal she was reaching for. And if Branwyn did, Tara would always post the bail.

"Educating myself. Self-improvement. You've seen some of the faerie videos, Grandma. We have to find a way to deal with how everything's going to change. Already changing. I've got a lead, I've learned some things, and I'm going to use them."

"And how does the large hammer fit in?" When Branwyn didn't answer right away, Tara added, "I felt something strange in your studio, Branwyn. You know I wouldn't say that lightly. But it isn't the first time in the last few weeks, so I'm inclined to pay attention. Be careful with it."

The taco line shuffled forward. Branwyn ran her fingers through her hair. "The hammer is just a hammer right now. I'd like it to be more, but… not a weapon, Grandma. I don't want to make a weapon, not this time, and the stone I'm working with wants so very much to be a weapon. To make other weapons" She twisted her hair until it hurt, then shook her hands out.

"Mph," said Tara. "And your goal is educating yourself, you say? Or is it using things you've already learned? You're not being truthful, dear."

"I want to win against the stone," Branwyn admitted. "Not winning might be... expensive." She didn't say that losing to the stone might cost her some of her identity, but that was what she was afraid of.

It was their turn to order and then wait for the food. Tara was quiet, only offering a few observations on their surroundings, and Branwyn's thoughts circled round and round the hammer and the stone. After they both got their plate of vegetarian street tacos and some of the delicious lime tortilla chips produced by the truck, they went to sit on a bench.

After a few bites, Tara suggested, "This stone. You could always walk away from the fight. Really walk away, not just take a lunch break. Unless the stone in question is going to chase you down."

Branwyn stopped, her taco halfway to her mouth. "Grandma," she said in shock. "You never walk away from fights. You've been part of so many. You and Great-Grandma both. You had goals and you went for them."

Tara snorted, then took a delicate bite of her taco. "Don't be a child, Branwyn. When was there ever any point to destroying ourselves throwing everything at a brick wall?"

"But—" began Branwyn, then didn't know what to say. "I've scaled some pretty impressive walls," she finally managed. "So have you."

"And do you think, oh heart of my heart, that the battles my mother and I fought started with us? No, you know better. You took all those classes in college." She placidly took another bite of her taco. "Sometimes the wall is just too high. Wasting yourself against it steals your power. You end up silenced, in an institution."

"But you don't *walk away*," argued Branwyn, still astonished.

Tara lowered her taco and gave Branwyn a long look. "There are always other battles. Life goes on, Branwyn. It's important that life goes on. It gives you the energy to walk back up to the wall sometimes and kick it a few times. Or cry on it, if the moment takes you. Either way, you last longer."

"So does the wall," muttered Branwyn. "Nobody should have to cry."

"Tears dissolve stone. We're women, Branwyn. We don't usually win brute contests of strength, but there are always other ways for the patient. Are you going to eat your lunch, or should I give it to somebody who will appreciate it?"

Branwyn stuck her lip out, then stuffed half the taco in her mouth. "I hate hearing you say 'We're women,' in that way."

"Don't talk with your mouth full. And I've worked hard so that you wouldn't have to fight the same battles. So that you wouldn't ever find yourself in a position where you think of being a woman as a weakness." Tara shrugged gracefully. "But here I find you throwing yourself into battle against something that feels as if it will swallow you whole. Against something you can walk away from."

"I *want* to win," Branwyn repeated. It would feel so *good* to win, to make the black diamond bend to her will and behave the way she wanted it to be.

Tara pilfered one of Branwyn's chips and crumbled it to feed to some curious crows. "You know yourself best." The way she took her attention off Branwyn made her feel like she'd been switched off, and Branwyn knew from long experience that the conversation was over. She tried to turn it to other directions, and Tara went along with her for the rest of their lunch. But she couldn't stop thinking about what Tara had said, couldn't let go of the shock of it.

And the worst part was the way her grandmother had ended the discussion. She'd done that over and over again while Branwyn was growing up, and it had become not just an indication of the close of conversation but a promised I Told You So. *You will understand later.*

It made Branwyn grumpy, but she did her best to manage it until she parted with Tara. Her grandmother kissed her cheek, hesitated, and then said, "Do you want me to stay with you while you throw yourself at the wall again? I really didn't like the way I felt in your workshop. It's not good."

Branwyn furrowed her brow. "You think I'll go right back to it? After your lecture?"

Tara smiled faintly. "Shall I stay? I might be able to pull you out if you get in over your head."

Branwyn made a face. "You have a plane to catch. I'll be fine."

Her eyes glinted again, as if Tara didn't quite want to leave, but she pulled away. "Very well. Good luck."

Once she was gone, Branwyn walked back to her studio thoughtfully. It was odd that her grandmother would offer to stay and help. Usually once she dropped the topic, she didn't mention it again until Branwyn did. That she thought it was worth bringing up again was worrying. Did she doubt her own arguments, or was she that worried about the stone?

In her studio, she looked at the stone, resting innocently on the work table as if it wasn't much of anything at all. The hammer really did look more *interesting* than the black diamond. It was a good piece of work. It drew the eye.

She put her finger on the stone and the awareness within it leapt to life, eager to once again sing to her of retribution and victory.

Branwyn remembered Tara's faint smile, remembered Tara arguing with her all through her childhood: arguing, then turning away and giving her words a chance to eat away at Branwyn's conviction.

She stood stock still, letting the memories wash over her. Then she laughed and turned away from the stone to walk back out of the studio. The black diamond was happy to see her, and that was a start. The rest would come, with patience and slow work, as long as she endured.

ETIQUETTE OF EXILES

When they released Penny from the hospital after the angel consumed her soul, she had a celebratory brunch with her family and friends. And then she went home, to her pretty little Craftsman house, where she lived all alone.

Her mother didn't want to leave her there, not so soon after she'd recovered. But Penny stood firm against the concern of her best friends and smoothed the wavy blue skirt her mother had brought her as a get-well gift. Today, Smile Girl could only smile so much. Too much had changed, within and without.

Once the door closed and Penny was left alone, she sat on the couch and stared into the blankness of the turned-off television. The paraphernalia of all her projects surrounded her: neat shelves stacked with books and paper, markers and pens, but they didn't offer her the same comfort they once had.

Before Branwyn had woken her at the hospital, Penny's last waking memory was of kneeling, surrounded by fire. She'd looked at a reflection of herself torn to pieces, screamed, and fallen to nightmares. Before that, she'd been dreaming of being cradled in *his* arms, safe and warm and beloved.

He was gone now, they told her. 'Gone,' the same way a dead fish flushed away was 'gone.'

She was safe from him, they promised

He'd almost destroyed her soul, they said.

She missed him so much, this angel who had used her as a chess piece and whispered to her of warmth.

Penny felt complete when he visited her dreams and like a perfect creature when he'd stepped into her mind. When he'd been burning away her soul, all she'd cared about was being with him forever.

Branwyn had saved her with a construction made from parts of a celestial machine, used it to give her a prosthetic soul. It was *nothing* like the peace of an angel's embrace. Lightning tickled her dreams. She heard whispers she couldn't quite understand, reminding her of secrets she'd never learned. Her friends and family blurred with colorful auras, and Marley *sparkled*. It was proof of just how much she'd changed.

They'd all three changed in the short time she'd been asleep: she, Branwyn, and Marley. But Penny hadn't asked to change, not the way they'd changed her. Not even the way he'd changed her either, not really.

Yet all this had come upon her, and it was far too late to go back again.

For weeks, somebody came to see her every day: Branwyn or Marley. Her parents. Other friends. Branwyn's mother, once. A reporter once. Only once. Penny smiled when she was supposed to, said what didn't matter. But she wasn't who she had been, and she couldn't convince those who knew her best otherwise. Her smiles weren't as easy, and she was so often distracted by what nobody else could see.

Once, at lunch with Marley and her mother, she saw a black bird on the back of Marley's chair, right inside the nice restaurant. It was strange and roused her to distant curiosity. She asked, "What is that bird doing on your chair?"

Marley frowned and looked over her shoulder, then shook her head. "What bird?"

Her mother looked at Penny with worried eyes. "I'm sure it's nothing. Branwyn and the doctors said there would be some… adjustment."

That was the only time Penny mentioned the odd things she saw. And she saw so *many* unexpected things now: the emerald serpents in her mother's hair, the blood smeared on Branwyn's face, and the stain on Branwyn's collarbone. A child down the street with wheels instead of feet.

Once, she saw a naked pixie flitting overhead and was shocked when her mother said scornfully, "These newcomers, they ought to learn proper respect. Wings are no excuse for not wearing clothing when everybody else is clothed."

Because the faeries were real, not figments of 'adjustment.' They'd come when her angel had gone, then gained ground when Branwyn's stepfather recorded a song. And what point was there in trying to make sense of what she saw, when faeries returned to the world because of a song? The universe no longer followed the rules she knew.

It didn't matter anyhow. When she was on the edge of sleep she could feel her prosthetic soul rubbing against the ragged edges left behind by her angel. She wasn't part of the world anymore, and she could never forget it. Even when she slept, the dreams that came were of distant, beautiful places that made her feel uncomfortable and lonely. During the day, she played idly with paper and markers, trying to recapture the pleasure she'd once felt while sketching clothes and coloring pictures. Instead, she drew a poorly drawn picture of a black bird, a child with wheels, and other waking visions. She threw them all away.

One day, her mother called her. "Have you been thinking about it? I really would like you to try this group, Penny." Her mother was using her bossy voice. "The one Marley found? It looks very promising. They are invested in helping people in your situation.

You see, the world adapts," Viviana added with a happy lilt.

"Which situation?" wondered Penny. The situation where she was some kind of metaphysical cyborg? Or the situation where she saw things nobody else saw?

Viviana paused, then said carefully, "It is a group for others who have had… dangerous encounters with the newcomers. Encounters they can't move past. And you've been moping, my darling. I think perhaps you are heartbroken. It would do you good to not be so alone."

Ah. Her mother meant the situation where somebody had almost destroyed her soul, and she still couldn't stop thinking about him. Viviana had worked out most of the truth about what happened to her with shocking ease, as soon as the first faerie sightings made it to the news. Marley had confessed the rest.

I'm always alone, Penny didn't say to her mother, because even now, she wasn't cruel. There wasn't even any point in arguing. It didn't really matter very much one way or another, and if that was true, why not yield?

"All right. I'll check it out."

The Clear Horizons support group met once a week, in a classroom in the local university's physics building. Both Marley and her mother emailed her directions, while Branwyn took her shopping the morning before.

In the midst of trying on cute batik patchwork skirts, Branwyn said abruptly, "Are you angry that I saved you?"

Penny furrowed her brow, staring at the mirror. Caterpillars crawled on both of herself and her friend, but only in the reflection. "No, of course not."

Branwyn scowled the way she always did when she was annoyed, so Penny tried a wry smile in return. It didn't seem to fly.

"Don't give me that, Penny. I saw what you dreamt about when I fixed you. And now—" Branwyn stopped herself, biting her lip.

"Marley is worried you'll fade away."

Penny searched for something reassuring to say. "I'm not sure I can now?" That apparently wasn't quite it, judging from the expression on Branwyn's face. "I'd never hurt people like that."

"But you miss him. You miss him more than anything." Branwyn's voice was raw as she added, "You wanted so badly to be with him."

Penny shrugged. "That's why I'm going to this meeting later today, right?"

Branwyn didn't push further. That was good. Penny had trouble when her friends pushed her these days. She couldn't cope, and if they pushed too hard, she'd just go home, turn off her phone, and lay in her bed to wait for her equilibrium to return. That was upsetting for everybody.

They parted ways. Branwyn had a project she was working on again, and Penny had a late lunch by herself. She watched people: watched them laugh and argue, watched how they strolled or stalked down the street. She liked people, even when they had six-legged dogs frisking around their ankles or vines twining their arms or seemed to be made of stone. She drew a rainbow on her napkin with the pens she always carried in her purse. People could be so clever and amazing. So strong, so unwilling to be defeated.

Maybe that wasn't always a good thing.

"And aren't you beautiful, here in the flesh?" came a man's voice. Penny looked away from the sidewalk to see that somebody had appeared in the other chair. She hadn't heard him show up or sit down and she frowned.

He sprawled like he'd been relaxing there for a while. His hair was black with orange at the tips, and his words had a light Australian accent. He wore expensive grey shoes, charcoal slacks, and a burgundy jacket. And he wasn't human. She could see that straight away. He didn't have any of the fuzzy light around him that humans had. There was a glint above his head, but other than that, he looked as vivid and real as everybody had looked, before her angel had damaged her soul.

"Can I help you with something?" Penny inquired politely. If it had been a human man, she would have just assumed he was hitting on her. But it seemed like anybody supernatural had something else on their minds.

"Yes, absolutely," he responded. His twinkling eyes were a bright, intense blue. "Fall madly in love with me? That would make this much easier."

"I don't think so." Penny's heart twinged. "I'm not really in a falling-in-love place right now, and you're not my type anyhow."

"Depends on how you look at it, doesn't it?" He grinned. "Sure, I'm not all noble, righteous, and misguided, but I *am* immortal, and I can certainly take all your problems away."

"Who are you?" asked Penny, curiosity overtaking a dull, distant surprise.

"Call me Blaze. I know who *you* are, Penny Karzan."

"And are you one of the—" she couldn't bring herself to say 'faerie,' because it sounded so strange on her tongue, "—one of the newcomers? From the other world?"

He twisted his hand in a way that conveyed the essence of a bow. "I am. I have the honor to serve the Duchy of Neverbank and its two most splendid Queens."

"Two Queens. My goodness," said Penny blankly.

He lowered his voice conspiratorially, "All of the Marches and Duchies have two Queens. It isn't always as romantic as it sounds."

"How sad," Penny murmured. "What did you actually want, sitting down at my table as you have? You may not be aware, being from a foreign place, but that's actually rather rude here."

"I already said," he responded happily. "I'd like you to fall madly in love with me. That would make it so much easier to steal you away to Fairyland."

He had an easy, friendly grin, with a thin, expressive mouth. She would have gone on a date with him in a heartbeat, back in the old days, just for the fun of it.

Instead, she narrowed her eyes. "This is about my soul, isn't it? It's not *me* you want to steal. Branwyn told me your people wanted the device she made to cure me. There was something about a door…."

That expressive mouth pulled to one side. "You have many attractions, it's true. Your soul is unique and would adorn the court of any Queen. But it's not just your soul. I did mention you were beautiful, didn't I?"

"Yes. Well, I'm not going to fall in love with you, so you might as well go away," Penny informed him. She felt a shudder in her soul, as if a nearby door had clanged shut. Blaze's eyes widened, and then he vanished, literally into thin air.

Penny sat back, startled. She hadn't expected him to obey her so directly, and almost as soon as he was gone, she wished she hadn't sent him off so abruptly. It had been rude, which she only liked to be after careful consideration. But after a while her thoughts wandered away, back to her angel, and she all but forgot the encounter.

The meeting with the Clear Horizons support group was in the evening. She'd refused all the offers to take her there and tried to discourage them from calling her later to check that she'd gone. She would go. She didn't think it would be any use. But yielding was easiest, and she liked people. She could simply watch these people and see what beauties they had.

The building only had a few scattered lights on. She easily found the classroom and peeked in. There were chairs arranged in a circle and only a few people sitting in them: a handful of young women, an older man in expensive slacks, and a younger man in new jeans with a university tee shirt. All of them had the blurs and crawling symbology she associated with humans. Everybody looked at her when she opened the door, and then the younger man sprang to his feet.

"Come in, come in. You're Penny, right? I'm Robert, the group's convener. Take a seat. We're just going through introductions."

Penny took a seat and listened as the circle of introductions completed, then introduced herself briefly, without giving any of her background. After everybody had a chance to state their name and, if they wanted, why they'd come to the group, Robert started talking about the origins of the group. His skin shimmered with sand that fell away and reformed as he moved, which was very distracting. But she picked up that they'd only had a couple of meetings so far.

It made sense; the faeries hadn't been around for very long. There were, Robert explained, many parties interested in those who had been emotionally victimized by the faeries. It represented an interesting field of study, due to the nature of the faeries. And the treatment was very promising.

By the time Robert said to Penny, "We do hope that you'll fill out some surveys about your recovery and your thoughts on the group," Penny thought he had been talking rather a lot for the facilitator in a support group. But nobody else seemed eager to talk. Maybe with a new group it look time for everybody to relax, and he was obligated to fill the time with chatter about university projects, government funding, and stories he'd read in the news about faerie sightings.

But eventually, in the second half of the hour, he quieted down. There was a long moment of silence, and then somebody bowed to the pressure to talk.

"I'm Jenzie," murmured a young, heavyset woman with thin,

pale hair and a printed sweatshirt. Lavender spirals literally crawled up her arms, and Penny wondered if they were some new magic effect or another vision. "I keep thinking about what he offered me." She held out her hand. It looked much older than her face, with knobby knuckles and heavy skin. "A way to get away from all the pain."

"Think about what brought you here," urged Robert. "Think about what made you refuse and decide to stay you. Think about your treatment."

Jenzie shook her head slowly. "Maybe I was just scared. Maybe what he offers is right."

"It's not right," said another woman, dark-skinned and dark-eyed, with a sleeping baby in a wrap on her chest. Something radiant moved under her skin, swirling over her legs and up her torso. "We're just trophies to them. They get inside our heads and make us think what they want, they take advantage of us, and it's not right."

"He said he wanted to save me," said Jenzie doubtfully.

"No he don't," said the second woman scornfully. "He wanted a new plaything."

Jenzie sighed and lowered her gaze. The older man (hair of metallic gold over his own greying cut) started talking about his own history, but Penny found herself looking at the women instead of listening, wondering if they felt what she felt. Wondering if it was possible that they understood. But they'd rejected offers. They were trying to escape from their supernatural lovers. The only reason she wasn't with her beloved angel was because he had all but died.

No, she didn't belong here.

The meeting concluded with a poor attempt at a rousing speech from Robert and an invitation to schedule their treatments online. As everybody was moving off, the facilitator caught Penny's attention.

"If you have a few moments, I'd love for you to fill out this survey. No identifiable information, but it would be a great help for us in customizing the program for the unique situations you're all dealing with."

Penny wasn't inclined to return, but it seemed like the least she could do. So he led her to a desk in the back of the classroom and gave her the form. It was a simple thing where she rated her feelings and opinions on various topics on a scale of one to five, and once again, reading the slant of the questions, she felt out of place.

While she went through the form, Robert put on a pair of amber-tinted glasses and inspected her, making notes of his own. When he met her curious gaze he said, "There's so much to learn. These are a recent—well, recently dug up—innovation." He tapped the frame of the glasses. Other than the color, they looked pretty ordinary to Penny. "They let us visually assess the faerie influence on a person."

"And what do you see on me?" asked Penny, more to find out if he was pretending than because she was really curious.

"Oh, you're totally different from everybody else. That's one reason I'm so glad you decided to join us. You've got something strange going on. Strange, yet familiar…. But it seems stable. Very promising." As he reached up to take the lenses off, a bit of light flashed against the glass and she realized his eyes were different behind the lens. Windows, she realized, windows to something within. Before she could see what, the lenses were being folded away.

"I hope you'll continue to attend?"

"I'll think about it," Penny said vaguely. As his face fell, she added, "I think you're doing good work here. My problems aren't quite the same, though."

He got a faraway look on his face. "Hard to tell that from one visit. I'll hope we see you next week."

Penny went home and sent texts to both Marley and her mother, assuring them that she'd attended the meeting and it was very nice. Then she curled up on her bed, pulling her covers high, and let herself drift into a daydream.

In her dream, Ettoriel hadn't died, been erased, or whatever dire thing had happened when he'd faced down Marley. He'd lost all his power and been banished to Earth, an ordinary human. He was somewhere in LA still, lost and in need of her love. And when she found him and provided that love, he once again held her close and she felt like she was exactly where she belonged.

She woke up to a noise in her room. Her light was still on so it was easy to see what had caused it: Blaze sat in a chair across her bed, little metal polyhedrons spinning in his palm. He wore artfully ragged jeans and a plain white tee shirt, and his hair was half orange and half black.

"What—?" she began, then stopped, trying to shake the cobwebs out of her brain.

"You don't undress to sleep?" he inquired, his eyes on his spinning toys.

"Maybe I was expecting you," she said tartly. She smoothed her wrinkled skirt and swung her legs off the bed.

He looked up and quirked a smile. "I don't think so."

"Well, I certainly will be in the future, Mr. Rude. What are you doing here? I thought I told you to go away."

"It wore off," he said casually. "And I do have a job to do."

"Well, this is not how you do it, whatever it is. You do not sit at people's tables and you do not invade their homes. That means you don't come in at all unless you're invited, since you seem hazy on the idea." He opened his mouth to respond and she didn't let him. "You don't grab them. You also don't kiss them or buy them expensive gifts. That's *also* unless invited or you have a close *reciprocal* relationship. Have some manners, please." By the time she was done with the little lecture, she felt much better.

He looked at her for a long moment. Softly, he said, "You should tell me to go away again. It's bad that you haven't yet."

It was, Penny realized. She ought to have screamed, called the police, demanded the Stranger leave her room at once. Instead she'd lectured him and smoothed her skirt, as if her appearance mattered. "Get out. Go away," she said automatically.

The door in her soul slammed closed, and Blaze vanished.

Penny sat on her bed for a while, thinking about Blaze's appearances and disappearances. Then she called Branwyn.

It rang a few times before Branwyn picked up. She sounded irritated. It was, Penny realized, 2:38 AM, and she began with, "Oh my God, I didn't even look at the clock before calling—"

"I was working," said Branwyn. "Don't worry about it. What's going on?"

Penny explained about Blaze's visits and the way he vanished when she told him to go away. "The weirdest part is the way I can *feel* him leaving. Like a door is slamming."

"Huh," said Branwyn. "That's... interesting. I guess your soul is still a key in some way. That would explain why they're harassing you."

"What can I do about it?"

"Keep telling him to go away?" Branwyn suggested. "If he doesn't get the hint, we can always progress to more drastic steps. I'm working on something right now— no, actually, I'm not. Not a weapon. But we can come up with something."

"If he wants my soul as a key, why doesn't he just kill me and liberate it?" asked Penny, surprised by the bitterness in her own voice.

"Maybe he can't? Maybe it wouldn't do any good. Or maybe," Branwyn finished, as if conceding an unwelcome possibility,

"Maybe he's just playing with you because that's more fun. If you want, you could go to our apartment. Marley should be there and she could keep you safe until we sort this out."

"No," said Penny. "I'll take care of myself. Thank you, Branwyn. Get some sleep, all right?"

She hung up and sat back on her bed again, staring at the place where Blaze had sat. After a while, she found herself half-asleep, pretending it was Ettoriel who had sat there instead. When she realized that, she roused herself just enough to put herself to bed properly, and fell into dreams of fire and broken mirrors.

Blaze didn't bother her again for a week, which was more disappointing than she'd willingly admit to anybody. But once, while strolling down Colorado Blvd, she saw a faerie following some boys down the street. She quickened her pace some, until she was walking behind the faerie, and then she whispered, "Go away."

And the faerie woman vanished, just like that, with nothing more than a tremor of Penny's soul.

It was a strange feeling. She understood the cause and effect of the power, but it seemed like some sort of cosmic joke that *she* would have it. She could send faeries away. Some people might have been very excited by that. Was she exorcising them? She ought to ask Marley. Marley would probably know.

She indulged herself with a moment of searching for 'exorcising faeries' on her phone and found lots of discussions about whether faeries were demons, or angels, or aliens, and what else might be real, with a side order of Catholic liturgy.

Then her interest waned, and the whole thing went back to being a curiosity, nothing more.

So strange.

Her mother called her to offer her a job as a production assistant. "It isn't good for you to be spending so much time brooding, my Penny. I know you have your artistic goals, and you know I support those, but I think for the time being you would be so much better in a structured environment."

Under your easy supervision, Penny thought. But her mother had every reason to be worried. Instead she said, "I'm not sure I'm ready for a day job yet, Mama. I haven't been working on anything creative lately either."

"What have you been doing, then?" She could hear the frown in Viviana's voice.

Walking, mostly. I visit coffee shops I've never visited before, in parts of the city I never go to, in case he's there. "Taking it easy," she said. "Doing some research on a future project, maybe."

She was lying. She couldn't help it. Her artistic goals were a lie, too: they had always been more about her self-image than anything else. She wanted to be a writer, be a designer, but her abilities to write and design were so limited. It took effort and vision, and she'd never managed more than the vaguest beginnings. Penny hadn't even realized it, until she'd woken up and looked at the props that filled her home. They were no different than the blouses and skirts in her closet: accessories for an identity she'd built for herself that never touched on who she actually was.

"Hmm," said her mother. "Perhaps you should do some art, then. As therapy. Oh, and speaking of therapy, will you be returning to the group tonight?" It was casually said, but Penny knew her mother. She embraced the topic shift, the chance to say the right thing.

"Yes, of course."

"Excellent. Perhaps you can open up some. And I will see you for dinner tomorrow."

"Bye, Mama." Penny put her phone on the bench beside her and stared at it. It was a nice afternoon, not too warm, and the air had a sparkle to it that usually only came right after the rain.

Music blared over speakers from the walking mall nearby.

"Oh, beautiful. You look blue. But I have a fix for that, anytime you want it."

Blaze stood beside the bench, wearing a crisp new pair of black jeans and a muscle shirt. The orange tips of his hair now threaded up along the black roots. He held an ice cream cone out to her.

She shook her head. "No, thank you."

"Your loss," he remarked. "Might I sit down beside you on the bench? Or is that also so very rude?"

"You may," Penny said. "Asking is polite, but it's also polite for me to say yes. A very different case than invading my bedroom."

"Ah, well. Mortal walls are all so permeable and fragile compared to the one I'm so used to throwing myself against. It's easy to forget about them." He sat down, leaned back and closed his eyes, turning his face to the sun. "So. Why so sad?"

"Why are you so interested in me? If you want my soul, why not just take it?" Penny asked. "I could hardly defend myself against somebody who thinks the walls of my bedroom are no more than smoke."

"Oh, but you're so interesting," he began.

"You don't even know me." Then, half-hopefully, she added, "Do you?"

He took a bite of his ice cream and looked at her with half-closed eyes. "A little. When I'm able, when I haven't been sent away, I watch you. And yes, I know that's wicked of me. Wickedness is rather my stock in trade."

Bleakly, Penny said, "You do want to kill me and steal my soul. That stuff about falling in love with you and going off to fairyland, that's just… you being wicked."

His mouth twisted in a strange smile. "No, it would be quite useful." He bared his teeth and took an aggressive mouthful of ice cream, so forceful that the rest fell off, onto his leg. He looked at it, then pushed it off onto the hot pavement and passed his palm over the remaining stain. It vanished. "Simply ending your mortal existence... well, nobody quite knows what will happen then. Perhaps you'll escape, just like this ice cream. Unless you choose to stay. And if there's one thing all of Faerie knows about the Gatekeeper, it's that she got that way by being willing to give herself up completely to love."

Penny stared at him, shock and humiliation struggling for supremacy. Finally she whispered, "Go away."

The door slammed and away he went.

"MY NAME IS JENZIE," began Jenzie once again. The lavender spirals on her arm undulated. "This week was hard."

Penny sat in her chair, her legs crossed, her hands clasped. She felt tight all over, like her body was made of wires and sharp angles.

"I mean, every week is hard," went on Jenzie. "But this time it was different. It was like... it first occurred to me that it might always be hard. I might *always* be wondering if I should be doing something different. He might always be out there telling me I'm making a mistake, and I might actually make a mistake, and then what would I be?"

"Aw, Jenzie," said Robert, spreading his hands as he leaned forward. "We're working on that, internally and externally, aren't we? If everything works out, he *won't* always be there talking to you."

"But he'll be on to somebody else?" said the woman with the baby and the radiance under her dark skin. "That's no good either."

Robert shrugged. "One day and one thing at a time. I'm glad

you're here again, Jenzie. I'll work with you after the meeting, and we can see if there's anything we can tweak in your treatment."

Jenzie nodded and silence fell for a moment. Then the older man in the suit and the hair of metallic gold cleared his throat. "I'm Henry. Still." His brief smile trembled and collapsed. "I saw Glory with somebody else the day before yesterday. I tried to say hello to her—I couldn't help it—and she looked right through me, like she didn't recognize me at all. It was devastating."

"That's good!" said Robert heartily. "That's a sign that the treatment is working."

Henry shifted uncomfortably, his eyes wide and wounded. "I gave up everything for her. I wrote my best work for her, and now I don't have her, or anything else. I don't even have the words...."

"She hurt you," said Robert. "Healing from that won't be quick. But I know you can do it, Henry. You'll write again, someday."

"How do you know?" Henry demanded. "We are the first people to deal with the fae in recorded memory. Perhaps she *has* stolen my art. You fumble around with your devices and this group, but you're just guessing—" The man caught himself, snapping his jaw closed.

Robert's eyes were wide and his hands moved nervously, but he didn't seem to have a response lined up.

The woman with the baby said, "Yeah, we're all just guessing. We have to start somewhere, eh, man? This group, a couple hours a week, and none of us are going to judge you."

In a more measured voice, Henry said, "I'm sorry. My temper isn't what it used to be either. I do appreciate the group. It makes it easier to deal with the news and my classes. Carry on, do."

Robert coughed, then said, "Thank you, Henry. How about you, Shandra? You've been talking a lot tonight but not about yourself." There were needles in Robert's voice, and the woman's hands came up across her baby as if shielding the child.

"Yeah. Yeah. Fine. I'm Shandra." The woman glared around as if expecting somebody to challenge her on that. "He brought flowers with the groceries yesterday. It didn't get him nowhere."

Robert frowned. "Why do you let him bring the groceries? It's leaving an opening, Shandra. You have to seal—"

Shandra gave Robert a scornful look. "You think I can stop him? He's a big guy, a lot bigger than me." She looked Robert up and down. "Or you. And you think I'm going to say no to help like that, so soon after losing my Pete and poor little Jordan? The bills don't stop even when you're dead, and my hours only stretch so far."

"He's trying to seduce you," said Robert patiently.

"I know that. Of course I know that. But he ain't going to make much headway with me. Least, not as long as I got Alyssa to bring up." Her fingers caressed the dark, curly-haired head resting against her chest. "And if something happened to her, I'd be dead too. Wouldn't care anymore about what *he* wanted. Or you, mister."

Robert gave her a look of mingled annoyance and frustration. "I wish you'd let us provide treatment. You see how it's helped Henry—no, not emotionally, that is a different problem—but his persecutor no longer even recognizes him." He checked himself. "But that's getting beyond the bounds of the group. I'll talk to you about it more later."

Shandra shrugged, then looked down as her baby started stirring. Once again, silence set across the group. This time, it pushed a very young person into speaking.

"I'm Miki," they said, their jaw sticking out in exaggerated belligerence. "My mom made me come. I don't belong here though."

Robert smiled tolerantly. "Why did she ask you to come, Miki?"

"Because I hang out on a fae-sighting forum. That's all! I've never even seen one up close for real. Yet. And it's not like just interacting with them makes you *crazy*. Plenty of people are working with them every day and they're *fine*. And I'll be fine, too."

Penny looked more closely at the kid. Little ink wings fluttered at their wrists, elbows, and temples. She wasn't quite sure if they were a teenage girl or a teenage boy, and figured that was probably the point. They seemed to have made some effort to appear androgynous, with their black hair in a sleek pageboy cut, and a baggy video game t-shirt over purple tights.

"That's the only reason?" asked Robert, in that annoying way adults talked to kids when they thought they had the answer already. Penny remembered it from her own days as a teenager, and she wanted to smack the facilitator for Miki.

"It's just a chat group," said Miki sulkily. "We talk about all kinds of stuff there. Everybody does. It's just the internet."

"Hmm," said Robert.

Penny found herself talking, just to cut Robert off before he could be any more irritating. "I know what you mean. I'm not sure I belong here either."

Everybody was looking at her, so she dug up a smile. "I guess I'll back up. I'm Penny."

"Why don't you think you belong here, Penny?" asked Robert indulgently.

Penny gave him a side eye, then looked at everybody else in the circle. "There was somebody. He came to me and... changed me and I didn't mind. I liked him a lot. And yeah, he was using me. My friends were worried and I didn't care, because I had everything I wanted."

The nodding faces in the circle made Penny want to run away. Instead she went on. "And then he died."

The nods stopped. "Died?" repeated Henry.

"How'd you manage that?" asked Shandra.

"I didn't think they *could* die," said Jenzie uncertainly.

"They can't," said Miki firmly. "He's tricking her, I bet."

Slowly, Penny shook her head. "I don't know if he died like humans died, but there was a fight, and he didn't walk away and he hasn't been around since. 'He's gone,' they told me. And I think they're right because when he... went, I got very sick. I almost died, they said."

"Do you miss him?" asked Jenzie intently.

"Oh yes," Penny assured her. "And that's why my own mother wanted me to come here. But he's *gone*." *And he wasn't a faerie,* she didn't say. It was there, part of why she didn't think she belonged here. "I'm not in danger from him."

"Might you be in danger from any of the others?" asked Shandra. "Sometimes a girl attracts all the bastards. Like they know she's got a weakness."

"I don't know," said Penny. "I honestly don't. Even if I had a weakness before—" she felt her cheeks flare with heat, because she *did* have a weakness and she knew it, "—things have changed now. Remember how I said he changed me? A consequence of that change is that... I can push the fae away." Suddenly the words started tumbling out. "There's this one who's been following me around lately, I think he wants to *kill* me, but all I have to do is *wish* and he goes away. He comes back later, and I *wish* again, and away he goes, like some kind of gorgeous, annoying ping pong ball."

Shandra chuckled darkly. "Neat trick, if it works."

Jenzie was wide-eyed. "He actually wants to kill you? You're not just assuming that's what he means?"

Penny's mouth twisted bitterly. "He wants to make me fall in love with him first and then kill me. Because, yeah, he thinks I have a weakness too."

Her audience bore expressions of mingled horror and sympathy. Glancing from pair of eyes to pair of eyes, shame rushed over Penny. She'd spoken up, she'd seized the spotlight, even though she was sure this group wasn't for her. Why did she do that? It was wrong of her. She looked down at her hands, wondering if she could apologize without derailing the group further.

Shandra said, "Hey. You did good telling us. And I think if you want to keep coming, we can be here for you. Maybe you're not like Jenzie and Henry here, but we've all got our own burdens. Sharing 'em and making 'em easier to bear is the whole point, eh?"

"True," conceded Penny and then folded her hands in her lap. She'd focus on others now. That was much better.

"Well said, Shandra," observed Robert grudgingly. Then he launched into his closing statement and Penny couldn't focus on *him* at all. She looked at Miki instead, thinking about parents and obsession. Robert finished up with, "And I'd like to speak to each of you privately, either right after today's session or on the phone later. Stick around if now is a good time."

Penny wondered if it would be another survey. She didn't have anything waiting for her except hiding under her covers and moping, so she lingered along with Miki, Henry, and Shandra. She was vaguely hoping for a chance to talk to Shandra, but Penny was the first person Robert fixed on as he turned around. He beckoned her over to the desk where she'd taken the survey before.

"As part of the attached study, I was wondering if you'd also be willing to provide a blood and tissue sample, so we can look for various markers and antibodies."

Penny narrowed her eyes. "That seems like an unusual request for a support group facilitator. What happened to just using surveys?"

"Well," said Robert uncomfortably, "We use those. But we're

doing a variety of research. And you're a particularly interesting subject."

"Yes, you've said. Well! I'll certainly think about your request." Penny wrinkled her nose as she smiled. "Tissue. Tissue always sounds so visceral, don't you think?"

"It's just a cheek scraping," he assured her.

"Oh! Well, that's good to know." She fidgeted with her bag. "Do you really think there's anything biological to discover? If anything, it seems like a spiritual issue."

"I'm sure there is," said Robert firmly, and she realized she'd steered the conversation back onto familiar ground for him. "Now that we know there's something to look for, we've discovered...." he hesitated, then clearly downshifted his word choices. "Unexpected forces acting in predictable, concrete ways. Like with those spectacles I showed you."

Penny smiled again. "Magic," she suggested brightly. "You're trying to avoid saying 'magic.'"

Robert frowned at her. "Hardly. Magic is, by definition, unexplainable and unmeasurable. I'm trying to avoid saying 'radiation.'" He shook his head. "In any case, it's quite plausible that some bodies are more sensitive to these forces. And if anybody would show changes as a result of them, I think that would be you, don't you?"

"Other people have wanted to study me," said Penny distantly, thinking of Branwyn telling her about Senyaza's intentions when she was all but dead. "But it's for a good cause, so I'll think about it." She gave him a nod and moved away toward the door. Miki gave her a blatantly curious look as they walked over to take her place.

Henry and Shandra were at the other end of the room, talking quietly. Penny lingered at the exit, rummaging in her bag as a polite excuse to cover her attempt at general eavesdropping. Robert set

Miki to filling out the same form he'd given her the week before, then picked up a tablet computer and walked down to the far end of the room to chat with the others.

Penny gave a tiny sigh of annoyance and turned to go. Then she turned back again. There was a prickling against her skin within the room but not in the dimness of the corridor to the outside. It had always been there, she realized as she moved her arm back and forth over the threshold: a faint tingle of poorly leashed power, hidden under the transition from dimness to bright, from cool solitude to the people sounds within the classroom.

She wondered if it was a coincidence. It was a physics classroom; whatever she felt could certainly be some leftover charge from earlier in the day

That was probably it. But it made her uncomfortable all the same, so she stopped trying to get more information and went home instead.

She took a shower, scrubbing away the memory of the tingle, then looked at herself in the mirror. Other than being a little skinner than she liked—sleeping for weeks was hard on muscle mass—there was no sign of the injury she'd sustained or the prosthetic she'd gained. She'd looked for some indication over and over again right after they'd explained what had happened to her. If it was something she could see, she'd feel better about it. She knew how to disguise and misdirect attention away from her physical flaws, and how to strut what she couldn't hide. But with this flaw, it didn't matter if she was naked or wearing knee-high boots and a belted fuchsia t-shirt dress. There was no hiding from those who knew what she was now.

The next day, she wore a patchwork sundress with panels of copper and bronze. Her mother thought it looked like it had been made from bad curtains, but Penny liked it enough to make up an excuse to get out of the house. She'd get coffee and a baguette somewhere, find some pigeons to feed, and admire how her dress caught the sun. And she'd try hard not to think about what else some people saw when they looked at her.

Blaze showed up as soon as she stepped out of her car. He came around a streetlight, wearing pressed dark slacks and an unbuttoned, baby blue shirt over a black tank top. Holding his hands out as if they were long lost friends, he advanced toward her. "What a splendid frock you're wearing!"

"Yes, it is," Penny agreed, but eyed him suspiciously and did not take his hand. "You're back much sooner than I expected."

"Oh, well, you didn't really mean it. A sign that I'm growing on you?" He caught her hand anyhow and kissed it. She let him do it, too conscious of her dignity and too irrationally pleased by the gesture to complain.

He released her fingers politely, and she walked past him, asking over her shoulder, "Are you going to stab me?"

"Are you in love with me?" He fell into step beside her.

Penny laughed breathlessly. "No. Not even a little."

He crooked a smile at her. "Ah, but I felt your heart flutter when I took your hand."

"That wasn't my heart," she informed him, then felt her cheeks burn. She lengthened her stride.

He kept up. "In a hurry, beautiful? Where are we going?"

Penny almost said, *Just trying to get rid of you* and didn't because as soon as she thought it, she knew it wasn't true. She could get rid of him anytime she wanted, at least for a little while. And she wasn't doing that, because he was companionship that wasn't interested in her welfare. She didn't have to keep secrets from him, and that made him almost comfortable to be around.

"We're getting some coffee," she told him. "And feeding the pigeons."

"Ooh, a date." He stuck his hands into his pockets.

"Hah, hah. Do you even have a wallet?"

"Nope."

Penny rolled her eyes and got him a small, blended frozen coffee. "Since you liked the ice cream."

"So considerate! Do we share? Two straws, eyes meeting?"

"No, I have this one." She showed him her cup.

"Yours is much larger," he said dubiously. "Why is mine so small?"

She gave him a sweet smile and didn't say another word until she'd made her way to some benches at the edge of a strip of greenery. Then she said, "You're working hard at trying to make me fall in love with you."

"You're *making* me work hard," he said reproachfully.

Penny frowned at her cup. "Am I? Does it normally work differently?" He shrugged and she pursued the topic. "I go to this group for people who have fallen in love with faeries and sometimes it happens so fast, so hard, it seems like the faeries must be doing something to them."

The corner of his mouth pulled to one side. "It's quite possible there're enchantments at work, although if they're resisting enough to seek help, the enchantments are very weak. But so many of your people are so enthralled by the *idea* of magic that it really requires very little to attract somebody who's already desperate to get away."

"Why haven't you just enchanted me? Wouldn't that be enough? Quick and easy, problem solved."

He pulled the straw from his frozen coffee and licked it. "You're not really enchantable anymore. Not by somebody with any sense of self-preservation anyhow. It seems like it would go badly." He grinned at Penny. "This is *technically* inconvenient for my allies, but turns out to be a lot more fun for me."

"How lucky," murmured Penny. Her thoughts went back to

Blaze's explanation of faerie enchantment of human hearts. "I can't imagine you're the only one who thinks it's more fun this way. Where's the pleasure in just having a treasure fall into your hand? And yet, there's something going on there." She thought of color wheels, of two markers from different color families laid down side by side, and the way the edges fuzzed together. Something nagged at her, something about fuzzing.

Her phone rang and she frowned when she glanced at it. "Speak of the devil," she muttered and answered it. "Hello, Robert."

"Hi, Penny," he said with an artificial smile in his voice. "I'm just calling to find out if you've made a decision about the tissue sample yet."

"It's been a day, Robert," she said gently. "I've barely had time to think about it yet."

"Oh." He sounded puzzled. "Haven't you? It's a pretty simple decision and we'd really appreciate the information it would provide. I could bring the kit to you."

"Well, at the moment I'm pretty uncomfortable with the idea, and this isn't helping me feel better about it." She rolled her eyes at Blaze, who leaned on his hand and watched her with wide, improbably innocent eyes as he drank his coffee.

"But there's nothing to make you uncomfortable in it. All we want is information. It's not like we're going to somehow extract your secret history, or use it to grow a fully functional clone in seven days, or anything like that. Haha."

"Yes, I saw that movie too," said Penny patiently. Her parents had produced it, but it wasn't something one liked to mention.

"Well, it's fiction," he said sullenly.

"And yet, there are so many ways a person's cells can be used in ways nobody anticipated at the time." She sighed. "Tell you what, Robert. You have your people draw up a legal agreement for exactly how my tissue will be used, and I'll have my lawyer check it out." It felt cruel, but he was asking a favor, and he was being annoying about it.

"Fine," he said, surprising her. "I'll have it at the next meeting."

Blaze reached the bottom of the frozen coffee and started rattling the straw

"Great. It's getting hard to hear at the moment, so I'll talk to you again then," she said pleasantly, then hung up and dropped the phone on the bench. "That man! Will you please stop that!"

Blaze stopped and precisely tossed the cup into a trash can a yard away. "I'm sorry. I was feeling neglected. It was a desperate cry for attention."

Penny turned her mouth down at the faerie. "This is probably your fault somehow. Once upon a time, I would have been happy to help this guy. But now, thanks to you, I can't help wondering where exactly it stops. I keep wondering if he wants to *dissect* me."

"That would hardly work. It's not like what makes you so unique can be accessed through your flesh, as delightful as your flesh is."

"Well, some people disagree. And they've got a whole setup dedicated to studying the fleshy side of magic.

The tips of his orange hair shimmered into translucent blue, but he stayed silent, listening to her.

"I can't believe he called me to nag me about this. And who knows where it stops? You came into my bedroom. Will he come into my bedroom? And God, what is he doing to those other people?" She thought of Miki, who hadn't sounded like they were there willingly, and Shandra, who didn't seem to have any trouble resisting her faerie suitor. "I mean, a support group to help people resist your charm, that's a great idea, but why does he have people there who don't want the help? It's weird." She realized belatedly that Blaze was staring at her with unusual intensity. "And why am I talking to you? I have to go. And so do you." She raised her hand as if to flick him away.

"Don't banish me, please" he said abruptly. "I have some things I'd like to do."

Penny hesitated. "Leave me alone for a while, then."

He rose to his feet, gave her an out-of-place bow, and walked off briskly. She watched him go, wondering if she ought to have sent him away. Probably she should have. Probably she ought to send them all away, each time she found one.

Brooding about that, she went home.

The next day, around three in the afternoon, Shandra called Penny. Penny didn't recognize the number but did immediately recognize Shandra's voice when she said, "Hello, is this Penny Karzan?"

"It is. Hi, Shandra." Penny stacked some papers on her design shelf, stuff she hadn't quite been willing to toss into the big recycling bin she'd lugged inside. "How's your day going?"

"Not so great. Sorry to bother you, but I saw your number on that Robert's paperwork and remembered it. I remembered your story about your fae guy, too."

"It's not a problem," said Penny warmly. "What can I do for you?'

"Uh, can you meet me? I think the help of a support group buddy could come in pretty handy right now. Especially yours."

Penny froze, then put down the rest of her papers. "Tell me where."

Shandra was at a frozen yogurt place in a dingy shopping center about ten minutes away, leaning against the wall outside, with her baby in her arms. She straightened up, patting the baby on the back. "Faster than I expected. Thanks."

"I was lucky." She was lucky she hadn't gotten pulled over for speeding, anyhow. Penny looked around. "What's going on?"

Shandra tilted her head toward the froyo place's window. "In there. Jenzie was going to treat me, and then *he* showed up. I couldn't get her to come away."

Jenzie sat at a table, her sheet of brown hair hanging down over her face. Across from her, leaning in, was a handsome, distinctly faerie male, with spikes of golden hair forming an unlikely halo around his head, and pointed ears straight out of a computer game. Blaze didn't have pointed ears, Penny thought distractedly.

"That's Helion," said Shandra grimly. "She doesn't want to be with him, but he doesn't care what she wants."

"A pretty good sign that he's not the right person for her," murmured Penny.

"Yeah, I told her the same thing and she's trying to be a good girl, but here he comes and he's damn hard to resist. So I was thinking…. I wonder if you could help?"

"Yes," said Penny decisively. "I can." She pulled the door open and went into the shop.

"—Honey." Helion was mid-sentence. "I want to know who else you've been with. I can *tell* there's been somebody else, I can see your soul fraying away." He glanced up at Penny and his eyes widened before he looked back at his target. "And you won't be lucky enough to end up like the Gatekeeper here. Not everybody loves you enough to take care of you like I will, once your soul is burnt away."

Penny gave Helion the same glance she'd give an out of place chair, then crouched down beside Jenzie, looking under her hair at her face. The other woman's body was still, but her eyes were darting from side to side, as if she was trying to will herself into getting up and going away. "Hey. Is this guy bothering you?"

"Yeah," whispered Jenzie. "You could say that."

"Want me to help?" Penny continued, ignoring whatever

bullshit explanation Helion had started spouting.

Jenzie's shoulders moved in a tiny little shrug, and Penny took that as a 'yes.' She took Jenzie's hand and pulled her out of her chair, giving her a gentle shove toward where Shandra stood at the door. Helion stood up too, so fast that his chair fell over.

The staffer at the counter said, "Hey, I'm going to call the police if this doesn't settle down."

Penny gave the staffer a radiant smile. "No need. You. Helion?" She channeled all her dislike and anger into her next words, every bit of will and force she could muster. "Go away, and *never* come back."

And away he went. The door in Penny's soul slammed very hard behind him, and Penny felt very, very good about it.

She turned around, away from the shocked gaze of the froyo staffer, to meet Jenzie's equally shocked gaze. Shandra, however, looked smug, which stopped confused remorse from taking the place of Penny's fierce pleasure.

"I *knew* you were the right person to call," said Shandra. "I *knew* it. Robert did something right, for once."

"Are you all right?" Penny asked Jenzie. The lavender spirals spread off Jenzie's fingers to the floor and she wanted to talk about it, but where to start? The colors fuzzing around her seemed strange, as if they were bleeding together with her surroundings. Was her soul damaged by something other than her erstwhile lover?

"I don't know." Jenzie twisted her hands together. "I don't know. I feel awful. I want to call Robert and see if I can get another treatment."

"Of course you feel awful," said Shandra. "He was awful. We can take you home, you can relax a bit, and you'll feel better."

"No, I want another treatment," said Jenzie stubbornly. She fumbled in her bag until she found a phone.

Shandra sighed. "Stupid Robert."

"I'll take her, Shandra," said Penny, watching Jenzie intently. Maybe if she could actually see the 'treatment' taking place, she could understand the rest of what was going on.

"I suppose she's not in any condition to go somewhere on her own," said Shandra, her disgust unhidden. "Go ahead. Right back to Robert."

With a wary look, Jenzie said, "You can drop me off, but you don't need to stay."

Penny fluttered a hand. "If that's what you want, but I don't mind waiting. I can bring you back after or take you home, whichever you want. Is the treatment hard? I don't want to leave you in the lurch."

Jenzie hesitated. "You aren't going to talk me out of it? Vanish stuff away? Shandra thinks the treatment's *bad* for me."

Penny didn't even glance at Shandra, keeping her sincere gaze fixed on Jenzie. "I don't even know what the treatment is."

"Oh, okay," sighed Jenzie, her shoulders slumping. She turned her attention to her phone and Penny let her gaze slide sideways to see Shandra's disapproval.

"It'll be okay," she lied encouragingly. "I'm sure they know what they're doing there."

"Mph," said Shandra. "I'm going home. Thanks for helping out, and have fun with Robert." She went out the door.

"He says I can come right away," said Jenzie, a bright thread in her voice as she put her phone away. "I told him what you did, Penny. He doesn't mind if you come, either."

"I didn't think he would."

The 'treatment' consisted of a pair of cuffs around Jenzie's wrist, plugged into a tablet computer that was in turn connected to a box the size of a child. Colored lights moved and flashed on the tablet screen, and Jenzie wept quietly as she looked at them. Her hands twitched in the cuffs. Robert stood beside her, wearing his amber glasses, watching both the tablet screen and Jenzie's hands intently. If he noticed she was crying, he was too accustomed to it to feel uncomfortable.

Penny, however, felt *very* uncomfortable with it. She didn't know if she saw what Robert did, but it didn't seem like something that any compassionate person could witness without being affected. The cuffs around Jenzie's wrists drained the color from her aura, intensifying the draw as Jenzie wept harder. It took all of Penny's willpower, and her promise to Jenzie, not to rip the tablet from her grip and fling it across the room. Instead, she stared at her own reflection in the mirror from her purse, looking at the way her own colors had been drained away,

At last, Robert reached down and tapped the screen to end the treatment. Jenzie's weeping had faded to just sniffles, and her aura was faded as if it had been left in the sun all summer. She looked up at Penny, wiped her nose with her hand as Robert uncuffed her, and said, "Thank you. I feel so much better now."

Branwyn wouldn't hesitate in breaking the device, Penny thought. It was tempting. There was no way it could be doing something good. Helion had been right; when Jenzie's soul was too drained for her to remain conscious anymore, she wouldn't end up like Penny. She'd just die.

But what good would breaking it do? There had to be software somewhere, and technical designs. Even if it was a prototype, that didn't mean it was one of a kind, with no backups, no earlier models, no later models.

Instead she patted Jenzie on the shoulder before drawing Robert away and out of earshot. Then, bluntly, she said, "What you're doing to her is bad. It's dangerous."

He frowned. "I have to disagree. We're acquiring enormous amounts of information and we're helping people feel better. And you yourself have clearly gone through something similar—"

"I am not a role model!" Penny flared. "I don't know what kind of information you're getting, but the cost is too high."

"*She* called *me*, begging for help," remarked Robert, growing more confident in the face of Penny's temper. "Tell *her* the cost is too high. Speaking of which, I'd like to interview you about what you did to her stalker?"

Penny stared at him for a moment, trying to decide if he was offering some kind of deal. No, no he wasn't, she realized. He was just that tone deaf. She resisted telling him to go to hell and instead said, "I don't think you'd do anything good with the information. Robert, I'm going to talk to the other members of the support group about what you're doing, and what the ultimate consequences are."

"Feel free," he said. "Nobody is required to participate. But you're not a particularly good example of the supposed dangers of the treatment, are you?"

"It's not even a useful treatment for keeping the fae away," pointed out Penny. "I still have one following me around. I still care about another one."

"But can they hurt you anymore?" asked Robert clinically.

"Yes," said Penny. "Yes, it still hurts."

"Ah," said Robert. "More information. Thank you so much."

Penny had enough. "Jenzie, do you want me to take you home? I have to go."

Jenzie, staring at her hands, shook her head slowly. "I'll take a cab later. Thank you for the ride here, though."

"Fine," said Penny. "Take care of yourself." Then she swept from the classroom door.

In the hall beyond, Blaze was walking toward her, his face cold and distant, his hair like blue flames. Irritated at the sight of him, Penny said, "Oh, splendid. Here you are. Now is not really the time." She raised her hand to swat him away and he darted forward, grabbing her wrist.

"Don't. I'm not here for you," he said roughly. She realized he was angry. His hand was very hot against her skin. "I've been watching what your Robert is doing."

"He's not 'my' Robert," Penny interrupted, more annoyed. She yanked her hand out of his grip. "He's doing something horrible, and he doesn't care."

"It's *wasteful.* Needlessly destructive." He cracked his knuckles.

Penny's mood improved marginally. "Are you going to do something about it?"

"Are you?"

Tossing her hair over her shoulder, Penny said, "Yes. I'm going to tell people and offer them something better. Real help."

Blaze raised one eyebrow. "Oh?"

Penny smiled at him. "What are *you* going to do?" She probably ought to not let the faerie hurt Robert, no matter how much it seemed like a good idea.

"I'm going to talk to him," said Blaze calmly, coldly, and moved past her.

Penny hesitated, then began walking down the hall toward the building exit. She heard the lab door open and close behind her as Blaze went through.

Shandra had everybody's numbers, and Shandra was happy to help her spread the word, especially since Penny had something to offer other than just gossip. It helped a lot when Robert didn't show up for the next meeting. It was like an admission of guilt. When the room stayed locked and they huddled outside in shock and bewilderment, calling a cell phone nobody answered, Penny had a solution. She invited them back to her house, made them all coffee and tea, and let Shandra take over the meeting.

The other woman didn't dwell too much on Robert's iniquity,

which showed a grace that Penny freely admired. Instead, Shandra started with Jenzie, asking if her tormentor had reappeared and inviting her to talk about how she felt about his banishment.

Blaze stayed away as well, and she might have claimed she was surprised by that too. But she wasn't. Nor was she surprised when she opened her door around a month later on meeting night, and Robert stood there, his eyes huge and vulnerable.

"Could I come in? The—the meeting is here now, right?"

Penny regarded him, then warned, "We don't have any of your special treatments. Just companionship and talking."

He flushed and looked down. "I know. He— he asked me to destroy the prototypes. I did. For him."

Silently, Penny stood aside, holding her door open. He entered the house, head still down. She took his jacket for him and pointed him toward where the others would be gathering soon. Shandra and Henry and Miki were already there, but there were other, newer members coming too. He sat down in a chair, his shoulders bowed, and Miki looked at him in unrecognizing curiosity; his demeanor was that different.

Penny left him alone. When Jenzie came in, she frowned and looked around worriedly, then went to the far side of the room. She'd been the angriest at the change in the support group, but she hadn't stopped coming and her soul was once again slowly suffusing with color.

During the meeting, Shandra called on Robert to introduce himself, as if she'd never seen him before. He shifted position awkwardly and said, "He left me, and I didn't know what to do. I found the flyer I'd made for the first meeting." He scrubbed his hands across his face. "It was amazing for a while, but I should have known I couldn't keep the attention of something like him. Like an angel without wings…."

"We share names here, so everybody can be safer. What was

his name?" asked Shandra gently, as everybody else shifted in discomfort or stared in fascination.

"Blaze," said Robert, and while he said the faerie's name, his features glowed with love. Then he sagged again and put his face in his hands.

"Do you think a treatment would help you feel better?" asked Henry, sweetly. Penny had met Glory, Henry's personal curse. Once. Briefly.

"Henry," said Shandra sharply, "The man's hurting. Be a friend or go away."

"I'm sorry," said Robert, raising his head to look at Henry. "I thought—I was wrong. Blaze showed me how wrong I was."

Shandra snorted. "One thing we learn here, mister, is not to trust anything taught by *them*. Now. Are you still seeing this Blaze? We can help if he won't leave you alone and you don't like that."

Robert shook his head. "He told me goodbye four days ago. He said... other things." The man's eyes filled with tears. "Cruel things."

The meeting went on, Penny sitting a little apart. She still thought about Ettoriel every day, but she didn't look for him. She didn't fall asleep wishing for him. At least not most nights. Sometimes, she thought about someone else.

When the meeting was done and she'd seen everybody to the door, she went out to her porch to take in the night air. She didn't have long to wait. Blaze came strolling down the sidewalk, his hair black once again and curling to his shoulders. His shirt was orange, his slacks charcoal and very new. He wore a cross around his neck. He raised a hand as he saw her and veered over to her house, exactly as if he'd just been out for a stroll.

"Very smooth," she approved. "Well done. By the way, if you don't have a wallet, how do you get all these clothes? I know those slacks aren't cheap."

He raised his eyebrows. "Is asking polite?"

"Tell me anyhow," she commanded. "We're practically friends. Asking is okay between friends."

"Oh. Well. If we're friends.... I don't buy them. But we're very, very good at copying."

"Hmm," said Penny. "Yes, you are."

He came up the steps of the porch. "I sent you a gift today. Did you like it?"

Penny shook her head. "No, no. You don't make gifts of something you've used up, especially when it's a person. That's not how we work. Besides, you weren't angry on *my* behalf when last I saw you."

"I was!" he protested. "Well, some. It was fuel for the fire. But sending you a penitent man—this was a gift and all for you. I didn't *have* to find that flyer of his and leave it where he would see it."

"You're terrible," she informed him.

"Yes," he said modestly. "Are you pleased?"

Penny hesitated, then didn't lie. "A little." She reached out and took Blaze's hand, lacing her fingers in his. "But you really were terrible."

"I sent him to a group that will help him," said Blaze dismissively, moving his other hand to her hip.

"Yes," said Penny. "And I'm going to help him. You're so very charming, Blaze. I've dreamt of you. But— Blaze. Go away. This time, don't come back."

The door slammed in her soul and away he went.

But he went away smiling.

THE WINTER WAR

There's this little old man who lives in a shack on the south edge of town. I have no idea what he is, some kind of brown. And he is *mean*. I mean, he's little, he's old, he's brown, he lives in a shack with the roof falling off, who can blame him for being grouchy, right? But Jen Klay told me once she got into an accident right outside his house and he came out to his porch and looked at the wreck and went right back inside again and, get this, locked the door behind him. That is *cold*.

But folks have reasons, right? Mama didn't raise me to judge. I know all about Boo Radley and I try to keep it cool.

I was out trying to earn a few bucks shoveling drives one day when the snow had let up some. We'd stopped trying to convince ourselves the snow was *done* for the season; nothing but June was going to save us from *this* winter and I think some of us had given up on that. I saw a book come out called *The Year Without A Summer* and I couldn't bear to pick it up and see if it had a happy ending. But people need to get to work and snow needs to get shoveled, so there I was, with my shovel and my snow boots, carving another day out of the endless white.

Somehow or other, I end up on the south edge of town, right near the old man's house. It's not exactly a clear day, unless your point of comparison is an outright blizzard. And hey, that was where we were. But I noticed the clouds parted over his street and an actual sunbeam hit the old man's house. I stood on the other sidewalk for a while, just kind of enjoying the hint of blue sky. Then I realized nobody had *ever* shoveled his walk.

There was absolutely no chance he was going to pay me, and I figured it would be wrong to ask him anyhow. But I had some cash already and, hey, Boo Radley, right?

Now, when I shovel old Mrs. Ee's walk, I don't bother to tell her first. I just get it done, and she wakes up to a nice surprise, and maybe later I get fresh cookies. Everybody wins. But the old man was just cranky enough that I figured I ought to make sure I wasn't going to get attacked just because he was confused about why I was there. So I go to knock on the door and let him know what's what before I get to work.

As soon as I step into the sunbeam, the temperature drops ten degrees, like cold is just pouring down out of the hole in the clouds. But I've got my muffler, I've got my mittens, I adjust them up, then go knock on the door with my shovel held in one hand.

He throws open the door immediately, like he's been waiting for me. Except when he sees me standing there, he jumps back, because I'm *not* who he's expecting.

He really is a shrimp, too: short and hunched over, with deep wrinkles around his brown eyes but not so many around his mouth. He throws a huge hand up, like he thinks I'm going to grab him and shake the change from his pockets. I guess mufflers do kind of make you look sinister.

I hold up my big snow shovel but before I can say anything, he says, "No! Go away! You shouldn't be here!"

Talking's hard in a muffler too, so I tug mine down despite the over-the-top cold and say, "Nah, I'm here to do it for free. A present, you know? I just wanted to let you know so it didn't shock you or anything."

He just stares at me, blinking in the cold. Then he glances up at the sunbreak, but he doesn't actually *say* anything else. So I shrug and turn away to get to work.

I've just dug my shovel into the crusted old snow under yesterday's powder when he says, "You don't want to be here, kid. It gets *cold* here."

"It's winter," I tell him. "It's cold everywhere. I'll be fine."

"Hah," he says, and slams the door.

Right about then, it gets just a bit warmer. Not enough to pull down my muffler, let's not get crazy now, but enough that I noticed. But the sun break sticks around and for a little bit it's nice, mindless, sunny work.

But sun on snow isn't something I can deal with for too long without a headache. I had sunglasses somewhere in my parka pockets, but digging them out was a hassle so instead I just took a break, leaning on the rickety post supporting the porch roof and resting my eyes.

I probably should have done that earlier, because I'd barely relaxed when I started seeing things. A breeze started making flurries out of the powder I'd sent flying and there were *people* dancing inside them, like sugarplum ballerinas or something, made of snow and sunlight and shards of ice.

They spun across the mountains of snow in the yard and twirled their way up the broken drainpipe, they fluttered against the windows and one of them dug her way up out of the snow I'd moved. I didn't move, not at all, because would you? If it was a hallucination, it was pretty, and if it wasn't, I didn't want them noticing me.

Some of them were as big as me, and some of them were the size of Tinkerbell, and the one that came up from under the snow, she was right in between. And they crowded up onto the old man's porch. One of them noticed me, I swear, but it didn't say anything to its friends and I was *glad* about that.

So at first I think they're coming for the poor old man and I wonder if I can use my shovel to turn them back into snow powder and ice. But they don't knock on his door or kick it down or anything, they just wait there. Sometimes they giggle, and it sounds like frozen leaves chiming.

Then the second batch of *things* shows up. These aren't sugarplum ballerinas. There's no dazzle to them, and I can't pretend they're just snow flurries brought to life, which is what I'd been doing so far. These things are made of old ice, the sort of ice that refuses to melt even after the flowers have come in and you're eating strawberries. They creak when they move. There are no pretty giggles, not even from the porch. One of them opens a maw and it sounds like a drum section when it talks. I have no idea what it said, but I'm not really concentrating because... Because ice piles are walking around, people.

One of the ballerinas attacks first, leaping off the porch with a sound like a frozen tree falling over, straight onto one of the ice creatures. Then the calm sunbeam explodes into a blizzard. Just like that, it's the kind of weather you never go out in without a rope. The wind is howling and there's snow everywhere, it's as white and terrifying as a blank page.

My first thought is that the storm is just within the area claimed by the sunbreak and if I can just get back to the street, I'll be fine. I'll be safe. But I don't know that and I do know a lot better than to go wandering into a blizzard. Instead I hang onto the porch support and pull my muffler over my face and hope like heck none of them decide I'm on the other side.

Then a hand grabs my shoulder. It's cold as frozen steel, and I'm sure it's one of the ice creatures. But it's not. It's the old man. Once he has my attention, he jerks his head toward the open door to his house.

Some things I don't need to be told twice. I fought my way

up the porch stairs, though I had to lose my shovel to make any headway. The thing was like a sail and the house wasn't doing anything to block the wind howling off the yard.

As soon as I'm inside, the old man slams the door and the howl of the wind cuts off. I go to tug down my muffler and he says, "Don't! You're all bundled up, that's good. Stay bundled up. I think you'll be safe." He rubs his hands together like he's cold and for the first time I realize that although his house is freezing, he's not wearing any kind of winter wear.

"The last thing I need right now is some dumb kid turning into an ice pop at my house, and at least in here you won't get skewered by an icicle." He laughs when he says this, but it's not a very nice laugh. "Just stay quiet and out of my way and you can go on home again once they're done out there." He gives me one final glance, then goes to the window.

The house is as much a disaster area inside as outside. There's food packaging everywhere, the stuff used by the local Meals on Wheels crew, and pizza boxes and sandwich wrappers. And there's books everywhere, too. Old paperbacks with the covers torn away, hardbacks with no jacket that are falling apart at the spine, library sale sci-fi books, textbooks that my mama used in high school, those big picture books that take over the sale rack at the bookstore. And there's two dictionaries open on the table, crammed in among the juice boxes and the chocolate milk cartons. There's an old TV in one corner, but it's almost completely hidden behind a stack of books. It's a little bit like a smelly paradise.

I'm not really sure what to do, so I sit down in the chair in front of the dictionaries. I knock the table, 'cause graceful is not the word for moving in snow gear, and a whole pile of juice boxes fall to the floor. They're frozen solid.

"Why is it so cold in here? Is your heat out?" I try to ask through my muffler, but what comes out is probably more like,

"Mmmmmrrrrrr."

Still, he glances at me. "Heat hasn't been on since the blizzard started. Since *they* found me. And I ain't going to apologize because you shouldn't have been here in the first place. Shoveling a man's walk. That'll give everybody the wrong impression."

The door slams open, and the old man jumps back from the window. One of the ballerinas is standing in the door and it doesn't take more than a glance to see that she's the lead ballerina, the one in the prettiest skirt with the tiara. Her eyes are like blue jewels and she looks right at the old man.

His eyes are bulging like somebody's squeezing him. I seriously think he's having a stroke or something. I don't know what to do, but I don't think anybody ought to be hurt by the icy stares of snow ballerinas, so I throw one of the frozen juice boxes at her. It slams into the wall beside her and she turns to look at *me*—which wasn't really a consequence I'd thought about—and then another figure steps up behind her.

This one is all sleek planes of the black ice of a bottomless lake. There's no pretty, whirling snowflakes here, just the foreboding of sudden death. She's the evil counterpart to the ballerina, although given the ballerina's eyes, I think 'evil counterpart' is probably assuming some things.

The ice queen puts her hand on the shoulder of the snowflake princess and says, "*Mine,*" in this slow, deep voice. Then they're fighting again, right in the doorframe. The poor old man is just standing there, staring at them like he's terrified, so I stumble over to the door and slam it closed, right in their faces.

It gets quiet again inside the house. After a minute, the old man shakes himself and says, in a normal kind of voice, "Stupid kid. I said I didn't want any human ice pops around my house. Just wait it out if they come back."

"What do they want?" I blurt as I sit down again.

He presses his hand to his heart and gives me a grim graveyard smile. "Me."

That's too much. I knock the chair over as I stand up again. "There must be some way to save you!"

His little smile turns into a really nasty look, and then that look changes into something sort of thoughtful. He glances at the books on the table behind me, then comes over to me and rights the chair I knocked over. He's not *moving* like somebody who's maybe having problems with their heart or their brain, which is good.

"Sit down. Shut up. You ever read books?"

"Well, I read *To Kill A Mockingbird* a few times," I admit.

His eyes get all narrow. "Is that the one about the idiot shut-in and the lawyer what liked the losing battles?"

I say firmly, "Sir, that is not a nice way to refer to Mr. Boo Radley." Then, because I was getting a little tired of how he kept acting, I added, "Especially for somebody like you."

"Hah!" He laughs, just like that, which I always thought was just a sound effect for comics. "Well, he liked kids and I don't, so we're different that way." He stares at me some more. Something bangs against the window and I jump, but he don't even blink.

Instead he says, "See this?" He holds out one of his huge hands and on it he's wearing a delicate silver ring.

"Sure, I see it. Is that what they're after?"

"Back in November," he says, like I didn't say anything, "Some people come to my door. The snowflake woman and her friends. They talk about this and that but eventually it comes out, they want me to join them."

I blink a lot. "What, like become one of those ballerinas?" It's a ridiculous thought and I snicker.

He just shrugs, and his eyes glitter so bright that it just sweeps my laugh away.

"Told them I'd think about it, and they said they'd give me a couple of days. The *next* day, the ice woman and *her* friends come by, and they tell me the same thing. They want me to join them. And I tell them to come back in a couple days, too."

I don't laugh this time, because he'd fit right in among the creaking, crashing slabs. "And now they're back?"

"Don't you listen? Why am I wasting time telling you this if you're not going to listen? That was back in November. It's after New Year's now. No, they came back right when I said." The old man starts grinning. "And I tricked 'em." He spreads both his hands and, on each one, he's wearing a ring. Delicate, silver filigree on one and heavy, black onyx set with diamonds on the other. "I joined 'em both."

He adds, after a minute, "They've been fighting over me ever since. I reckon this whole blizzard situation has been them fighting over me."

Finally, I say, "Wow." I think about that a while, then I say, "I heard the orange trees froze in Florida, and the Lakes aren't going to melt until July, and the jet fuel for the airplanes turned to ice."

He just shrugs again. "Might have happened anyhow. It's winter. It gets cold."

"You have to stop it," I insist. "You can't just go around two-timing winter queens. You've gotta choose one of 'em and give the other ring back."

He grins. "I don't know, I think they kind of like it."

I stand up again, so I can look him in the eye instead of looking up at him. "You said you didn't want human ice pops all over your lawn. What do you think will happen if they keep fighting like this? Another ice age, I bet. Ice pops everywhere."

"Won't be on my front lawn," he says, stubborn as a mule.

"Another ice age and the whole world's going to be your front lawn. Come on, man! You didn't want me to freeze to death on your porch, or in here. Don't be so—" I stopped.

"Don't be so cold?" He barks a laugh again.

"Don't be so cold about everybody else." I can be stubborn too.

He taps his fingers together. "You read, kid. You ever try writing?"

"What?" He changes subjects so fast I'm having trouble keeping up.

"You ever try writing down a story? So that other people can read it?"

"Not since seventh grade. I had to keep a blog on the internet. But I didn't have anything to say."

"Well, now you do." He looks at me like I'm irritating him again. "Stop gaping. You go out there and you write down the story of Old Man Winter, eh? Me, in this falling-apart house, me, who the winter queens came to. Nobody ever wanted to give me a chance but them and I tricked 'em and look how they love it."

I give him my best suspicious look, the one I save for the kids I'm babysitting. "You going to go out there and stop this?"

"Fine, fine," he says, and he puts his hand on the door. His hand's trembling, though.

"You stay in here, you're nobody," I tell him. It's mean, but he's cold, and apparently mean is what cold likes best. He'd know, right? "You're just a guy pretending. I don't have to write about Old Man Winter, just some mean, old guy who wouldn't let me shovel his walk."

He glares at me, then flings the door open and steps out into the storm.

I go after him, at least to the door, because hell yeah, I want to see what happens next. But all I see is the whiteout. Then, less than a minute later, the whiteout ends with a snap. The wind dies.

The *storm* dies. And the old man is nowhere to be seen.

Well. I don't really know what happened, I don't know which ring he chose, but the big storm circling half the country broke up that day. It stayed winter, of course, and it hasn't been a nice winter for anybody. I know it's April now, and I'm finally getting around to writing this in the hopes that the winter will finally start backing off. I could use some spring.

The problem with an angel's magic coursing through your veins is that it just *does not quit*. Take getting falling down drunk. It's hard to get properly drunk when that angel magic is just working away repairing all the damage you're trying to do.

All the same, Simon had gotten pretty good at it over the centuries. He and his magic had come to an accommodation. But it scared the natives.

He sat on the curb outside a grocery store, the afternoon sun shining down brightly, and tried to remember why he was there. Oh yes. The nice little clerk inside had refused to sell him more booze. And it was afternoon now. Last he remembered clearly, it hadn't quite been dawn.

They'd arrived during the twilight, as the town shimmered like a mirage around them. But he didn't want to think about that.

He eyed the gas station across the parking lot blearily. But in a town like this, it probably dispensed moonbeams instead of proper fuel. He'd rather drink the water.

The face of a woman swam before his mind's eye as the angel's magic did its dirty business. The face didn't belong to the grocery store clerk. It was another woman. She was the reason he was in this damned town, and it wasn't the fun kind of reason, either. It had been a job. She'd wanted him to bring her into Eden Falls.

Into this town stolen away from the world by faeries.

It had been tricky, right enough, but he'd managed it. Just a lick of wizardry and some persistence, and they'd fallen right through the emptiness at the end of the highway.

Simon stopped remembering then. That was another skill. It was a good skill, but it worked better when he had something to drink. So he pushed himself off the curb and managed to roll to his feet.

A hand gripped his arm supportively and he peered down. It was the little clerk, in a knit hat with a flower and a backpack over her shoulder.

"What, you off work already?" Simon tried to say.

She said, "I was worried about you, so my boss let me go early. They'll be all right. The question we're all wondering about is: will you?"

"Oh, I'm just great. Peachy." He considered. "Not like you, though."

"Clearly not," she said, amused. She had fine black hair like Simon's and pixie-like features. "I'm a bit curious about that too."

"Dunno. I was waiting and waiting. Didn't happen. So I went to the bar down the street. Real friendly barkeep there. Proper-like. Everybody knows your name. But not my name."

She gave him a bottle of water. He regarded it doubtfully. Drinking it seemed rather contrary to his goal, but she was looking at him so expectantly. Once he'd finished it, she started walking with him, gently pushing him along by his elbow. He let her, because he hadn't any idea what to do next. Coming up with an idea required looking in places he didn't want to look.

The water and the angel magic did their horrid work, and he said, "Ah...." just as she released his arm.

"There's a men's room right here. Go take care of business and splash some water on your face, and then maybe we can figure out what's wrong?"

"Good timing," Simon mumbled. They were at a small, lush park with a playground visible amidst trees that radiated health. Even the damn trees were happy here.

"Try your best and everything will work out," she said cheerfully. "It all works out."

This was the first time anything had worked out for Simon since he'd entered Eden Falls. Maybe it was the girl; maybe things were working out for the girl so she didn't have an even bigger mess on her hands.

The water was very cold, and didn't help him feel any better. Of course, the girl had a very different idea of what Simon needed to feel better than he did.

He left the bathroom, and the girl was still waiting there. "What's your name? I can't keep thinking of you as 'this girl,' or else I'll get you confused with the other girl."

She giggled. "I'm Tammy."

"I hope you're not going to sober me up too much. I get mean when I'm sober."

"I'm just trying to solve a puzzle," she said earnestly. "You shouldn't be here. Not like this."

"Doesn't living here bother you?" he asked, rubbing his fingers against his temples. "It sounds like you understand exactly where you are."

"It's Eden Falls." She shrugged. "Who's this other girl you mentioned?"

"Came in with her. Came here because of her. She wanted to be here," he said bitterly. "Carolyn Astin."

"Oh, her. I know where she is. Shall we go talk to her?" Tammy took his elbow again, like somebody used to guiding people around.

"Don't much see the point," he said. "She paid me in advance. Of course, a lot of it's in my bank account back in the real world."

"Hard to access now," she agreed. "But you seem to have some kind of unresolved issues with Carolyn. Let's go find out what they are."

"How do you know where she is? She only just got here." He paused, thinking about that. "Unless I've been drunk a lot longer than I thought."

"Oh, you hear a lot of gossip working at the register of a grocery store in a town like this. Everybody's passing the time of day with you. She's getting set up at the Stonefire Apartments. That's our local nest of artists. It's about a ten minute walk away. Do you think you can make it?"

Simon thought about that, then ventured, "No?"

"Liar," said Tammy cheerfully. "Come on." She pulled him down the sidewalk, past the park. The avenue beyond looked just like an ordinary small town, except that everything seemed clean, even the faded signs.

"It'll be a lot more than ten minutes," he warned her. "You've got better things to do than drag a man like me someplace he doesn't want to be. I'm pretty heavy when I fall down."

She flexed her free arm. "Stocking shelves has made me buff. Try your best, Simon!"

"That's such a stupid slogan," grumbled Simon.

Tammy ignored him to greet a middle-aged man strolling down the sidewalk. "Afternoon, Peter! Did you see that episode of Tanglewood last night?"

Peter shook his head and smiled. "Had a date, Miss Tammy. I'm going to watch it tonight." The man's gaze lingered curiously on Simon, but he didn't say anything.

As they passed, Simon frowned. "Wait, you get TV signals here?"

"Sure, some of them. The popular ones."

"Popular with *who*?"

Tammy elbowed him and grinned. "The faeries, of course."

"I hate this town," Simon said bitterly.

Tammy said again, "Liar," then waved vigorously at somebody crossing the street.

"How do you figure I'm lying?" Simon asked indignantly.

"Well, you're still here, aren't you?"

"Hah, you think it's easy to get out? It took over a week to make our way in. And I've hardly been in any condition to do that kind of work to get out."

She didn't respond, maintaining her pressure on his elbow with a careless ease. Instead she studied the sky. "It might storm later. Do you like thunderstorms?"

Simon's father had worked as a storm god for a while. "No," he said shortly. "They make me itch."

Tammy gurgled with laughter. "Of course." She sniffed, then pointed at a red, brick building with a massive mural of a castle on the near wall. "Hey, look, they're having a building barbecue. That's great, we can get some food in you."

"Did you ever consider," said Simon, with as much dignity as he could muster, "That I was trying my best to die of alcohol poisoning? Your bloody town is broken that way."

Her expression turned serious. "Not normally. There's those who want to die in the way they choose, and Eden Falls is there for them, too."

"Then why are you meddling?" wailed Simon.

"Because you're complicated, Simon Mitsukuni. That's awfully interesting. I like interesting and Eden Falls provides."

"Great. I'm here to be your fix-it toy. Just perfect." He made a token effort to yank his arm out of her grip. She was barely half his size; a token effort should have been enough. Would have been enough if he'd been at his best.

It had been a long, long time since he was at his best.

"There's your girl," said Tammy, far too excited about it. She waved at a group of people standing around a barbecue on the side lawn of the illustrated building.

"She's not my girl," explained Simon, for what felt like the ninth time. "She was just a client." Maybe all the other times had been in his head.

But Carolyn looked over, put down the plate she was holding, and came over to them. "Simon!" she said. "You're still here?"

Smiling, Tammy released Simon's arm, said, "You two talk," and wandered over to the other people.

"Sure, I thought I'd see the sights." Looking at Carolyn was like anticipating a drink of the best Scotch.

She'd been a client, but she'd also been an artist he'd followed long before she approached his group for help. Her work, written and inked, had spoken to him: spoken to him of what he'd lost, spoken of his own misery and shadowed pain. And then he'd brought her here, where there was no misery and only as much pain as one liked. He felt like he'd murdered something beautiful.

She looked at him a long moment. "It hasn't touched you yet, has it?"

He shook his head. "But it's got you. It got you right away. I saw your face change."

Carolyn sighed at a pleasant memory. "Yes. I feel so amazing now, Simon. It was a struggle just to sit up some days, you know? And now the burden is gone. I feel like I could fly. Thank you."

"Try your best," parroted Simon, because he didn't know what else to say. Then he did know. "What about your art? Is it worth giving up your art for?"

Carolyn's eyes widened and then narrowed. "Oh. You're one of those who think I can't make art if I'm not unhappy." She took a step away from him, as if she'd finally noticed his reek.

Mulishly, Simon said, "Can you?"

Her chin came up. "Yes. Of course I can." She laced her fingers together. "It won't be the same art, but my style has always been developing, hasn't it? And even if isn't the art everybody else wants, I'm a person, not an art machine. I deserve to be happy, don't I?" Her eyes were wide again, pleading, and Simon felt a small, shameful pleasure that even in legendary Eden Falls, he was capable of ruining somebody's joy.

She hadn't talked to him much on their journey in. She'd been reserved, thoughtful. She was a far star: beautiful, distant, and inspiring. She hadn't seemed miserable to him. He hadn't known quite what was going on in Eden Falls until she'd told him, hadn't realized she wanted to stay until she'd walked away from him.

He wondered now if she would have talked more if he'd talked first. But he hadn't talked either. He would have said something stupid if he'd tried. But maybe if he had found a way, maybe if he'd given her the opportunity, she would have given up her quest, gone back to her life in the outside world where she was a celebrity, beloved by thousands.

Probably not. He'd never successfully talked anybody out of a dumb decision, not even himself. It was a good excuse for drinking.

He found himself peering over Carolyn's shoulder, wondering if there was an ice chest full of beer to go along with the barbecue. Beer wasn't his favorite, but in a pinch anything would do. He was feeling the pinch right now.

Carolyn was still staring at him, as if she wanted him to bless her choice. Him. That was crazy. "Sure," he told her. "It seems nice here. Well done. You found a great place. 'Scuse me, I need to get me one of those."

He stepped around her and headed straight for the table of

drinks he'd identified. He had one in his hand and half-empty before Tammy appeared in front of him, lips pursed and eyes laughing. "Did you two sort things out?"

"Don't tell me a keen young thing like yourself wasn't listening," he accused.

Her nose wrinkled. "Maybe a little. I'm not sure what you talked about made much sense."

"She's famous," he said. "You can go see her stuff on the internet if you want."

"You know, the internet doesn't much work here anymore. You try to go to a website and you get these moving lights and pretty music instead. It's nice."

"Unlike the internet. God, this place really is paradise, isn't it?"

"Aww," Tammy said and tugged him over to a broad-trunked tree at the corner of the building. "Sit here in the shade and you'll feel better." She handed him another can. This one was full of fruit juice, the nonalcoholic kind. He slumped against the tree.

"What was it like, when it happened? When the faeries stole this place away from the world?"

Her gaze went distant. "It was just a town, you know? Everybody just trying to make it through the day and hoping like hell tomorrow wouldn't be as bad, and convincing themselves that yesterday was worse. Except for the ones who didn't think about their days at all, even to appreciate what they had. And then, one day, everybody woke up and things really were better. The toast didn't burn. The milk didn't spill. The babies didn't have colic. Nobody ached anymore." She regarded him seriously, her brown eyes wide. "There's still pain, sometimes. But it's a sharp pain, and it fades quickly, leaving the… the pleasure of not being in pain." She blushed, and he wondered what kind of things went on in paradise after dark.

"You met any of them?" He swigged some of the fruit juice. It tasted like it needed a couple of years in an oak barrel. "Any of the faeries who did this?"

"Yes," she said, and that was all.

He prodded, "Are there a lot? What are they like?"

She resettled herself on the grass, tucking her legs beneath her. "There's some. A circle. The magic comes from the circle. They're strange, mostly. But kind."

"This ain't kind," Simon told her. "This is *unnatural*."

"Well, I think it's kind. Carolyn seems to like it. So does Peter, who we met walking over here, and Cassie, my manager at the store."

"And none of you mind what's been taken from you? Makes me sick."

"What's been taken from us?" She sounded honestly puzzled by the idea.

"I don't know. Something. This sort of thing don't happen without a price."

She was quiet, so he finished off the fruit juice and threw the can across the lawn, then watched as one of the barbecuers ambled over to pick it up and put it in the trash.

"Don't you *want* to be happy?" Tammy finally asked, in a small voice.

"I don't think that's even possible," he answered sourly, then glanced at her. She looked childlike in her bewilderment, and it struck him, right in his aching heart: a sharp pain that didn't fade.

"Yeah," he whispered. "Yeah, I do. So why aren't I? Why won't the magic work for me?" He stopped, then started again. "I waited. I waited for hours, didn't drink a drop. But being sober didn't help." He laughed bitterly. "Being sober never helps. You and this damn juice."

"Well, the magic can't work for you," said Tammy gravely. She put her hand on his. "But if you want to be happy, I'm sure you can still find a way, Simon."

He wondered suddenly when he'd told her his name. Had he shown her ID in the grocery store when she'd refused to sell to him? He hadn't. They'd never gotten that far.

She looked at him with eyes older than the dawn and realization lit like a spark in a dark room. He knew who she was. What she was.

He gripped her hand in both of his. "Please," he begged. "All I've ever wanted is to stop hurting so damn much."

She put her free hand on his hair, like a benediction. "You can't. You're beyond the magic of Eden Falls. You know you are. Your angel blood takes you beyond our touch."

He stared into her bottomless eyes, wishing he could drown in them. Then he scrubbed at his own eyes and stood up, drawing her up after him. He said, "That's okay. That's fine. What you're doing here is wrong anyhow. They're not human anymore, now are they?"

Her eyes searched his face as he kissed her hand. He drew the knife he always wore behind his back. Then, silently, he called on the angel magic he couldn't escape, called on the power of a storm god father, called lightning from a clear sky. Her eyes widened as she realized what he was doing, her mouth opened to cry out, to stop him, but the thunder rolled and he could not, would not, hear her. Her fingers closed tightly around his hand, but only because a body spasms when struck by lightning. Only because of that.

Simon broke the circle of magic chaining Eden Falls.

Nobody thanked him.

10 WAYS TO GET RID OF AN UNINVITED VISITOR

I am an old woman. You all know that. There's lots of stuff I just don't have time for anymore. That includes the Strangers. You know the ones. Showing up in shopping malls and on the YouTube, all flash and dazzle. Some people are worried about what their arrival means but I have enough on my plate. My schedule is booked!

But apparently the Strangers didn't get the memo. One of them has been poking around the outside of my trailer. Pretty enough, if you like that kind of thing. But I do not. It's just plain weird having him out there. He smiles at me when I come outside which is all wrong. So I did some research on how to get rid of the Strangers. This is what I've found.

1. Garlic on the outside windowsill. I can confirm this does not work. Not with his sort of Stranger anyhow. He just collected all the cloves.

2. Keeping the trash indoors. I don't know who suggested this but they are stupid. Sorry. While the Strangers may share a few physical characteristics with raccoons and coyotes, they are not those. He has never even looked at my trash.

3. Salt around the outside of the trailer. This at least got his attention. He knelt down and tasted it. And he stepped over it

with a giant step. It didn't stop him from knocking on my door and leaving banana bread on my doorstep though. I assume he stole it from somewhere.

4. Not speaking to them. I tried to do better than this and not even look at him. Didn't work. He's out there across the street singing. Nobody should be able to sing like that.

5. Standing on the porch and saying in a firm voice, "Go away, you're not welcome here." He took that as an invitation. AN INVITATION. He came right up to my porch and started talking about some New Age gibberish (And I am sorry, Margaret, but you know it sounds like gibberish if you're not up on all that crystal stuff).

6. Call the police. You see how desperate I am? I actually called the cops. They did not help. Of course. They had some nonsense about having more important fish to fry than a Stranger who was acting like a good neighbor. If they came out here and saw the way he keeps watching me, they'd change their tune— wait, no they wouldn't. Pigs.

7. Iron around the house. Everything I read said this should have worked. I put some nails across my walk. He LAUGHED when he saw them. Then he picked them all up, put them in a bag on my porch and told me it was dangerous for the mail girl. He said if I needed any help with a project, all I had to do was ask.

8. Silver. Where is an old lady like me going to get silver? Besides, given what happened with everything else, he'd probably steal it.

9. Insulting them. Apparently this works in Sweden. But not here. The less said the better. Moving on.

10. Saying "thank you," for every little thing they do. The Twitter gave me this advice. It would never have occurred to me. It just goes to show how unnatural these Strangers are. I started thanking him, sweet as sugar, every time I saw him. He gave me

this hangdog look after the second time like he couldn't understand why I'd do such a thing. The fifth time, he stomped away. It's been a whole day Stranger-free now. Sweet relief! Thank you, Twitter!

10 WAYS TO HAVE COFFEE WITH A FAERIE

I had this problem a few weeks ago. Maybe you remember it. A Stranger kept hanging around my trailer. I am too old for nonsense like his, so I started working on getting rid of him. The only thing that worked at all was being very polite to him. Basically, I had to thank him every time I saw him. Well, status update. That worked for a while but then it got a little complicated.

First, that banana bread of his started showing up outside my door every day. And cookies. And some kind of little quiches. I caught him leaving them once at dawn. I explained (as politely as you can through gritted teeth) that I did not need some kind of Stranger Meals On Wheels yet. He just gave me a grin that I will be writing a stern letter to my Congressperson about, and ran away.

Then I started feeling some guilt. I think it was all the thank-yous that did it. It is hard for me to say thank-you as much as I was without feeling it. I don't know how all the grocery store clerks do it all day! Maybe it is because they're doing the same thing all the time? But the Stranger was all over. The more I thanked him, the more aggressively he did stuff I had to thank him for. He watered the plants outside my fence. Now they have big puffy crimson blooms. In February. Unnatural!! (But pretty. Guilt.)

So. Now I have a new problem. If I keep thanking him without doing something decent in return, I won't have my self-respect. I have to take steps.

In case you ever find yourself in this situation (and I hope for your sake you do not), here is a list of ideas for how to handle the situation.

1. Take a tray of coffee out to the porch. You can offer him a hot drink when he comes by. He always comes by.

2. When he wanders by shirtless and dazzling like some tumblr boy, do not get flustered and holler at him to put some clothes on before you warm him up yourself. You'll mean with coffee. It will be misunderstood.

3. I hope by the time he is on your porch, he is wearing a shirt. If not keep your eyes on his face. Except when you're pouring the cup of coffee. Hot coffee hurts when you miss the cup.

4. When he takes your scalded hand, stay calm. He can't make it worse and you do not need a cardiac arrest too. Perhaps he is a doctor. After a minute, the burn doesn't seem that bad anyhow.

5. Once coffee is poured, a bit of chat is mandatory. Miss Manners says so. Unfortunately. Stick to safe subjects like the weather.

6. For some Strangers the weather is personal. Go figure. Move on to something else. It may all come back to the weather. His job? Related to the weather. His family? The weather.

7. You can try discussing the garden. This may be uncomfortable because of his tendency to make flowers bloom in February, but at least you can let him know you appreciate his work. Do it carefully or he will give you that should-be-illegal smile again.

8. In desperation, you'll find yourself gossiping about other neighbors. They probably deserve it as the good Lord knows they gossip about you.

9. When the conversation turns to politics, you might discover that he has interests other than the weather and trailer park inhabitants. This is probably dangerous. But thrilling. Who else talks to you about your political activism off the internet? Nobody, that's who, especially not handsome young men.

10. Grudgingly allow that it might be all right if he comes back again another day for more coffee and chat. But not too often, mind.

10 WAYS TO PUT A FAERIE TO WORK

These Strangers sure are everywhere these days. Some of them have been doing kind of scary things. Others are more helpful. Perhaps you've found yourself with an overly helpful Stranger on your hands and are at a loss at how to put him or her to work. Here are some ideas.

1. Sort out your old boxes. Any Stranger who cares enough to be helpful will love this. Warning: they may draw certain conclusions from your stuff. These conclusions may be right. Just blame magic.

2. Weed your garden. I highly recommend this. Their ways are strange but you will never have unwanted weeds again.

3. Clean your house. I'm personally not so sure about this one because the day I can't clean my little trailer is the day I'm ready to be laid out. But for busy folks like moms with small kids, it is a very efficient plan.

4. Escort you to a demonstration. It's always good to have a little extra security at these things, especially when they can stop the cops from getting too handsy with a wave.

5. Adjust the location of your house by a few inches. It's probably best if you're not inside. Or around. Drop a hint, then go to shopping for an hour. Then don't ask too many questions.

6. Be your copilot on a cross-country trip to crash a conference in DC. Do not let him drive. Not even if it's an automatic. It is bad.

7. Bring him along to hold your hand as you go to an upsetting meeting with your doctor.

8. Go to Athens, Greece to see the sights. Hint: The Strangers have access to very fast travel. I only wish I'd known that before we drove to DC.

9. Let him carry your parcels in Rome.

10. Get a lift to the blogger meet up in NYC. So much better

than flying. Note: This may lead to embarrassing questions. Embarrassing for you, not him. He has no shame and positively wants them to think ridiculous things. We are just friends! Anything else would be so inappropriate.

10 WAYS TO REFUSE A FAERIE

I'm not going to go into details, but I got some bad personal news recently. The sort of bad news we all face eventually. And I don't really want to talk about it, thanks, so let's not drag down my comments with depressing stuff, please.

But I also got an offer. It's an offer I can't quite believe but I've got to refuse anyhow. And just plain "no" isn't good enough. I mean, there's plenty of situations where that's all that's necessary. But sometimes you want to let someone down easy, because you care. (There, I said it, all right? You commenters can just hush now.) And whatever you say is going to last longer than you are, so maybe you make a list, like this one.

1. I've lived a good life. Even better since I met you. But I'm human. This happens to us.

2. It is not natural. Just like flowers in February. Sorry. I know you're good with nature but it is natural for things to wither. Everything has a season and all that.

3. It isn't right. I'm not the only person out there with this disease. Why should I get the miracle? I know you have some considerable affection for me but that doesn't change the fact that other people are suffering much worse than I am right now.

4. In fact, I have friends in various stages of illnesses. How can I look them in the face? And don't you look at me with those eyes. I'm the one who has to live with myself after.

5. And speaking of your affection, you're immortal and beautiful and you don't want to be saddled with a cranky old lady

like me forever. Go find some movie star.

6. I am terrified of this illness. Accepting your offer would be running away. If I'm brave I can maybe help others be brave too. I've been wanting to do that my whole life.

7. This is just denial speaking. I read about it. If we wait long enough, we'll accept it.

8. Of course I don't want to die. I wish there was a cure for the whole mess. I mean, beside your way. Which is unnatural, not fair, and so, so kind.

9. What would I do as one of your kind anyhow? Besides things that make me blush, because you can't do that ALL the time. Sure, I'll be leaving a lot of unfinished work done. I was making real progress with the Oversight Committee campaign and your people need some kind of advocate still and that blogging conference wanted me as a speaker. That's a lot of work, really.

10 ….You know what? Looking over this list… I changed my mind.

11. Yes.

HER DAUGHTER, PINNED TO THE SKY

The Queen of Stone sat in state under the mountain, in a hall of sparkling crystal and cleft souls, and watched stained glass visions of the world above. She watched dancing waterfalls and lovers kissing. She watched the sea crashing into the shore and a solitary runner. She watched a crowded marketplace and a riot. None of it pleased her. The panes became fixed and cold, and she turned to look at the hall's glittering ceiling far above, her gaze yet more distant.

Her court didn't notice at first, engaged in the intrigues and whispers that filled immortal hours. But her handmaiden knew the signs. She knew, too, what to do when that scarred face and those empty eyes searched for the sky beyond the stone. "Your Majesty, perhaps we ought to check on the mortal's window again. It was your favorite, do you remember?"

The Queen of Stone lowered her gaze to look once again upon her screens. "Her mother cried."

"I've watched, Your Majesty. It's better now."

But when the stained glass that channeled the vision of a mortal woman came once again to life, she was speaking with another mortal: this one with faded hair and a lined face. An old mortal.

"Her grandmother," said the Queen, her harsh voice crackling. "No better. Take it away."

The handmaiden flushed in chagrin. "She'd been crafting a

hammer when last I checked, Your Majesty."

"She is a mortal. We know mortals. Their activities change rapidly."

"Yes, Your Majesty." The handmaiden watched her mistress raise her eyes to the ceiling again and turned her own gaze to the floor. Beyond the silence of the stained glass screens, the rest of the court shifted, whispers fading as they noticed where the Queen's gaze was directed.

The handmaiden wondered hopefully what they might to do to pull the Queen's attention back from where it must not go. It was their responsibility as well, one reason among many they all gathered here. Or so the handmaiden trusted. But one of them turned to the reflective wall and walked through it. A pair of courtiers retreated, bowing, down the hall.

Fleeing. The handmaiden turned her attention away from the cowards and back to her Queen. "Shall I play for you, Your Majesty?"

"Do not," said the Queen of Stone. "Music is a cruelty now. It makes you all free, while I am...." She trailed off and one hand moved restlessly, as if to take in all of herself.

"You are our beloved Queen, Your Majesty," said the handmaiden sternly. "We would do anything for you."

"So beloved," said the Queen harshly, sardonically. "Let me alone to look upon the sky, then."

The handmaiden exchanged glances with those courtiers placed closest to the throne: those who both pleased her the most and most wished to be of service. But none of them, not one, was willing to disobey their mistress's command.

The gentle rustling and chiming of the court faded into silence. Another courtier moved as if to leave and the ringing of his crystal gown drew the court's eyes. The court's eyes, but not the Queen's. Shamed, he stopped where he was. Together in silence, they waited.

The Queen's fingers tightened on the arms of her throne. Her eyes widened. "I see her. She is alone. How could we have— oh, I must—" The Queen's skin heaved tectonically as rarely used muscles moved. Her gown crackled. A vast pressure grew, as if the whole world was about to fly apart.

The handmaiden took a quick, restless step forward. "Would you like to rest, Your Majesty? We could move you. You might find your private chamber peaceful—"

The Queen looked away from the ceiling at the handmaiden, her eyes glowing. But her skin stopped heaving, and the pressure on their world faded a little.

"I *told* you to let me be. If you don't want to be spun back into the pumice that adopted you, *be silent*." The edge in the Queen's voice momentarily shattered the handmaiden's will, and she sank to her knees, staring at the floor.

When she recovered herself enough to look up, the Queen was once again staring at the roof.

"Please don't," whispered the handmaiden. "Don't hurt yourself—"

The Queen raised a hand without taking her gaze from the ceiling and the handmaiden felt the bonds that bound her to a body fraying.

Even if that was what it cost her, she had no other choice. "Your Majesty, you mustn't—"

"Sorry I'm late," said a cheery voice from the hall's entrance. "It takes me a bit longer to get around. But I'm here now and with a gift for Her Majesty."

The fraying of the handmaiden's bonds stopped as the Queen's head lowered, her attention momentarily diverted.

It was Tarn, the Duke whose Duchy had been dissolved into the mists of the Backworld, thanks to ambition and compassion and a doorway he couldn't manage. The handmaiden knew him of old and no longer liked him. As the murmuring court cleared a space between him and the Queen, she saw what he had brought with him and liked him even less.

He held the hand of a mortal child, a boy, who looked at the floor rather than at the wonders who surrounded him. The court murmured and the handmaiden sprang forward. "How *could* you? How could you do this to her *again?*" She moved between them as if she could obscure her Queen's view of the child, vainly.

"Bring your gift forward, Tarn," commanded the Queen. "Let me inspect it."

Tarn tugged on the child's hand and the child raised dark brown eyes to the Duke. "What?"

"Remember, I had somebody for you to meet? Come, little one. You'll like her."

"I like the ground," remarked the boy. "It shines. What kind of crystal is it?" He took an obedient step forward.

The handmaiden looked away, holding her arms across her chest to contain her fury. As they passed by her, Tarn murmured, "We do what we have to, my lady, as distasteful as it might be."

"You stink of mortal's death," said the handmaiden coldly. "Stand away from me, if you please."

One of the courtiers who had left returned smiling, and she realized he hadn't fled at all. He had sought this out, gone to Tarn to push this mad plan. She wished he'd been a coward instead.

The Queen said, "What is this, Tarn?" and the handmaiden wanted to press her hands to the ears to shut out the farce. She couldn't turn away, though, couldn't take her eyes from the child's sweet face. The fire had come upon them again and they would all suffer until it was ashes once more.

"A mortal child, Your Majesty," said Tarn, sweeping a bow. "He is homeless and alone. I heard other children describing him as 'stone-like' and thought you might enjoy meeting him."

The Queen's blank eyes stared down at the child. The child stared back. "Why are you a statue? What are you made of?"

"I had a child once," murmured the Queen. "Once and oh, so many times since. But once of my own." Her eyes raised again to the heavens and the handmaiden felt her blood chill. What if even this step, as repellant as it was, did not serve? What if this time there was no stopping the Queen of Stone from rising from her throne and ascending into the sky to tear the world apart?

The little boy touched the Queen's gown. "You *are* stone," he said happily. "Me too." He started clambering up the Queen's skirts, oblivious to the direction of her attention.

The court's murmuring became a mix of horror and amusement, as it suited the courtiers. Tarn was amused, the hateful creature that he was.

The handmaiden alone was yet afraid: afraid of the Queen rejecting the child and afraid of the Queen accepting him. She watched her mistress's face intently.

The boy made it up to her lap and leaned back against her chest. "Crystals," he said in pleasure.

"Look beyond the crystals, child," said the Queen.

"What for?"

Her arms came around the child. "Beyond the crystals is your eldest sister. They took her and pinned her to the sky. And one day, when you are grown, you will rescue her."

Tears in her eyes, the handmaiden went to prepare the necessary chamber for the Queen's new son, just as she had so many times before.

BOOK 3

THE ENDLESS SILENCE OF FORGOTTEN THINGS

The sky is black. The ground is fertile with the ashes of the dead, but nothing grows in the clearing where they died, where they burned, where they were devoured. Nothing grows there. Not anymore.

The trees around the clearing, though. The trees thrive. They have been watered with blood and grief. Their trunks are twisted and gnarled, but their greenery is lush with the strength they draw from their roots.

The sky is black. The ground is ash. The air is a conspirator, pressing down on the ground. Nothing grows in the clearing and nothing moves: not vibrant leaf or swirl of cinders. Movement is akin to life and the barrier here between life and death is too easily crossed.

Silent night.

Roots stretch deep. They do more than probe for water. They do more than anchor. On the other side of the soil is another world, a winter world where the roots are leafless branches hanging down over the caverns of the dead.

This is an endless place, and tiny: bounded by roots and broken mirrors. What enters does not leave. How can anything leave, when the only movement is the slow growth of roots in the hollows of the dead as they transmute the ash?

But now—now the air moves. A breeze, drugged by the silence, traces a path through the ash. Slowly, slowly: the best effort of that which has forgotten how to dance.

Silver traces cracks in the sky like lightning. The breeze freshens; the membrane between the clearing and the sunlit world trembles. Something terrible presses against the blackness.

The wind strengthens, raking fingers through the glossy leaves and kicking the ash into a whirlwind. Bell-like thunder follows the silver lighting and something terrible comes through.

A figure stands on the edge of the blackened clearing, a yew and a sycamore at his back. The ash surges over his shoes as the wind settles like a mantle over his back. He surveys the clearing for a long moment, looking at the ground as closely as the trees, at the nothing as well as the something.

"Speak with me," he commands, in a voice of bronze.

But nothing stirs in the clearing. It is a place of the dead, and the dead do not answer back.

The figure listens to the silence. "Very well." He puts his hands in his pockets and leans on the yew behind him. He is gaining— something. The trees bend toward him and the ash shifts as if on a slope, as the earth itself distorts under him. He is a black hole and he is gradually pulling the clearing into himself.

When the roots twitch from their elaborate patterns in the spaces below, that which waits in the clearing ignores the visitor no longer. Shadows grow from the trees, orienting like needles on a compass until they layer upon each other in the center of the clearing, where the ash is deepest. A shape forms among the shadows and the ash, and the *pull* the visitor has exerted upon the clearing reverses as once again the spiritual forces come into balance.

As the visitor appears as a young man of business, dark-haired with his shirt sleeves rolled up, so the ghost appears as a schoolgirl, with shadowy hair to her waist and eyes of static. She balances on one foot for a moment then braces herself on the charred earth.

After equilibrium returns, it is some time before the visitor once again breaks the silence. "It would be better if I didn't stop."

"No," says the girl, the word bobbing up from the depths of silence, "It wouldn't."

"I first heard a whisper of what grows here when I was on the far side of the stars. The earth itself groans under the strain."

The girl whispers, "Before I was born, my mother clutched her back and vomited through her nose. And yet she lives still, in all her grief." She spread her hands and ash spins around her, through her.

The man with the wind as a mantle kneels down and plunges his hands deep into the ash and the earth, until the surface seethes around his forearms. His sleeves remain clean. His awareness goes deeper yet: into the hollows cradled by the roots and the strangeness that grows between them. "It is an atrocity," he says, but he doesn't pull away.

The girl watches him, her hand upraised to cup a fragment of ash that flares to a cinder. "We know you."

"Oh? And what do you know of me?" Tendons move in his arms as his fingers move under the earth.

"You are the executioner of angels. You have committed endless atrocities."

He pulls his hands out of the earth and sits on his heels, tilting his head to gaze at the ghost. "Not endless," he says, and his voice is mild. "I've kept count. I remember them all."

"And yet they do not end. Those you have cut off from their names continue on, broken and breaking." More sparks flare in the ash and scarlet glints in her eyes. "What we've suffered could be laid at your feet. Just as our vengeance is."

The leaves tremble as if a hand has been pulled back to strike.

His mantle of wind rises around him, which fans the embers into tiny flames. But she does not move. He listens to that which he just touched, listens for premature movement, for the howling of an atrocity lunging for its doom.

He hears nothing.

The girl with static eyes and coals on her fingertips smiles. "We are patient. Our vengeance will not be destroyed so easily. If we are patient, he will come to us in the end, he who murdered us, who commits horrors day after day."

Trouble touches the brow of the executioner of angels. "He was corrupted before I took his name. It was all I could do to limit him. I assure you, he would be worse if I hadn't."

The coals on her fingertips make a fiery pattern through the drifting ash as she shrugs and spreads her hands as if to encompass the clearing. "And yet you seek to stop what we do here."

"You're immortal souls," he points out as he rises to his feet. "Chaining yourself like this, to this purpose, goes against all that was built into your nature. And what you do cannot succeed. He is as immortal as you are."

"The executioner of angels," she repeats, savoring the phrase.

"Yes. Trust me to know. There are better places for you. Even my mansion is better." A wry expression twists his mouth. "Mostly unoccupied, too."

"You make a joke," she says, as if identifying a distant landmark.

"An offer. Abandon what you do here and know peace."

Her mouth twists in disdain. "And how would we know peace beyond this place? Would you strip of us our hatred? Destroy our memories? Make us into preserved blossoms to adorn your home?"

"The mansions of heaven have a way of providing… perspective." He holds out his hand.

All the ash flares bright as her rage ignites. Her hair lifts from her back, her feet lift from the ground. "Perspective? Perspective on how our lives were shortened? Perspective on how we suffered?

Or perspective on how we are not important? Perspective on how your kind, guardians of the world, does not care, does nothing to stop him and those like him? On how you create monsters, then leave them to play in the wreckage of our bodies and hearts and minds? We do not *want* your perspective."

He steps back, back from her rage, until once again he is leaning on his tree. "You want retribution."

Surrounded by her scarlet rage, the ghost stares through him, as if that which she is connected to grants her vision beyond what is possible. "We wanted justice. We must, it seems, make our own." The embers die again, all but those at her fingertips and burning at the ends of her hair. "You can destroy what we build here, if it pleases you, but you cannot stop us from building anew."

He looks up at the fractured sky, beyond the cracks. "There is that which could stop you. That which was made to stop you."

Her voice is once again a whisper. "Not to stop us. Not to stop this. You never expected that we might be a danger to your kind. Are you afraid now?"

The man thinks about the question and then smiles. "No more than I should be." There's something wrong with his reaction. Something is off.

The ghost's mouth is a slash as she stares at the man. Then her expression changes, and for a moment the static of her eyes fades to reveal a very human surprise. "You don't actually want to destroy our work."

"No," he says, smiling still. "I want to learn. Teach me what you do, and in exchange I will protect you from the others."

She hesitates, this representative of the clearing. Then the ghost and the angel exchange secrets: the method of the machine for the means of calling the executioner. When it is done, the angel departs.

The sky is black. The ground is ash. All is silent. And under the earth, vengeance grows.

FAR CITY CHEER SQUAD

The feral city was a far cry from Neverland but the lost ended up there all the same. Criminals, runaways, or lovers, sometimes all three, and most of them were little more than kids. It had been that way for uncounted years: the homeless hiding in the streets and alleys of a city that barely tolerated them, while dodging the hunters prowling for a moment's entertainment.

All this might have been true in any city in the world. But the feral city was different, because nobody lived there except for the runaways and the hunters and their monstrous prey. It was a strange place, full of both wonders and terrors. But the wonders—buildings made of crystal, twenty foot tall sculptures of roses, weird and elaborate water fountains—never lasted, while the terrors seemed to be eternal.

And then one day, the hunters left.

Once the rumbling of their collapsing tower had faded and the crimson dust had been swallowed by the city, once their monstrous prey returned to the snow-and-blood forest, the runaways considered it a reason to celebrate. But too soon their joy turned to something else. They'd started as runaways, criminals, lovers, but in the feral city they all became scavengers. It was the natural path if you weren't a hunter and you avoided being prey.

It wasn't like the hunters had ever valued their kills. They hunted so many things: monsters and big game and small game and children—and most of those were good eating once the hunters had taken what trophies they wanted and ridden away.

So. Once the dust of the hunters' doom had faded, once the joyful dancing had become weary sprawling, the scavengers realized they were once again getting hungry.

They went out to look for food. At first it wasn't too bad. There were many kills, and few other scavengers, and sometimes the city itself, in its pure randomness, brought forth bounty.

"I'd give anything to find that spaghetti tree again," said Izzy wistfully. He was a scrawny, dark-skinned boy wearing a tattered Seahawks jersey and carrying a canvas bag that was sadly empty.

"Oh come on, man." said Ramone. "You never found any such thing." He—and he fought like a demon for that 'he' when others expressed their doubts—was quite a bit shorter but a lot less scrawny than Izzy. He tapped the pavement with the twisted remains of a metal signpost, clanging out a simple pattern as they strolled down one of the broad avenues of the feral city. There were never any cars to worry about, police or otherwise, and now that the hunters were gone, only hunger to fear. Hunger didn't care if you made a lot of noise.

(The city sometimes did. But as long as they didn't go inside the city's buildings, they were usually safe. Everybody learned that pretty quickly when they came to the city. The whole idea that indoors was safe and outdoors was dangerous was the first of many ideas turned on their head in the city. The idea that Ramone should have introduced himself as Ramona was another.)

"How did I get the bag of spaghetti then?" demanded Izzy. "I don't lie, jerk."

"What we really need," said Ramone, ignoring Izzy blithely, "is for Miss Zellie there to get herself over to the shitty real world and bring us back some chow."

'Miss Zellie' was half a block ahead with her boyfriend Cam, checking down alleys for edible remains, for signs of small animal life, for weeds and randomly generated trash. She'd eaten all of it in her time in the feral city. But when she heard her name she stopped and turned around, putting her hands on her hips. "Would you guys stop following us? And you too, Eden!" She raised her voice so she could be heard by the two girls a block behind Ramone and Izzy, too. "I'm not going to lead you to some promised land of roast chicken so you might as well piss off and go look down another street."

Ramone groaned. "Roast chicken. Like, that rotisserie stuff. Oh man, and pizza. Come on, Zellie! We're starving here and you got the gift! All you need to do is pop over, grab some stuff and pop back. Nobody'll notice quick enough to catch you."

"Did somebody find food?" demanded Eden, sprinting up with Deena beside her. "That weed stew Zellie made did not go very far, let me tell you."

"You're so welcome," Zellie said nastily. "I didn't want to share it with you anyhow."

Izzy said, "Don't listen to her, Zel. We need you. We're going to end up bones ourselves without you." Most of the inhabitants of the city just wandered in one day and never could figure how to get back out again. The city was a maze from which there was no exit.

It was different for some of them, though. Like Zellie. She could walk between the real world and the feral city just by changing her pace. She went other places, too, like the snow-and-blood forest that bounded the city. Almost everybody could get there if they tried, but it took longer, and Zellie could go much farther, because she didn't seem to be afraid of anything.

Zellie looked away. "What we *need* is to scour this city until we find a park or a backyard or something where we can plant some seeds and take care of ourselves. This climate is good for that. It would work."

"Hah!" said Ramone. "And that would last just as long as Izzy's stupid spaghetti tree, which didn't last longer than spit in a frying pan."

"We need to make friends with the city," said Cam quietly. Cam said things like that. He was slim with silky brown hair, and intensely nearsighted. His glasses had shattered the first time he'd had to run from the hunters. Zellie said that even when he'd had them, he hadn't quite seen things the same way as everybody else.

Ramone ignored Cam. "And even if it did last, we'd still starve long before anything was ready to eat, Zellie. Even radishes take a few weeks and believe-you-me, you don't want any of us living off radishes, anyhow."

"It's not like we're shacking up together, why should I care?"

"Sunny says we all have to take care of each other," Deena piped up.

Zellie scowled. "Like I care what that *tourist* says."

"I've been thinking about a plan," Cam went on in the same quiet voice, and Zellie turned to look at him. Everybody stopped wheedling then, because there was no point. When Zellie paid attention to her boyfriend it was like everybody else had been switched off. It was a trait generally agreed on as totally disgusting and super sweet at the same time.

"A plan for what?" Zellie demanded.

"For how to make friends with the city. So that it helps us out more. So we can tell it we like spaghetti trees and stuff."

"The city isn't a dog, Cam," said Eden impatiently, her stick-like arms crossed. "We can't tame it with bacon."

"Oh god, bacon," moaned Izzy. "I'm so hungry."

"It's not a normal city, Eden," said Deena earnestly. "It has a voice, if you listen."

Cam gave Deena an encouraging smile. "I think all cities do. But this one's special."

"Well, yeah. It's all post-apocalyptic empty," said Ramone.

"It doesn't have any food," Izzy added.

"It's *ours*," said Deena.

"It's a bunch of cement and stones," mumbled Eden. "I think I'm gonna faint." She swayed dramatically and Izzy absently put a hand on her elbow.

"It's alive," said Cam. "And it thinks we're an enemy. But we're not. The hunters were the enemy and now they're gone, so we can all be friends." He beamed.

Zellie sighed and repeated, "So what's your plan?"

Cam said, "We just have to wake it up and talk to it. I've done a little talking already." He hesitated. "But we're going to need food to do that. A lot of food." He gave Zellie a little smile.

She put her hands over her eyes. "I don't know how to get a lot of food. Just because I can walk back over to Normaltown doesn't mean I end up in front of an all-you-can-steal buffet."

Confidently, Cam said, "I have a plan for that too. It'll totally work. Only…." He hesitated, worry darkening his face.

"Spill it," said Zellie grimly.

"Only for *this* plan to work, we have to go inside."

Silence fell as everybody stared at each other. *Inside* was bad news. Nobody wanted to go inside. But between that or starvation? Or worse, returning to the real world? Well, it took some thinking about.

"I CAN'T BELIEVE that you want to start out making friends with the city by doing something it *hates*, Cam." Zellie squeezed Cam's hand as they walked to one of the persistent landmarks in the mercurial city. "That's not *you*. You're the nice one."

Cam shrugged self-consciously. "I hate getting vaccines, but they're good for me in the long run."

They stopped outside the vast block-sized building they called the Mall. It wasn't a very original name, because it looked like a mall. It had big windows on every floor, and they were almost arranged like somebody rational had been involved. It had big glass double doors, too. Looking through them showed a huge cavernous space, lit only by the windows, with a concrete floor and not a speck of furnishings. A mall, before any tenants had moved in. Or any internal floors had been built. With freestanding ladders leading up somewhere above.

Nobody knew exactly where the ladders led, because once you went inside one of the city's buildings, things changed quickly.

Cam said, "Ouch, I'm going to need that hand, Zellie." He stared at the glass door thoughtfully.

Zellie relaxed her own hand enough that she wasn't crushing Cam's anymore. His nearsightedness *must* be a benefit when dealing with the city's horrors. But he was very brave, too, she certainly knew that. She wouldn't be where she was now without him.

Ramone and the others trailing behind them stopped on the other side of the street.

"You can do it," called Izzy encouragingly. "Nobody'll notice you fast enough to report you."

"Doesn't matter if they do," said Eden. "They're never going to find their way back here."

Zellie didn't bother to correct them. Besides, maybe they were right. But she was scared, all the same. Not of going *inside*—well, not *much* afraid of going inside—but of what would be waiting for her on the other side.

But Cam said they had to do this, Cam said this would make them safe in the end, and she trusted Cam. "Let's go."

"All right," said Cam softly. "You do the walking and I'll do the talking, just like we've done before. But don't take the big step until I say go, or we'll have to come back and try again."

"What if it doesn't let us back again?" asked Zellie, suddenly struck by a new worry.

"Zellie," said Cam softly, looking at her with his dark eyes. "Nobody can stop *you*."

Zellie forced a smile past her dread, squared her shoulders, and pulled open the door.

When they stepped inside the Mall, the air was cool and dry. Motes of dust floated in beams of light, enough dust that the freestanding ladders were just gawky alien forms in the shadows. Two steps in and the air warmed as the humidity rose. There were mannequins deeper in the shadows, draped with blotchy cloth and posed in impossible ways.

Cam and Zellie moved cautiously, continuing to hold hands. Despite what he'd said, Cam was quiet for the moment, waiting for the bad stuff to start happening.

Twenty steps in and Zellie was about to remark on the unusual quietness of the Mall when a gong sounded and the floor vibrated beneath them. A mannequin twisted its head upside down to watch them pass. The cloth wound around its neck was stained with red and black. It dripped onto the floor, the black devouring the red and pooling around the mannequin's feet. The pool sent out tendrils that crept around the ground toward their feet.

Zellie shivered and stuck her chin out. She might have run from this the first time she went Inside, but it wasn't anything now. "What now?"

"We keep walking. This isn't where we want to be. If we cross here, we could end up anywhere with a big building. Nah, I have to make it clear that there's only one place we'll be getting off." Cam's gaze, always faraway, focused on something only he could see. His mouth twitched as he whispered something just below Zellie's hearing.

Zellie eyed another mannequin, which opened its hands. Strands of something slimy reached down to the ground and started humping along it, like earthworms made of snot. There was shuffling behind them but when she looked over her shoulder all she saw was the door out, still open, about a mile away. If they ran, they might make it to the door. Or a nightmare might eat them first. Even odds.

They wouldn't run, though. They had a job to do. Zellie lengthened her stride, pulling Cam along behind her. She was hungry, too. The stew she'd made from weeds and bones had been a long time ago. She wouldn't have gone back without Cam asking it of her, no way, not for a stack of pizzas. But she was excited about the prospect of real food again all the same.

A mannequin carved of lavender wood opened its shroud and teeth rained down from a gash in its belly. All wood, but the paleness was disturbing. Zellie slowed, unable to look away from the teeth scattering across the floor. Her grandmother had kept all her baby teeth for a reason and nobody but Cam had ever understood how creepy that was.

Zellie's foot slipped on a stray tooth that rolled too close and she went down to one knee. As soon as she fell all the mannequins turned toward her, all through the gloomy building-cavern. They rippled closer. Even the ladders shuffled closer, except they weren't ladders anymore, but elongated men with their hands bound to their sides. One bent in the middle, a skull-like head with bulging eyes swooping down toward Zellie and Cam.

Zellie didn't scream, because she'd worked hard learning not to scream. She took a step to the side, yanking Cam hard after her, then stopped and flung up her free hand. "Cam," she said urgently. "We have to get out of here soon." She'd only stopped because running now would be worse.

"Keep walking," Cam muttered. "I think I'm getting somewhere."

The mannequins were uncomfortably close to a crowd around them and the skull-like face dove again, but Zellie started walking again, just fast enough to escape the edge of the crowd before it closed around them. As a mannequin reached out for her with a clawed hand, she dodged away and the mannequin howled and collapsed into a pile of limbs that reformed into another worm-like creature. Zellie kicked it apart and pushed on ahead.

They left the mannequins behind, moving into a vastness that seemed impossible: no columns, no supports, no visible walls, just an endless high ceiling and an endless cement floor.

Cam kept on muttering to himself, talking to the city or the building or God. Zellie knew he could get results; they'd survived together this long because he could get results. But they were never what you'd call 100% reproducible, just better than the average result when somebody begged the city to feed them, save then, find them.

Then large cubes appeared in the distance, stacked on top of one another. "Now," breathed Cam. "Here."

Zellie promptly took a Big Step, and another, and another, dragging Cam with her. After the third Big Step, the cubes popped into pallets stacked with boxes. Noise and light and life erupted around her. They were *inside* a store. A big store. One of those big warehouses her grandmother had always scorned.

Cam looked at her, smiling tiredly. "We just need a cart."

"And we need to hurry. We can get back from here? Do we have to go outside? I don't want to—" she stopped herself uneasily, looking at people passing by with their carts.

"I can *definitely* bring the city back if you can get us across," said Cam confidently. He looked around. "I'm going to need some help navigating, though. Misty weird cities, I'm great! But this place seems to have a lot of corners...."

He looked little-boy-plaintive and Zellie wanted to kiss the expression away. But—later. She looked around, figured out where the front of the store was, and then led Cam to an abandoned cart near where somebody was checking membership cards at the entrance. There were cameras there, too, and Zellie tried to stay away from them. Her initial feeling of triumph at working together to *get somewhere* was fading rapidly under a bad feeling.

"Cheese, maybe? And nuts."

"Hold on to the cart," Zellie said. "I'll guide it. We have to hurry." People were looking at the two of them. Their clothing was old and torn and they weren't exactly clean but Zellie wasn't worried about that nearly as much as other things.

They shoved their way through the crowds—it must be a weekend back in the world where that mattered—and found the dairy aisle, grabbing this and that as they waited for knots of people to unravel. The cheese aisle was huge, full of enormous rounds and long bricks of hard cheeses. Zellie piled pounds and pounds into the bottom of the cart. Then they moved on to the dried fruit and the nuts, and one aisle over, canned tuna and crackers.

"Down here!" pointed Cam. "I can smell stuff we need." It was perpendicular to the food aisles and contained sporting goods, of all things. "You grab socks! We always need clean socks! I'll get some other stuff!" commanded Cam, and fumbled over on the other side of the aisle. Puzzled, Zellie grabbed an armful of sock packages and then raced after Cam as he kept pushing the cart down the aisle. He rotated it awkwardly.

"Pasta and breakfast cereal!" crowed Cam, pointing at what could only be a blur of colors for him. He darted over and grabbed what turned out to be a giant-sized box of Pop-Tarts. "Och and there's cookware down there!"

But Zellie was looking somewhere else. On this side of the warehouse she could see a large display of garden supplies. "Seeds," she breathed.

There was an odd coughing sound behind her, but she was so enraptured by the idea of seeds that at first she didn't recognize it. "Come on, Cam. We can grab some trail mix as we go over there!" Cam dropped a bag of chocolate chips into the cart and latched on. She started pushing.

The coughing sound came again. This time it cut through Zellie's distraction. She looked around, dreading what she'd see, but all she saw was people. Nobody she recognized.

It didn't matter.

"Dear child," said a sad, wispy voice, from the other side of the aisle of pastries, and it was followed by another rattling cough.

Cam heard it too. His face went pale. "We need to go."

Zellie was breathing hard. She felt cold with terror. "We need those seeds. Hop onto the back of the cart, Cam! We have to run!"

They ran, Zellie pushing both the heavy cart and Cam as fast as she could. She was strong and tough, but the rattling cough and the wispy voice followed her. "Don't run, child. You must know I'm sorry."

The garden section was close. There were wheelbarrows, bags of dirt—surely they had to have seeds? People weren't moving out of the way. Somehow the voice was getting inside other customers' heads, too, making them look around for Zellie and Cam. Terror gripped Zellie's chest. She couldn't seem to get enough air, but if she stopped moving they'd catch her and they'd hold her—

"I've been sick with worry, child, ever since that horrible boy lured you away from me. Terribly sick. How could you do that to me?" The rattling cough started again and just kept going and going.

There! A big mixed selection of vegetable seeds, heavily illustrated with happy children and grandparents. "Grab it," yelped Zellie, and Cam windmilled one of his arms to knock some boxes into the cart. "Now, let's out of here!"

A uniformed employee appeared at the end of the aisle, with a walkie-talkie in one hand and a concerned look on his face. They couldn't go that way. Zellie needed room to take her Big Steps. Momentum was important.

She pivoted the heavy, awkward cart. It was slow, ridiculously slow. Cam jumped down and pushed with her, and they started running the other way down the long aisle. Three more employees were at the far end. It didn't matter.

She fumbled for Cam's hand and as soon as her palm met his, she pushed hard with her exhausted, aching legs and took a Big Step.

The aisle flickered around them. She took another Big Step and the flickering increased, like she was playing a new game on an ancient computer.

"No, no, child," rattled the voice, and the flickering slowed down.

"Go to hell!" yelled Zellie and pushed as hard as she could. The final Big Step took her over the boundary point and the aisle snapped from something real into long, wavy lines that vibrated with her pounding feet.

Dust rose up around them and the air changed. Everything was once again dim and grey, filled with crowding, unfriendly shapes.

"We want to get out!" cried Cam, and a door opened in the floor under their wheels. They fell through....

and rolled the cart out of the Mall. The door slammed shut

behind them and the blinds slithered down.

"Oh my God," said Izzy. "Oh my God, you did it!" He took two steps toward the cart, then stopped himself.

Ramone didn't wait. He darted across the street, grabbed a box of crackers and broke it open. "Hey, you okay? Was Inside that bad?"

"It's always bad," said Zellie shortly. "It was worse when my grandmother found us in the warehouse, though."

Eden hissed and said, "Wow, that's shitty luck."

Zellie snatched the box of crackers from Ramone's hand and tossed a stack each to Deena, Eden, and Izzy. "Wasn't luck. I told you before my grandmother's a witch."

"Don't eat too much," said Cam. "We need this food for later."

"Do we get to eat it then?" asked Izzy, eyeing the Pop-Tarts.

"All you want," Cam promised. "But the first thing we have to do is round up everybody in the city."

———

THERE WERE no more than two dozen mortals scattered across the feral city, and they hardly ever got together in one group. It was dangerous. Even after the hunters vanished, it was dangerous, because the city didn't like it. When enough people gathered in one place, the Inside started coming out.

But Cam was right in thinking food would lure them together. Zellie brought him wood from the red and white forest that bounded the city, and he built a fire in the Fountain Plaza, another of the city's stable landmarks. He fried onions, and stewed apples and sugar in the bent ruins of a street sign, muttering to himself about the cookware that Zellie's grandmother had stopped them from acquiring.

Slowly, the others trickled in: Ramsey, the eldest at the ripe old age of twenty five, solitary and gifted the same way Zellie was. Rani, fifteen-years-old and never, ever in the alleys of the city, no matter how cold the night. The dreamy, scruffy twenty-year-old who answered only to Chairman. Sunny, the young woman Zellie had dismissed as a 'tourist,' and Dev, the creepy thirteen-year-old boy Sunny had decided to adopt. And others, too, those Zellie had only seen at a distance. They all came, edging up to the shopping cart full of food that Ramone and Eden guarded jealously.

Ramsey put down a case of beer he'd acquired on his own. "I hear we're having a party." He looked better fed than the rest of them, which wasn't really surprising given his gifts. But he'd come all the same, Zellie noticed. Probably because Cam had wanted him to come. Cam could charm a girl from an ivory tower and a hermit out of isolation—but the real test was coming: could he charm the city itself?

"Oooh," said Chairman, zeroing in on the beer. "Man, it has been a long time."

"Take it slow," said Ramsey, amused. "Eat something first."

Cam frowned at the beer. "Definitely eat something first. Ramone, break out the cheese."

Ramone grumbled under his breath but did as he was asked.

"Cheese and beer! Perfect!" said Chairman, and slung himself onto the rim of the fountain. It was big and round, with an unrecognizable stone shape in the center from which water trickled. The water from the fountain was always fresh and cold and good: an essential mercy in the feral city.

Ramsey drifted over to Zellie. "So what's this about?"

"Didn't Cam tell you? He's got a plan to save us all." Zellie watched Cam smile at Sunny and Dev as he stirred the stewed fruit.

"Yeah, he said that much. I was hoping for more detail. Having a party is nice, if crazy dangerous, and I can't see how it'll help."

"Maybe it wouldn't in a normal city," said Zellie. "But this place isn't exactly normal, is it?"

Cam gave the spoon over to Sunny and wiped his hands on his ragged jeans. "All right, everybody. This is a kind of ritual we're doing. We have a snack now, and then we play a game, and after that, we feast."

"What do we do when the Inside comes out?" asked Izzy nervously.

Cam pointed at Izzy like he'd said something clever. "That's exactly what we're waiting for."

Eden scowled. "What, and then we scatter? Maybe we ought to feast first."

"Nah," said Cam. "If we eat too much we won't want the game. And the game is important."

Dev sagged against Sunny. "I'm so hungry, though. If I don't eat soon I may *die*." He looked at Cam with the big brown eyes that might have worked on adults back in the normal world but never charmed anybody in the feral city. Well, nobody but Sunny, but she'd clearly never acquired the survival instincts of a real runaway.

Ramsey said, "You eat better than most of us, you little beast."

"I'm a growing boy," said Dev, smirking. "Sunny understands."

Sunny, who was watching Ramsey instead of what she stirred, said, "He's still a kid. Obviously."

"So what *do* we do once the Inside comes out?" demanded Eden. "What exactly is the *point* of all this?"

"The Inside coming out is what we *want* to happen. And once that starts, just... ignore it. Leave it to me."

The murmurs of the gathered runaways faded as everybody stared at him, flabbergasted into silence.

"*Ignore it?*" demanded Ramone.

"Once the city eats you, can we run away then? Or should we still keep ignoring it until it eats the rest of us?" Eden asked acidly.

"The city isn't going to eat Cam," said Zellie sharply. There was no way the city would eat Cam. Zellie wouldn't let it happen. She'd grab him and run, first: to another part of the city, to the blood-and-snow forest, even back to the real world if she had to.

Cam gave everybody a bright smile and went over to the shopping cart. He dug around for a few moments, spilling boxes and bags onto the pavement. Then he pulled out a cardboard cube. In it was a pair of brightly colored balls. "Not quite basketballs, definitely not soccer balls, but I think they'll do if we can manage to have fun."

"Wait a minute," said Izzy. "When you say you want us to play a game, you mean a *ball game?*"

"Wow," said Chairman. "Great idea or best idea? I want to be goalie!"

"Hey, it'll be fun," said Sunny. "I recognize those balls from PE class!"

Chairman was the most enthusiastic of them, although Sunny came close on his heels. That made the two of them the team captains. Everybody else grumbled and complained as they got sorted into teams. Cam pointed out the two sides of the plaza that would serve as the goals.

"Do we each get one of Ramsey and Zellie?" asked Eden. "That would be fairest, since they're both cheaters when it comes to getting around."

"Nope," said Ramsey. "Zellie and I will be the referees." He handed Zellie one of the whistles that had been in the packaging.

And the game began. It was a little bit like soccer and a little bit like basketball and entirely made up by Ramsey and

Zellie's whims. About half of the potential players stayed on the sidelines—the 'field' wasn't big enough for two *large* teams, and Cam encouraged them to root for their teams. They got into it, screaming and laughing in a way the city had never heard before. A whole hour passed, with plenty of breaks for squabbling and ball theft and laughter, before Ramsey declared that the next point would decide the game.

The ball flew over the ground: blocked by Izzy, kicked by Deena, who passed it to Eden. At the far end of the field, Chairman jumped up and down in delight as Eden drove it past Sunny's hapless defense, past Ramone's guard, and over the brick they'd established as goal.

Everybody hooted and howled as they stomped their feet and rushed toward Eden. The conquering hero fought off a hug from Sunny. "Come on, girl, cut it out, you're on the other team, have some self-respect."

Sunny released Eden into the arms of her adoring fans and put her hands on her hips. "I don't think I've ever seen her so happy," she said to Zellie.

Zellie twisted her mouth. "This isn't exactly Disneyland, Sunny."

"Still. Oh, hey, is it time for supper? Hurray! I'm starving." Sunny bounced over to Cam and Zellie followed close behind.

Cam was standing on the fountain edge, waving his arms in the air. "Time for food, everybody! I've put stuff out so everybody can get something!" As the clamor died down and people turned to look at him, he dropped his voice. "And please… don't let the party spirit you're in fade, *even if we have guests.* Very important."

Some of the runaways gathered were smart enough—or hungry enough—not to glance around. They headed over to the spread of food on the fountain edge, Izzy and Chairman in the lead.

But Eden just couldn't resist looking to see what Cam was

talking about. Zellie darted over beside her as she turned her head, scanning the edge of the plaza. The distant sun was just starting to set, and crimson fingers of light crawled around the buildings and cast long, distorted shadows. Glimmering shapes stood in the shadows, things with eyes that glinted like marbles and white grimaces for smiles. Something tapped the pavement, *clack clack clack*. Stiletto heels, maybe.

"If you ruin this for him, I swear to God, I'm going to drag you straight to Hell, Eden," Zellie whispered.

"I'm afraid," Eden whispered back.

"They're over there and I'm *right here*." Zellie gave Eden a little shake, then pushed her toward the food. Then she resolutely turned her back on the observers and moved to grab something to eat herself.

It wasn't hard to imagine why the others were able to ignore the eyes in the shadows. They'd all been creeping closer and closer to the edge of starvation for days, and if Cam hadn't passed out snacks before the game, his entire plan would have fallen apart. But now after the exercise and excitement of a game, supplies that could have been rationed out to last weeks were going to be demolished in an evening.

Zellie snatched up a broken end of cheese and was about to bite down when she realized Cam wasn't eating. His mouth was moving, and he was looking off into the shadows to the west. Slowly, he hopped off the edge of the fountain and began weaving through the feasters, pushing them lightly this way and that. He didn't move any one person more than a few steps and he didn't stop them from bringing whatever they were devouring, but somehow when he was done there was a pattern: two rows, not quite aligned.

Cam walked down the aisle between the two rows and Zellie followed behind. He was quietly chanting a little song, a children's song. He turned at the end of the aisle and looped around the group, then began again, chanting still. Slowly the others started to notice him. Some of them shifted uncomfortably, but full bellies contradicted their sense of danger. And others—Ramone, Deena, Ramsey, Sunny—seemed relaxed.

Zellie made them less afraid too, she knew. Everybody knew how protective she was of nearly-blind Cam. She heard Izzy whispering about it as she followed Cam down another circuit. If *she* was letting Cam do this, what was there to fear?

But they had it all wrong. Cam was the one who'd saved her. She tried to take care of him, but if he wanted to catch a tiger by the tail, she had no ability to stop him. All she could do was help him get the rope.

The shadows grew longer. The eyes within them glowed more brightly. They were, Zellie felt, running out of time. If Cam couldn't get this done before the shadows reached the fountain, none of them would be here in the morning.

Cam's pacing got faster, and his chanting got louder. Everybody put up with it, even though most of the kids thought he was crazy. He'd fed them well; he'd earned the right to be crazy. Some of them fell asleep, curled up on the paving stones. Dev, his head in Sunny's lap, looked almost innocent.

Zellie rubbed her eyes. The glowing eyes in the shadows were moving. They weren't eyes any more, but a dazzling galaxy of lights. Then, with an electric hum, the lights collided into a burst of golden glory.

Cam's chanting faded away and Zellie took his hand. The coalescing light shifted and changed, thinning out until it formed a fiery, complicated glyph in the air. Some of the sleepers woke up and scrambled to their feet, nudging the others awake.

The glyph hovered there, flickering and shifting, humming like a wire.

"Now what?" inquired Ramsey casually.

Cam pulled his hand away from Zellie's and walked toward the spirit he'd summoned. When he was only a couple yards away, the barely-audible humming changed, becoming staticky.

"Hi," said Cam gently. He held out a hand. "Nice to meet you."

The spirit's flickering intensified and the points of the glyph of light pulsed in agitation. Then there was a sharp, unpleasant crackle and the spirit fled, darting down the street and vanishing into an alley that exited into the depths of the city.

Cam stood looking after it, his hand still out. After a moment, he looked down at his hand and shoved it into his pocket. His shoulders hunched.

"What just happened?" asked Izzy plaintively.

"We didn't get eaten," said Eden happily. "That's great."

"Not yet," said Ramone. "Looks like there's a new monster in the city, though. Great job, Cam!"

"Shut up, Ramone," said Zellie as she stalked over to Cam. She turned him so she could see his face. "Are we done?"

He reached out to her face, running his fingers over her cheeks. Then, his own face drawn with exhaustion, he said, "I guess so."

Zellie put her hand over his, then clasped it and turned to lead him away.

"Hey!" said Ramone. "What now? What are we supposed to do now?"

"I don't care," said Zellie. Cam didn't say anything at all.

"What about the *food*?" asked Izzy.

"Do what you want with it," said Zellie, then stopped. She left Cam standing and ran back to the cart, where she dug out her package of seeds. Then she went back to Cam and took him away to the corner of the city they called home.

"MAYBE I DIDN'T SCREW up," said Cam, a few days later, as they wandered the city together on Zellie's endless hunt for a permanent garden. "I think the city's changed, don't you?"

Zellie gave him a sidelong look, then thought about it. "It's colder. And we haven't come across anything really weird since the party. No fire hydrant spraying rainbows, no glass pavement, no cloud-mural houses."

"And the spirit is still around," said Cam. He sounded happier than he had in days. Zellie couldn't share his cheerfulness. 'Colder' wasn't a good thing and neither was the lack of weirdness, not for her dreams of a garden.

"And the spirit hasn't attacked anybody, either. Not *really.*"

Zellie turned to look directly at Cam. "Deena wouldn't agree." The other girl had burns all over both her hands, because she'd been foolhardy enough to try to imitate Cam's approach to the glowing spirit. It had done more than bark that time; it had bitten.

"I'm sure she just frightened it, sneaking up on it like that."

"Everybody's having nightmares now, too," said Zellie. She wasn't—not about the city, anyhow—and Cam wasn't, but she'd seen the circles under even Ramone's eyes and listened impatiently to Eden describing in graphic detail the horrible dreams of being devoured from within.

And she wanted not to care, but she couldn't escape the haunting idea that they'd broken the city. She didn't like it, and not just because it hurt her dreams of a garden. The city seemed eternal and endless: they were mites as they ran around on its ancient roads, and whether or not it had intended to be kind, it had sheltered all of them as they hid away from the real world. Breaking it, and taking it from all the other runaways, was an uncomfortable thought.

But she didn't know what to do about it. Deena had tried to reach out to it when she'd encountered it in the plaza again, and now Eden was scouring the city to beg Ramsey to carry her to a hospital.

"It's confused," Cam went on, oblivious to Zellie's worry. "It's been sleeping for so long and we woke it up and this isn't what it expected. But you've noticed how often we see it? It's following people around."

"You say that like it's a good— did you hear that?" She'd heard coughing from one of the alleys, she was certain. That's what she'd been dreaming of since the food run: her grandmother finding her again. The witch's spells had found her at the warehouse, and now her grandmother knew she was still alive, but somewhere beyond the normal world. Could she find her way to the feral city?

Well, Zellie had.

"It's just Izzy," said Cam soothingly. "Hey, Izzy! What's up?"

Izzy waved from the alley where he was panting. "Eden found Ramsey. He's going to take Deena to a hospital. But he wants you around in case that spirit thing shows up again while he's traveling."

Cam shrugged. "Okay. Come on, Zellie."

Zellie looked around apprehensively, then followed Cam and Izzy.

They went down the alley, between red-painted walls with alien writing and turned down a street where every structure had wood-paneled upper stories over concrete ground floors. The stable part of the city had always formed a sort of skeleton, with the strange discoveries in the spaces between the reliable streets and alleys. The whole city had been stable for the past few days, though. It was like walking through a corpse.

The others were waiting in the same Fountain Plaza where they'd summoned the city spirit. The shopping cart was still there, though only half full now. Zellie was surprised nobody had run off with it entirely. Did they think she would be angry?

Eden had her arm around Deena's shoulders. Deena's hands were wrapped in socks from the shopping cart and her head was down. Ramsey stood nearby, talking quietly with Sunny. Dev played with a stick nearby. Zellie wondered what Ramsey was worried about; there weren't quite enough people to attract the city's attention, at least not until Izzy brought them.

Sunny waved and pointed out their arrival to Ramsey. He came over. "There's something going on."

"The city's dying," said Zellie, and tried to ignore the shocked look Cam gave her.

Ramsey gave her a funny look, too, then shook his head. "Not that. Something else. Something with the shadowland." He didn't think of the way he traveled between worlds as a Big Step, but as a change in perspective that put him into a dark place. It was why he only ever seemed to travel in order to come back with a mind-altering substance. "I keep hearing a rattle when I start to step over."

Ice raced down Zellie's spine and her hands spasmed into fists. "No!" She dragged in a breath. "No. You must be imagining it." She wondered if the blood-and-snow forest would be any safer, with its monsters and its endless chill.

Ramsey shrugged. "Could be. Wouldn't be the first time. But I thought it'd be good if you two were both here."

"The city is just confused," interjected Cam. "It's not dying." Zellie was grateful that that idea had distracted Cam from Ramsey's other concern.

Ramsey gave Cam a cool look. "But Deena could be."

"I'm fine," mumbled Deena. "I should have known better. One should always know better than to try and reach for glory."

"You're not making any sense," said Eden irritably. "Ramsey…."

"Yes. Cam!" said Ramsey sharply. "If your precious spirit shows up, keep it away from us." He scooped up Deena in both arms and closed his eyes.

Zellie watched carefully. She knew Ramsey could do the same thing she could do, but she'd never really studied how he did it. Now, with his ridiculous, terrifying stories of a rattling sound on the boundary, paying attention was essential.

The light faded around him, as if a cloud passed between him and the already-hazy sun. He lowered his head, cradling Deena against his chest as she started whimpering. The fading light became growing darkness. Then, with a silent flicker, he simply vanished.

A heartbeat later, something else took his place. Zellie couldn't see it, except for a shimmer in the air, but she could hear the rattling cough, she could smell the rotting teeth, and she could feel the twisted pressure of her grandmother's attention.

Her hands went cold. Cam quietly said, "Well, darn." Then he raised his voice. "Everybody get out of here."

"What is that stink?" asked Eden, wrinkling her nose. Izzy backed up, and Sunny frowned and grabbed Dev's hand.

"Dear child...." The witch's voice crackled, and Eden turned to look at Zellie, the set of her eyes changing as the witch crept into her mind, just like she'd moved into the mind of the warehouse employees.

"Go!" said Cam again. "Somebody get Eden and Zellie out of here." Nobody moved, and he shouted, "Everybody, come on!" Acid etched his voice as he said, "What are you doing here, you nasty piece of twine and bone? Zellie doesn't want you. Nobody wants you. You should have died a century ago."

Eden's lips pulled away from her teeth. Then Dev yanked her hair hard and she screamed.

"Dev!" said Sunny in a shocked reprimand.

"Grab her!" Dev urged. "Or leave her but let's get out of here."

That was enough. Sunny and Izzy both took Eden under a shoulder and carried her away

Zellie barely noticed. She cowered behind Cam, feeling the force of her grandmother's rage as it focused on Cam instead of anybody else. She wanted to run away so badly, but leaving Cam to face her grandmother alone would be unforgivable.

"How can you let him say things like that to me? After I sacrificed so much for you? Terrible girl!"

"I'm not," Zellie whispered.

"Run, Zellie," said Cam softly. "I'll be fine."

Zellie's fragile self-control broke and she fled, leaving Cam taunting her grandmother behind her and her grandmother hurling insults at her back.

Zellie went down paths she didn't recognize in her attempt to escape, but she didn't take a Big Step. She didn't leave Cam behind entirely, though she knew that was fear and not courage. She had no courage.

At last, when her muscles failed her, she found herself in a court paved with emerald-flecked glass bricks, in front of a vast, ash-colored mansion with windows like hollow eyes and an iron fence painted vermillion. The bricks reminded her of when the city had been warmer and stranger, before Cam had woken the spirit. That meant she wasn't surprised when the spirit itself edged around the house.

The tangled lines of light didn't seem as bright anymore, and the spirit drifted along closer to the ground. Zellie, still panting, rolled to her feet and backed away, but it didn't seem inclined to pay attention to her. She watched as it moved up to the window of the mansion, then passed through. The light passed behind the windows like a ghost. Zellie watched for a while, trying to see what Cam saw. She couldn't, though. It was an alien made of light and a manifestation of something frightening and dangerous. If it was the city, it was unfriendly and wild. What could they possibly do to reach something so very different from them?

At last the light moving behind the windows winked out. Zellie was unable to avoid thinking about Cam and her grandmother, then. After pacing back and forth for a few minutes, she went home.

It might have been a garden in a different city. It was fenced on one side and bounded on two sides by tall townhouses. If it had even a little soil and greenery, it would have been a garden. But instead it was pavement, cracked here and there. Zellie had done her best to expand the cracks, but it was harder than it would have been in other cities. She grew dandelions, because dandelions would grow anywhere, and they helped the pavement crack apart.

She'd learned that from her grandmother, long ago. She wished she'd learned it somewhere else.

A pile of rags and leaves and branches covered with an old sheet was shoved against one of the walls. Cam sprawled out on his back, his eyes half-open as he stared up at the sky. Zellie almost tripped over herself dashing over to him.

He drew in a ragged breath as she fell on him. "Hey," he said, his voice creaky. "Glad you got away."

"What happened?" demanded Zellie, snuggling up to him. "Is she gone?"

Cam reached over and brushed hair away from Zellie's face. "She's still around. Eventually she got bored yelling at me and went off to find somebody she could actually possess."

Zellie thought of the other runaways in the feral city and wondered why her chest hurt. She was safe and Cam was safe and that was what mattered, right? They'd have to move on, of course. Safety didn't mean much if her grandmother's projection was roaming the city even while they slept.

She ought to start gathering up what little they had, turn her attention to convincing Cam they had to leave. It would be a challenge; he liked the feral city. He'd put so much effort into trying to tame it and if he gave up easily on projects like that, why, she'd still be with her grandmother, deluded by her lies.

She ought to start moving. But she didn't. Instead she rested her head on Cam's chest, listened to his heartbeat, and wondered what would happen to everybody else. She'd warn them, she decided. It was the least she could do.

"GREAT," said Ramone. "Now we have *two* new monsters to kill." He kicked the curving spiral swing set at the Snail Playground that he and Izzy lived on opposite sides of.

Zellie boggled at him. His attitude was just as alien as Sunny's had been. The woman had given her a little smile and said, "I'm sure everything will be okay. I know you can handle this."

Dev, despite being a creepy little brat, at least reacted in a sane and sensible way to the news that an invisible witch with mind-control powers was roaming the feral city. "This is why I hate people," he'd muttered, right and proper.

And Eden, too, had been appropriately angry and upset. "My body stopped listening to me, girl. I know now. I'm staying the hell away from you, any weird shimmers, lines of light, or old person smell. And if I starve to death in the process, I'm going to haunt you. You brought this bitch here, you have to deal with her." That last part was troubling, but the rest was a sound, healthy reaction.

"How the hell are you going to kill anything?" Zellie asked Ramone. "I didn't see you slaying any Huntsmen or giant lions or anything."

"Well, shit, what else are we going to do?" Ramone climbed up the slide. It shimmered like a seashell and stayed slick and cool on the warmest day. On cold days, like today, like *every* day had been since the spirit of the city was awakened, it crackled when touched. "Your man did his thing and now everything's gone to crap. If we can kill that spirit, maybe the city will come back to life."

Zellie stared at him incredulously. "Did you see what it did to Deena?"

"Well then, why are you here? Where's Cam? Did he finally get eaten?" Ramone perched at the top of the slide, then stood up, shading his eyes.

"He's resting. Resisting her takes a lot of energy. I just thought you should know about the witch," Zellie muttered but Ramone had stopped paying attention to her.

"Hey, that's Rani! She got something...." He slid down the slide and bounced to his feet. Rani was another of the city's inhabitants. She'd been at the party, and she was somewhere lower on Zellie's list of people to warn.

The other girl bounced into the playground, carrying a bag fashioned from her jacket. Loaves of fresh bread peeked out. The smell made Zellie's mouth water.

"Where did that come from?" Ramone advanced on Rani with his hands out and she gave him a loaf.

"The spirit," said Rani happily. "I was looking for food and singing a song my auntie used to sing while she baked. The spirit showed up and I didn't run away because I thought maybe it was listening to me. And it *was*, and when I was done, it sort of did a little dance and made this big pile of bread appear! And then it ran away."

Ramone paused in stuffing the bread in his mouth and said, "Wait, was it a song *about* baking? Do we just gotta sing to it to control it?"

Rani shook her head. "Not about baking. Just this song my aunt sang. In Hindi." She sang a line from it, then offered Zellie a loaf of bread. "Take some, there's so much. Take one for Cam too. Is he unwell?"

Zellie took the loaves. "Ramone will explain," she said dully, bewildered and unexpectedly afraid of Rani's discovery. "Ramone... if you encounter the spirit... remember Deena too." She turned and walked away. That was it. That was the best she could do. And it wasn't going to matter: they were going to get burned trying to control the city, or they were going to get possessed by her grandmother, or maybe even get caught in some awful clash between the two.

She felt sick, her stomach twisting around so much that she couldn't risk wasting the bread by eating it right then. Instead she took it back to her hideout. Cam had gone, but she felt so nauseated by fear that she couldn't even be concerned about him. Instead she curled up on the makeshift bed and tried to squeeze the anxiety away.

Zellie remembered how Sunny thought everything would be okay. She was an idiot tourist, she'd never really lost anything, but her faith was reassuring until Zellie remembered that Sunny's faith depended on *Zellie* doing something about the problems.

She must have meant Cam. Cam was the one who solved problems. Zellie would wait for Cam to come back, and he would figure out how to make everything okay, even if it meant they had to run away again.

But the shadows lengthened and Cam did not return. Zellie refused to think about it and did her best to fall asleep instead.

Her grandmother coughed nearby. "Didn't I tell you he'd abandon you? Just like your mother did? Everybody will always abandon you, sweet child. Except for me. You're the one who abandoned me."

Zellie covered her ears and rolled to her feet. "Shut up!" She looked around wildly, trying to spot the source of her grandmother's voice.

"Don't you talk to me like that, you ungrateful brat. After everything I've given up for you! Shame on you!"

Zellie stumbled out of her hideout and down the street, blindly trying to escape the witch's voice. She thought of other voices instead.

Sunny whispered, "I know you can handle this."
Eden breathed, "You have to deal with her."
Ramone said, "Now we have two monsters to kill...."

Her eyes, half-closed against tears and dust, flew open. She veered to the right, went up some steps and flung open the door to a tall building the color of fire. Inside it was bright instead of dim, with lights blazing in burnished brass fixtures along a richly paneled corridor. But it was cold, too, cold enough that Zellie's toes felt it immediately through her ragged sneakers.

Zellie waved her hand, feeling for the prickle of the Inside's attention, then took another few steps inside as her grandmother's cough rattled behind her. "Don't you take this to somebody else's house, child. Do you want to be put in jail? That's what will happen."

Carefully Zellie moved down the corridor, achingly alert for any movement or strangeness. Any minute something would happen and the Inside would attack her. If she was quick and clever, maybe she could divert it onto her grandmother. It was the best she could come up with.

But nothing happened, except that it was cold. Even the lights were cold and there was no reaction, not even a flicker, when she touched one. That was mysterious, but not the least bit threatening. It was odd. Zellie thought about the streets that no longer changed and wondered if the city really was dying.

But the Inside didn't seem to be slowing down the witch at all. Her stinking breath reached Zellie's neck when she stopped to investigate the frozen lights, and her rattling voice continued to hurl a mix of insults, threats, and pathetic pleas.

"That's right, keep walking. But nobody will ever love you. You'll see. You'll ruin it just like you always have, and you'll come running back to me, begging me to forgive you. But why should I? No, I'll tell the truth about you to anybody you manage to delude. I have a duty not to let you hurt people."

"Shut up," said Zellie. "Go away. You don't know anything."

"I know you, child. I'll make sure everybody else does, too. Or you could just come home. We could start over. You could apologize and I'd let you have your old room back. I've been busy turning it into a workroom, but I'd make the sacrifice for you. I do try to be a good person, unlike some people."

The rattle crept inside Zellie's head, giving her a headache. She'd spent so long blind to what her grandmother was doing to her, believing all her lies and distrusting her own emotions. But what if Cam was really gone? What if the others in the feral city all turned on her, caught and twisted by her grandmother's voice?

No. She wouldn't go back again. Death would be better.

The bright corridor shuddered around her. Tiny holes along the bottom of the walls opened up: fanged mouths opening and closing, just big enough to snap a hand or a foot clean off. The walls themselves rippled like the sides of a great beast, inhaling and exhaling. A twisted joy swept through Zellie. Maybe she and Cam had hurt the city somehow, but it wasn't dead, not yet.

She moved faster, breaking into a jog. The corridor opened up into a series of small square rooms, each one a little bit larger than the next, with fanged maws stretching across the floor in random patterns.

"Oho. I see. Oh yes. Look at you," rattled the witch. "Look at you, invading this creature. You live on its back like a flea and then you creep inside. You are terrible. Poor creature. Let me help you, poor creature."

Zellie wondered if the city would get inside her grandmother's mind or her grandmother would get inside the city's mind. She really, really hoped they'd manage to devour each other.

The final square room had a door made of brass and red wood, and it opened like another maw when Zellie approached it. She could see the teeth and the tongue beyond. But she heard a voice, too: Cam's, and she plunged through.

She emerged into the dim, clouded evening, into a large courtyard. Three tall buildings formed three sides and the final wall had only a broken hole to serve as a gate. The sea-green and white paving stones fitted together to form a design that was both blossom and beast. In the corner sizzled the white-light lines of the city spirit, and a few yards away crouched Cam, talking to the thing.

Zellie's grandmother was right behind her again, the exhalation of her cackle a foulness against Zellie's hair. She could see the shimmer of her presence, feel the clutch of her hand. She was so very happy to see Cam again, to witness proof that he was exactly who she thought he was, but she didn't hesitate. The spirit of the feral city was a burning spirit. It didn't like what it perceived as a threat, whether that was a gathering or an invasion or simply reaching out. It had burned Deena. It could burn her grandmother, too.

She leapt forward, driving herself at the spirit. She could see the lines of the spirit reacting to her charge, twisting, turning, brightening. Then, as a crackling thunder boomed around her, she took a complicated Step, twisting herself sideways through space. A forest of crimson and snow flickered around her and a parking lot full of people and a reeking house she knew and hated. She saw a wrinkled old hand on a crystal ball.

Then her complicated step completed and her leg kept twisting under her until it snapped. She fell to the ground as light and thunder raged around her.

Then the light faded and the smell of blood overwhelmed the smell of ozone. The green paving stones were slick with red, and streaked with black and glossy white—but mostly red. Zellie hurt so much she couldn't breathe.

The lines of the city spirit rearranged themselves over her and she tried to scoot herself away. Then Cam was at her back, holding her. "Shh, you're okay."

"My leg," Zellie whimpered. "My leg."

"It's still there. Maybe you broke it, doing what you did, but it's okay."

Zellie kept her eyes on the light. It was moving closer, and it was already so close. It was going to swallow them; she'd seen all the fangs. "The blood...."

"I don't quite know what happened there. I couldn't really see," Cam admittedly candidly. "But it's not yours. Was it your grandmother? I thought I heard her." He glanced around. "But not anymore, I guess. Too bad for her." He scarcely paused a moment before breathlessly barreling on. "I've been thinking about this spirit."

"We have to get away, Cam. Help me stand up?" Zellie's teeth chattered together.

"Not yet," he said gently. "I know what has to happen with the spirit, Zellie. And I can't do it."

"Oh, Cam," she moaned. The pain was making her dizzy and the smell of blood made her stomach revolt.

"It's lonely, you see," Cam went on, his hands tight on Zellie's shoulders. "I've never really been lonely before. I've always had family who loved me. Friends. And you. I've never been alone like the city is. It's totally separated from the people meant for it. I could never really *commune* with it because we don't overlap enough." Cam's voice became tender. "But you know what it's like to be lonely, Zellie. You were *so* lonely when we met."

"What—what?" Zellie couldn't quite get her question out.

"You have to let it touch you, Zellie. So it can understand what we need. So it knows it's not alone." Cam supported her, holding her, giving her his strength. The wavering lines of the spirit tangled themselves together fretfully. "No Big Steps, no running away. No grabbing at it. Just let it reach for you and know you."

Zellie remembered Deena's hands and looked around at the remains of her grandmother. She'd been sliding backwards through the goo of her grandmother. And Cam had caught her. Cam loved her. Without Cam, she'd be alone. She'd trusted her grandmother once. She trusted Cam now.

She closed her eyes and held out her arms open to the spirit.

Lines of light wrapped around her, penetrating through her flesh and into her core. It hurt a little, but compared to the pain of her broken leg, the experience was a warm tickle. Then the light reached into her emotions and she no longer knew whether it was pain or something else.

She wondered if she could communicate with it. But no words came to her, heard or spoken, only a *feel*, like music. It *was* lonely: lonely and afraid and desperately out of place. For a moment she felt as if it was kindred, like she'd found a frightened dog in an alley that wanted to be taken home and fed.

But only for a moment, only for the time it took for her to perceive the rest of the entity: vast and alien and old. It had been there far longer than any human city, waiting for the fulfillment of a promise. Its thoughts were mannequins spilling teeth from their gut, crystal sculptures weeping music, a playground made of seashell. It wasn't out of place. She was. The knowledge was profound and absolute: *She did not belong there.*

And yet—it *was* lonely, as she'd once been lonely. Cam had seen that much. It looked at her and *saw* her, for the first time: saw more than an irritation in its skin, saw a mind, small and foreign and hungry. It saw and it moved against her soul as if it would fill her, It would edge out her dreams and will and flesh until she too was nothing more than blood and a memory.

Then the force withdrew and her leg screamed in pain and Cam's arms were around her. The creature of light and lines was gone.

Zellie blinked and coughed. There was something she had to say. Some message she'd understood.

Oh yes.

She croaked, "We really... *really*... need to stay out of the Inside. No matter what."

"I think that will be okay...." said Cam uncertainly, looking around in wonder. "Is it getting warmer?"

Zellie looked around too. The pavement was no longer slick with blood. It wasn't even pavement. The blood had sunk into the stone, melting it into dark, rich soil. The whole courtyard was earth now.

Something tickled under Zellie's left hand. She moved it and a green sprout poked up. It grew rapidly: a young tree with unfurling silver leaves.

Cam helped her move to the edge of the courtyard, just in case. The tree matured, although it stayed delicate. It wouldn't block the light for the rest of the garden, thought Zellie hazily. That was good.

"You were right," she said shakily.

Cam said fondly, "*We* were right. Zellie, it's a garden for you."

THE WILD HUNT GOES TO SCHOOL

This is home now, Mom," I said, waving the pendant my mother haunted around the foyer of the elderly farmhouse Jen had purchased.

A mist shivered around the pendant, and my mom whispered sleepily, "Where are we?"

I looked around and then went out onto the porch. Boxes and crates were stacked high in front of ancient patio furniture and the accumulated garden junk of decades. "Kind of the middle of nowhere, really. But the dogs like it, and I think I do too."

"Are you alone?" My mom's voice stayed wispy. She wasn't really awake, but the more often I talked to her, the more she'd remember when she did wake up.

"Nope. This is Jen's house. Her farm. I'm staying with her for a while, and some of my other new friends are just down the road." It had taken a while to find exactly the sort of place Jen wanted: with a farmhouse and pastures, and another house available a mile away, with a high school close enough for me and a college relatively nearby for Amber. But she'd managed, and now here we were.

I went down the porch steps and around the side of the house, where Jen leaned on a pasture fence, talking on a cell phone. Theoretically, it didn't matter where we lived when duty called— the magic that bound us together would bring us to our task no matter where we started. But we hadn't tested that yet, and we all had reasons to stick together. The only one of our little crew who didn't live nearby was Brynn, who, being fourteen years old, lived at home with her family in Pasadena. But she was on her way for a visit now, bringing along some pretty important cargo.

Jen waved at me and continued her phone conversation. I put my mother's pendant around my neck and ducked between the rails of the pasture fence. It wasn't in any better repair than the rest of the farm, but it shouldn't matter. We'd find out soon enough.

My dogs sprawled in the afternoon sunshine around Jen's feet. They loved it here. They hadn't been sent back into my shadow since we'd first arrived, and I half-expected they'd choose to stay on the farm when I started school in a few days. There was plenty to keep them busy: the pastures, the rotting barn (first on Jen's repair list), and in the distance an overgrown grove of fruit trees and berry bushes, with all the wildlife that implied. We'd already been over it once, and it was a perfect playground for three supernatural dogs.

A hand snaked through the grass and curled loosely around my ankle. I looked down at Yejun, who was also lying in the tall grass. My reflection looked up at me from his new sunglasses.

"Hi," I said. "How's the view?" I meant the view of the tangle of magical leylines he saw constantly, but as soon as I said it, he smiled and I blushed.

"Nice," he said. "How's your mother taking the change?" He let go of my ankle and tucked both his hands behind his head.

I closed my fingers around the pendant. "It will take a while. But she understands the most important fact: neither of us are with *him* anymore."

"Good," Yejun said. "That's good." My reflection kept staring back at me. It made me nervous. I kept remembering his hands on my shoulders when he'd offered to help me kill my father.

And then I remembered the goodbye kiss I'd given him before returning home again....

I dropped down into the grass. If I was lying beside him looking up into the blue sky with its puffy clouds, it wouldn't feel nearly as strange as looking down at him did. Plus, the dogs would get involved and stop things from being awkward. As soon as I hit the ground, Grim realized something great was happening, slid through the fence rails, and wiggled into a prime position between Yejun and me. His ears twitched invitingly.

"There's a time and a place, Grimwhiskers," said Yejun sternly, but he scratched Grim anyhow.

"The others are almost here," called Jen. I rolled to my feet again, sniffing.

"Not that close," I pointed out when I couldn't detect the scent of Amber's slick, yellow sports car.

"Close enough that you shouldn't get distracted," Jen countered, an odd look in her blue eyes.

Yejun's voice drifted out of the grass. "We were just looking at the clouds, Jen. Relax."

Those stupid sunglasses. Maybe he hadn't been looking at me at all. I was embarrassed and annoyed and irrationally pleased. This was the sort of thing I *wanted* to be worrying about. I was nervous about starting school again, too, and that also made sense. I was a teenager, right? These were teenage things. It was cool.

I caught the scent of Amber's car and, a moment later, its occupants. A bit after that the vehicle turned onto our empty road, and I ran to the long driveway. Brynn scrambled out almost before the engine was off, throwing herself at me as all three dogs danced around, barking.

"Look at you!" said Brynn, clinging to me. "Are you doing okay? Do you like it here?"

I gave Brynn a squeeze around the shoulders and then pushed

her away. "I've answered that in text about a thousand times already, Brynn. And on the phone. And video chat."

"It's different seeing you in person," she said blithely. "You might have been lying to stop me from worrying or something." She'd had a haircut since I'd last seen her, and all her clothes were brand new, including the long-sleeved shirt that didn't fit her style at all.

"As if she'd ever do that," said Yejun, behind me. He was brushing grass fragments off his slacks.

"Exactly," said Brynn, and looked around. "This is good. This will be a good place for them." Then, as Amber and Cat finally got out of the car and started unloading what seemed like an awful lot of luggage for a short visit, Brynn pulled her shirt off.

She had a tank top on underneath, revealing the intricate tattoos of horses that covered her arms and shoulders and back. "Can I let them go now?"

Jen said, "Yes. If it doesn't go well, you might have to call them back, but there's no reason to delay. We got this place for them."

Brynn nodded and walked over to the pasture. She climbed up the first two rails of the fence, hooking her knees over the middle rail, then raised her arms.

The wind picked up, spinning in a little vortex around her. With a sound like the horn section of an orchestra warming up, color streamed off Brynn's body and the horses of the Wild Hunt took form. When they touched the ground, they were already running, racing each other. The ground vibrated with thunderous hoofbeats.

I held the dogs steady beside me. They were excited to see those they already regarded as old friends, but I didn't want to make the horses nervous their first moments in their new home—and all they could possibly associate my dogs with was the Hunt itself.

The horses didn't smell quite like horses. There was a little of an equine scent even ordinary humans could detect, but to me they smelled more of magic. Not really a surprise, that. Even before Brynn had started carrying them around as tattoos, they'd been more magic than natural.

But they'd started out as real horses once, long ago. They'd been born, they'd eaten grass and run and lived. Brynn had insisted they deserved that again, and Jen had agreed.

They reached the trees at the edge of the pasture and wheeled around. The black horse and the sunset-colored horse were in the lead, while a brown horse dropped to the back as if determined to keep everybody together. But it was only for a moment, really, before they returned to where Brynn waited at the fence, kicking up dust as they stopped a few yards away.

Only one came forward to nuzzle Brynn's outstretched hand: a silver mare with a black mane and heavy feathering around her hooves. The others hung back, some nosing at the grass and others watching the rest of us warily.

"What's her name?" asked Jen softly.

Brynn shook her head. "They don't have names. Not anymore. They lost them when they were made part of the Hunt."

A line appeared between Jen's brows. Then the brown horse pushed through the crowd to plop his nose in Jen's hand. He had an extremely long, flaxen mane with a matching tail and he was gorgeous, like a little girl's toy brought to life.

Jen's frown lessened. "He says I can call him Earth Horse. And that the others are Gold Horse, Silver Horse, Black Horse, Red Horse and Sunset."

Brynn turned pink. "Uh, yeah, I've been thinking of them like that. Sorry," she said, darting a glance at the remaining herd.

"I'm pretty sure 'Earth Horse' isn't an approved color term for horses *or* tattoos," said Amber. She climbed through the fence and held out her hand to 'Red Horse.' He was the tallest and sleekest of the bunch and looked like he'd match Amber perfectly.

Then Gold Horse edged over to where I was. He lowered his nose to each of my dogs, who were all sitting by my side vibrating with excitement. Finally, he lifted his head and looked at me with topaz eyes. I held out my hand, but he didn't touch it.

I remember you, said a voice in my mind, strange and sweet as a harp. The magic of the Horn bound the whole of the Wild Hunt together, including the horses, and through it we could hear their voices, if we chose to listen.

The previous Huntsmen hadn't listened. I was determined to do better.

We hunted down the old masters together. You didn't fall off.

I was trying to decide if I ought to explain myself, when he went on, *And the dogs are part of you, as we are part of the Horn. But now we are all its slaves together.*

My open hand curled closed. Gold Horse lowered his head to snatch a mouthful of grass, then came up again. *The grass is fresh and real. Is this your place? Will we stay a while?*

"Yes," I managed, still trying to pull my reeling thoughts together. "Quite a while. There will still be work, but also playing."

At that, Grim gave on being a good dog and leapt forward, barking sharply once and wagging his tail furiously. All of the horses looked at him, then returned to communing with their chosen riders.

Will you learn to ride? Gold Horse's sweet voice became plaintive. *I didn't like having a lump to balance on my back.*

I covered my face with my hands, which had to substitute for running away to find a bed to hide under. "Yes. I'll learn to ride."

"I *know* how to ride," said Amber, apparently having the same conversation with Red Horse and irritated by it. "I had a horse for three years."

Cat was gazing into the eye of the mare called Sunset, his hands clasped behind his back. "They have discriminating standards."

"They're entitled," said Jen. "They're our elders and our teachers in this job we've taken on."

"Well, yeah," said Amber. "Obviously. But you're not supposed to let horses think they're the boss…." She trailed off, biting her lip as Cat touched her elbow and shook his head. Then she pulled an apple out of her bag and offered it to Red Horse. He ate it sedately.

"At least I know how to be a good apple-fetching monkey," she said, resigned.

You will train soon? Perhaps after I've enjoyed the grass? It will take some time and it would be good to be ready before duty calls.

"How often does that happen?" I wondered. No supernatural calls had disturbed the day-to-day rhythms of life since we'd accepted the obligation, and I'd wondered if it might be years between Hunts. Technically the Wild Hunt existed to hunt down corrupted ghosts: souls of the dead that had become twisted and destructive. I'd spoken to ghosts all my life, and I'd never met even one of those.

Soon, said Gold Horse, just as Yejun said, "She says she can hear something coming on the wind." He had both his hands on the black mare's head. Only Brynn looked as comfortable with her mount as he did. I was jealous, because I knew he had no more riding experience than I.

I reached out for my dogs and our shared sense of smell. Together we could smell the color of Amber's lipstick, the rain coming next week, and Cat's controlled yearning for Jen. Scenting corrupted ghosts was right up our alley.

But there was nothing like that around. Just ourselves and the horses and the farm.

"Their sense of time is a little messed up," Brynn volunteered.

"'Soon' could mean anything. Anyhow, why don't we let them run and you can give me the grand tour?"

"Yeah," I said, still uneasy. "The grand tour." I'd hoped it would be longer before there was even a hint of our duty. I'd liked the thought of having a family around me, for no reason other than being a family.

I wrapped my hand around my mother's locket. Then Brynn caught my arm and Yejun smiled at me and I remembered that they'd liked me before the Wild Hunt bound us together. I did my best to push down that old voice that told me how alone I was. It had always sounded like my father before. But these days, I was slowly starting to recognize that, while he may have put it there originally, the voice now came from far closer. And it was still a battle, every time.

Gold Horse nibbled on the top of my head. *You will learn to ride,* he said, as if offering a comfort. And, unexpectedly, it helped.

We gave Brynn the tour, and Jen talked about her plans for various parts of the house and the farm. Then she said, "No time like the present," and set all of us to work. I wasn't quite sure what she was doing with Cat and Amber and Yejun, but she ordered Brynn and me to sort through the junk on the porch.

"So what's up with everybody?" asked Brynn as she knelt down to carefully pick up a box of nails that had spilled out years ago.

I found an old toolbox to investigate and wondered what exactly Brynn was really asking. She was almost as up to date on our lives as I was.

She didn't leave me at sea long though. "And by everybody, I mean you and Yejun. What's up with you and Yejun?"

The toolbox was crammed full of old, good tools. A hammer. A set of screwdrivers. A mallet. I picked up a crooked wrench. "Cat and Yejun live down the street. You can get the grand tour there too, but it's a lot smaller." It wasn't really an answer, but I wasn't sure how to answer her.

"Yeah, why is that? It seems very Girls Dorm, Boys Dorm. It's got to be cheaper and easier to have everybody in one house, and you've got the room here."

I shrugged. "I guess Jen is old-fashioned. She didn't really explain herself. She doesn't, usually. She just announces something in that quiet way she's got, and we all do it."

"Hmm," said Brynn, and tugged at a nail rusted to the planks of the porch. I rolled a screwdriver over to her and she used it to get the nail free. "What about her and Cat? They definitely had something going on before. Do they, like, go on dates now or anything?"

"Usually Yejun and Cat come over together and go home together, but we haven't exactly been here long. And we've been busy. Nobody's been thinking about dating." That was a big, stinky lie, and even Brynn could smell it. She gave me the exact same look my dog Nod gave me when he thought I was being an idiot: kind of patient and resigned and exasperated. And like Nod, she didn't actually call me on my bullshit.

"Well, the Boys' Dorm is probably for the best. It takes the pressure off. Boys need to go brood sometimes. Or at least my brothers do." She looked at me directly. "So what's *going* to happen?"

"I don't know," I said. I wasn't really used to being in a position where I liked a guy, he liked me back, and there was nothing really to stop us from having a relationship. It was as uncomfortable as Gold Horse demanding I learn how to ride. They were both new territory.

"Do you *want* to spend time with him?" Brynn asked carefully. "Look, I can't read your mind. I can't even read your scent." Then she looked self-conscious. "Actually I maybe could read your mind.

According to the horses. Because of the Horn. But they think it's a bad idea for mortals. But I *wouldn't*, anyhow. That means you have to talk to me."

"Yeah," I admitted. "I do. Want to spend time with him, I mean."

"Okay," she said. "Where can I get rid of these nails?" And just like that, we were done with the topic.

After dinner, we went out to work with the horses. There's something about getting riding lessons from your own horse. Every mistake and every correction made me cringe, because I was worried about hurting him or being a useless burden. I had trouble with the idea of being a rider, a *passenger*. I was used to moving on my own feet. Relaxing on Gold Horse's back was a challenge.

Brynn sat on Silver Horse, watching the rest of us. She'd clearly already been taking the lessons we were getting. She sat on Silver Horse like she'd been born there, and the last time I'd seen her riding, she'd been almost as awkward as I was. That was hopeful. I'd take it.

"Apparently you're all divided between 'lumps' and 'masters,'" she shared as the sun dipped below the horizon. "Neither of those are a good thing. But it'll be easier tomorrow."

"What are we supposed to be?" asked Yejun. He was sweating, which made him smell even better than usual. (What can I say? I share my soul with some dogs.)

Brynn hesitated, then said, "Partners. You're an extra pair of eyes on the horse's back, higher and more mobile. You've got to learn how to move and communicate like you're part of the horse."

"That should be easy via the Horn," Yejun grumbled.

Brynn shrugged. I could smell a surge of anxiety rolling off her from which I concluded she really wanted the horses and the people of the Wild Hunt to get along. "They like it if we do it the way they want. The non-magical way. Silver Horse explained it to me very nicely. Are things not going well with Black Horse?"

Black Horse rested her chin on Yejun's shoulder, then blew in his ear. He smiled reluctantly. "She's gorgeous. But not really as good at explaining things as Jen is."

"Well, they're horses," said Jen, in that gentle way she had of pointing out the obvious.

"It'll be better tomorrow," said Brynn confidently. "Once you've slept."

She was right. The next day the basics came easier, which meant in the afternoon we started on harder stuff: learning to not be a lump *and* to listen *and* to communicate all at the same time. Even with frequent breaks, we were all sore by mid-afternoon when we returned to working on the house.

As we had an early dinner, Jen said, "If you insist on going to school tomorrow, you ought to head to bed early."

There'd be a later supper too, at least for me. I burned a lot of calories even on the quietest of days, and the last few hadn't been that. But for the moment my appetite faded.

"Why don't you want me to go to school? You didn't keep asking Amber if she was sure she wanted to go to college." My father hadn't let me go to school, either. I didn't like seeing any parallel between Jen and him.

"Amber needs to stay busy," said Cat, and Amber gave him a sharp look.

Jen's lips thinned, and she looked down at her plate. "I'm sorry. I didn't realize I was being so obvious."

I felt guilty and confused, but I rushed on. "I just want to know why. High school is what kids my age do. Brynn is in high school. Yejun went to high school."

"I didn't finish it, though," he admitted. "You couldn't pay me to go back. I'll get the GED, thanks."

"Yeah, but you have…." I hesitated, trying to find the right word.

"A handicap?" he said equably. "Yeah. Though it isn't really worse at school than not. There's just a lot of boring and assholes at school and not much fun. But hey, I can see why you'd want to go if you haven't. It's fun to try new things," He gave me a little smile that made my heart beat faster.

Jen sighed. "I wanted to be supportive. It's hard starting new schools, especially when you're a junior or a senior. I don't have good memories of that myself."

"Way to poison the well, guys," said Amber, slicing herself more pot roast. Just between Amber and me, we probably went through an ordinary family's weekly protein budget in one day. "AT's tough. She'll be fine."

"Not all schools are awful," added Brynn. She wanted to reassure me, but I could smell that she was worried. "My high school is awesome."

Jen bit her lip and then shook her head. "You ought to go to bed early. Get lots of rest."

"I'll make you a lunch!" said Brynn, brightening.

"I'd like that," I admitted, and we exchanged smiles. I already had friends. Yay. How bad could school be?

The next morning I walked to the bus stop while almost everybody else was still asleep, because high school starts at a ridiculous hour. Yejun was waiting at the stop, looking enough like a delinquent that the few other kids—all younger than me— were staying far away.

"Hey," he said, as I approached him. "Good luck today. I hope it's like Brynn's school."

"You don't think it will be, though." I wasn't guessing; I could smell his doubt just like I'd smelled hers the night before.

He shrugged. "Small town schools, man. You don't hear good

things. Doesn't matter, though. You'll be fine either way. And… while of course, like a good schoolgirl, you've got to get to bed early this week…. Want to catch a movie Friday night?"

I looked at my reflection in his sunglasses. It was smiling. "Yeah," I said. "That would be great. Let's do that."

So that was a good start to the whole week. Unfortunately, it didn't last.

It didn't get *bad*, exactly. Not the way Jen was clearly afraid of, anyhow. I was starting school in the middle of the year, as a junior, in a small town where everybody had known each other their whole lives. The other kids mostly noticed me to ask questions I had to give really vague and deceptive answers on. *My mom and I moved to town to stay with some friends. I'd been homeschooled before. Nope, no church. No, my mom didn't have a job, but we were okay.*

I think some of them read *something* between the lines, because they would suddenly stop asking questions. Other kids—the younger ones who found me at lunchtime—just didn't stop, though. Nobody really wanted to be my friend. On the bright side, nobody developed an instant loathing for me either, so that was good. But when Brynn went back home on Tuesday night, I missed her.

And then it got worse, in the way I'd least wanted.

On Thursday, even the kids who had noticed me had something else to talk about: one of the other juniors, a girl in my math class, had been hospitalized because she'd tried to kill herself. That was pretty bad, but what made it awful was hearing that if she'd succeeded, it would have been the fourth suicide that year.

During math class, when everybody else was hugging each other and making cards to send to the hospital, I stared out the window. I wondered if any of the suicides had left ghosts around. I hadn't seen anything, but I definitely hadn't been looking. Thinking about it, I'd realized I'd been *avoiding* looking: seeing ghosts was one of the ways I was different, and I was trying to so hard not to be different.

Guilt nagged at me. I opened my mind a little, paid attention to my nose, and looked around the room, then out the window. And there were ghosts. More ghosts than I expected to see at a high school and recent ghosts, too. One stood in the corner of the classroom, and two in the courtyard in front of the school—and that was just what I could see immediately.

The ghost in the corner was a boy, looking sadly at an empty desk. I wanted to go talk to him, but I also didn't want to look like a crazy person. So I didn't. I just looked at him, hoping that he'd notice me and come whisper to me. It was a stupid hope. Ghosts didn't work like that. When something changed around them it could take them days or months or years to notice. It's why, every day, I had to explain to my mother where we lived now.

When the bell rang, I left the classroom, ignoring the twinge of shame I felt as I passed the ghost. I couldn't talk to them while everybody was around. It wasn't happening. I was going to fit in. If they had a problem they needed my help with, they'd eventually notice me and say something.

By the time I got home, I was worn out by wading through the other students' stress as well as my own turmoil. I'd had to keep my head down and focused on my books in order to avoid seeing ghosts I refused to engage with. I went to the kitchen to make myself a sandwich for a snack. Heart, one of my dogs, followed me in from the porch. She sat down and looked at me with liquid brown eyes. I could feel her compassion across the bond that joined us.

But it wasn't compassion for me, I realized. Or even for the ghosts. She could smell the living kids at the school: their grief and their fear. Their *fear.*

I'd been so caught up in the ghosts, my shame and my desire

to fit in that I hadn't paid attention to other details. I'd focused on the smell of the books and the ghosts and ignored the fear of the living people.

It was too much. I left my unmade sandwich on the counter and went to the laptop Jen had bought me, to find out what was going in the way most immediately available to me.

It didn't take much eavesdropping on my fellow students' social media accounts to realize that they knew their school was haunted. None of them could see the ghosts I saw, though. They knew it the traditional way ghost stories had been passed down: bad dreams, legends, and dark events. Something evil lingered at their school, and it was driving kids to suicide. It had been there for years: the story kids told each other and adults ignored.

I couldn't get more details from the poking around I did. They weren't explaining it to outsiders, just talking among themselves: a ghost, a curse, and every day the risk that going to that high school would kill you.

At last, I found somebody who knew the hospitalized victim and was saying something direct and public. Not a student, not somebody who believed in ghosts, but it didn't take much social media arithmetic to figure out what he meant when he posted, "Please, kids, you don't need to get suicidal over a guy." Especially when his comments were filled with people from my school declaring, "She didn't."

The front door opened and Jen, Cat, and Yejun came in. They worked on magic in the afternoons, way out in the far field. Today they were home earlier than I expected. Jen had an odd look on her face.

"AT," she began, and then stopped when she saw me. "What's wrong?"

"Did you *know* something was going on at my school? Is that why you moved here?" I demanded, standing up.

Slowly she shook her head. "No. Did something happen? Is that what the horses meant?"

"Something—a ghost, a monster, I don't know—is making kids kill themselves. We have to deal with it. We have to stop it."

"The horses did say something was coming," said Yejun, lowering his sunglasses to look at me over the edge.

"They said it was *coming*," I snarled. "This has been going on for *years*. So, you know, maybe there's something else 'coming.' I don't care. We have to fix it."

Jen blinked, then said carefully, "Earth Horse said the wind that brought you back also brought back the howl of the corrupted ghost. I just came to check with you. I can use the Horn. We can solve this."

I stared at her expectantly. Then Cat said quietly, "Manage your own monster, if you please, AT." I switched my gaze to him, and then wilted as I processed what he said.

"I'm sorry." My vision clouded with a crimson burst of self-hatred, and Grim and Heart both whined behind me. I was part monster and I could never let myself forget that.

"We all have our crosses to bear," said Cat in that same even voice, and I remembered that of all of us, only he'd had to promise his horse that he would control himself.

"I'll get the Horn," said Jen, with a briskness that hid her anxiety. She vanished elsewhere in the house.

Yejun said, "It'll be fun. We can see if it'll really bring Amber and Brynn out to play. I bet it won't. I bet they'll have to Skype in."

The image of the other girls Skyping into a Wild Hunt was so incongruous that even though I was horrified by myself and the situation, I couldn't stop myself from laughing. Yejun quirked one side of his mouth in a return smile.

Then Jen reappeared, holding the Horn. It curled in a glittering golden spiral. It was no longer infected with something evil, but it was still enormously powerful and twisted at right angles to the rest of Creation.

"Let's go outside," Jen said. "I can feel something within the horn. The call, building. I think you identified this before the Horn did, AT. We're ahead of the game."

"I wonder if we can learn what sets it off," said Cat as we trooped out into the fading twilight. "It would be good to know, so we can exercise some control over the process."

The horses waited for us at the pasture fence, lined up precisely. Jen led us over to the fence, glanced at us solemnly, then put her mouth to the Horn and gave it voice.

I felt the song of the Horn before I heard it, in a place so deep inside I didn't know it existed. I'd thought my bond with the dogs came from my heart but this—it was like I was nothing *but* the song of the Horn, set free to wander the world. I was a shaped chain, and I was Cat and Jen and Brynn and Amber, I was Gold Horse and the other mounts.

I was Yejun, too. Our thoughts mingled and I gasped. It wasn't words or even sensation, just an overwhelming sense of *him*, drawing my focus in a way the others didn't. I wanted—

Within the coils of the song, Gold Horse moved between us, calling my dogs to join him. I blinked, trying to see the real world again. Gold Horse really was beside me, and over his back I could see Amber and Brynn becoming nearly real. As real as any of us right now. Their expressions of surprise faded as the power and the mission overwhelmed mundane concerns.

Our bodies had been suffused with the magic of the horn. It radiated through us. We were the Wild Hunt and we *did* have a task before us. There was something to hunt. A mist settled around us as we mounted, dividing us from the world.

I whistled to my dogs and they cast around until they found

the scent the Horn taught them. Once they set off after it, we rode. Tree, earth, sky: none of it mattered when the mist dream of the Wild Hunt cloaked us. We were an elemental force and nothing could stop us.

From the sky, and revealed by the roiling of the mist, the high school I attended looked different. The buildings were shadows on the land, cast by lines of a sick glimmering light that twisted together into a knot behind one of the old 'temporary' buildings.

The dogs slowed, circling. This was definitely the place the Horn had identified. The ghosts I'd observed from my classroom, along with more than a dozen more, all looked up at us as we descended. They were bound along the lines of sickly light: trapped and damaged by whatever had led them to their deaths.

That was against nature. It was a core law of Creation that souls couldn't be tampered with, except as they permitted. *We* were the only exception to that law, and it took the touch of something beyond Creation to empower that.

There were ways to slide around that metaphysical law, though: all the many ways people had always been convinced to work against their best interests. Faith, hatred, and love were only a handful of the possibilities.

"*Love*," whispered Jen, and I saw what she saw: the pair of ghosts entwined behind the temporary building at the heart of the knot.

"*Oh,*" said Amber as she saw the trap that had caught so many students: the two original ghosts using the vulnerable as tools to help them in a grotesque reenactment of the maelstrom of emotions that had led to their deaths.

"*Tangled,*" muttered Yejun, his free hand moving reflexively. The ghostly lovers had their own talents, obscure and unfamiliar to me.

I saw the ghost of the boy in my classroom. He looked up

at me, seeing me clearly, alone among all the ghosts. His mouth opened in a cry for help.

I didn't want to see more. I leaned forward, urging Gold Horse on. My dogs dashed ahead and the others followed me. We descended to where the violation originated, the noise of the Wild Hunt a cacophony of doom.

And we cut the violation away, we cured the crime, we cauterized the wound. The two originating ghosts never even looked at us as we swept around them and tore them to pieces.

Flames sprang up around each unraveling strand of the souls, and the Horn sang a hot, hungry song that called the fire into its bell. The sick light that bound the other ghosts flared to incandescence, then became cinders, ashes, nothing.

Most of the ghosts fled away, some fading, some climbing the sky, some literally running from the school. The one who had seen me stayed, caught by other bonds private to his own life. He watched us, still terrified, until we flew into the sky again.

The magic stayed with us until we returned to the farmhouse, and even once we'd landed and dismounted it was slow in ebbing away. It made me feel confident and unafraid. I'd had a problem and I'd solved it and it was wonderful.

Idly I wondered what else I could do while I felt so good, so *connected*. I remembered touching Yejun's mind before—

Once again, Gold Horse inserted himself between us. I ran my hands over his neck, frowning, but he turned his head away from me, refusing to respond to my silent inquiry.

Then Brynn said, „I… don't know. Was that *right?*"

It cracked right through my confidence.

"We're supposed to deal with bad ghosts. They were bad. We dealt with them," I said. "How could it be not right?"

Brynn bit her thumbnail as she stared at the ground. "I just… wonder what made them bad. They were… hurting. I could feel it. What if there was another way we could have fixed it?"

Cat said to Brynn gently, "Duty is sometimes harsh."

Jen gave Cat a sideways glance, and something passed between them. His brow furrowed.

"I just keep thinking of your mother, AT," said Brynn earnestly. "About how hard it is for her to understand when things have changed. But she *can* learn, you've said. If you make the effort. Maybe we could have helped those two ghosts change."

I stared at Brynn incredulously. Light shimmered around her frame. The final dregs of Horn magic were fading, taking her back to where she'd been called from.

"We couldn't have," I told her. "They were beyond recovery. That's what the Horn's call means."

"I don't know...." she repeated, and then she and Amber both vanished and we all came back to reality with a spirit-jarring thud.

I knelt down and buried my face in Nod's black fur. He licked my ear and panted, tired from all the running around.

"Hey," said Yejun softly behind me. "Back to normal life, yeah? School tomorrow, no ghosts, movie at eight? Uh."

I looked up to see Black Horse had shoved her head hard into his back. Suddenly I was sure: the horses didn't want Yejun and me thinking about each other that way. The way that the two broken ghosts had thought about each other.

Frustration boiled up in me, and I bounded to my feet and over to Gold Horse's side. "Hey, let's go for a ride, just you and me," I said to the horse. "We have to talk."

Yes, said the horse and I flung myself onto his back. Almost as soon as I was up there, he started running, around the pasture fence and into the fields beyond.

It was different than riding as part of the Hunt: earthbound and relying on bone and blood to move us. Different, but the *reality* of it was intoxicating. The contrast between the two worlds balanced against each other.

We were far beyond Jen's land when Gold Horse finally stopped. His sides heaved and we were both sweating in the night air. He stretched his noise to the wind, flicking his ears back at me. *They never had this.*

"They?" I asked, confused. I was still thinking of Yejun and the ghosts and Brynn's weird concern for them.

Our previous masters. They never ran on the earth of Creation, felt the mortal wind, or tasted true rain. They flew on wings of power and hunted in dreams and devoured souls without ever really experiencing the world they were first bound to protect.

"Oh." I slid off the stallion's back and moved so we could see eye to eye. "Why do you keep getting between Yejun and me?"

Gold Horse had topaz eyes: almost the same color as my father's, but so different in shape and wisdom. For a moment I wasn't sure he was going to answer, but then he heaved a dramatic sigh. *You are part of the same chain, the two of you. If you make a loop, the chain will eventually knot and warp and you too will lose the feel of the wind through your mane.*

"Uh. You think if Yejun and I see a movie together, we're going to end up just like the previous Wild Hunt?"

Gold Horse's skin rippled in an eloquent shrug.

"What about Cat and Jen?" I demanded.

Earth Horse and Sunset have their own burdens, although there are differences.... Golden Horse's mental voice was delicate.

"This is really stupid," I complained hotly. It wasn't like the horses could stop us from... forming a loop. Not really. Could they?

"I'll be careful." Then I blushed, because that sounded like I was talking about something I knew I wasn't ready for. "I just want—"

You want what mortals have, said the horse gently. *Find it with mortals. Stay connected to the world, and keep our bonds pure.*

"I'll think about it," I said slowly.

When we went home, I passed Yejun walking along the side of the road by himself. He had a hunted expression that made me think he'd been having a similar conversation with Black Horse, and when he saw me, he waved before looking down.

I took the hint and didn't stop to talk. I wasn't sure Gold Horse would have let me anyhow.

That night, I slept like a log. A log filled with wormy nightmares and burrowing bad thoughts with chitinous wings of horror that flickered in the spaces between deeper darkness. I woke surrounded by my dogs, my face pressed against Grim's chest, Heart on my legs and Nod at my back. I ached like I had after one of my father's gentler training sessions.

Gold Horse was probably right, I realized. If all I wanted was a movie and to get to know Yejun better, there was no reason to put the trappings of romance onto that. And workplace romances were the sort of thing you were supposed to avoid, right? Yejun was a coworker, in a way. I had to keep that in mind.

But I spent a while thinking about him anyhow because it was a lot better than thinking about what else had happened the night before. It was the ghost lovers that had consumed my dreams, mingling with my vague feelings for Yejun and drifting into other, uglier things.

My father had wanted me to mate with somebody, had hoped that my children, taken from me at birth, would be easier to mold than I'd ended up. I'd been afraid of any relationship: a kind boy would have been destroyed, one way or another, and one of my father's servants would have been... worse. Yejun was just as safe from my father as I was now, which was one reason he was so attractive to me.

But if it did go bad between us—what would happen? Would we twist the whole Wild Hunt around us? The horses' concerns *weren't* stupid. Even mortal love, without law-breaking power behind it, could warp the world. It made sense to be careful.

When I finally rolled to my feet to get dressed, I felt like I'd made a decision. I couldn't really bring myself to think about a mortal boy, but Yejun and I could, at the very least, wait a while. I just hoped he'd understand.

I worried about that as I ate my bacon and eggs. Jen sat across me, eating a bagel and some melon, and staring into the depths of her coffee. She was just as shocked as I was when Brynn walked out of Jen's office, looking rumpled and determined.

"Hey!" said Brynn. "It turns out I can summon myself to the Horn. Can you get the others here, please? We have to talk." She thought. "I'll go get Amber."

"No need," said Amber creakily from the staircase. "I got back the hard way at midnight. You show me what you did, right now. I really hate that drive."

Jen put her phone to her ear and said, "Brynn is here. Yes. Why don't you come over with Yejun?" Then she put her phone on the table, folded her hands in her lap and stared fixedly at Brynn.

The burning determination in Brynn's eyes didn't flicker as she stared back at Jen, and I started to get a bad feeling that slowly grew to overshadow my worry about talking to Yejun. When he and Cat arrived, I barely glanced at him.

"AT, where's your mom?" asked Brynn, once the guys had settled themselves around the kitchen.

My hand was already closed over my mother's pendant. I tightened it protectively. Then slowly, I took it off and held it out to her.

Brynn took it gently, cupping it in the palm of her hand. "Denise," she said, and her voice had a sweetly commanding echo I'd never heard before.

My mother's ghost shimmered into existence around the pendant. She looked to me first, the usual anxiety on her face. Then she looked around, saw the others I'd introduced her to so many times before, and her anxiety faded. Finally, she looked at the girl who had summoned her and said, "Hello, Brynn. Thank you for being my daughter's friend."

"Thank you for having such a brave, wonderful daughter," she said gravely.

My mother smiled. I scrubbed at my eyes and wondered what Brynn was doing.

"What can I do for you, Brynn?"

"You've already done it, Denise. Thank you." Brynn held the locket out to me and I snatched it back, bringing my mother back to me. She looked a little puzzled, but brushed her hand through my hair comfortingly as she faded away.

"She remembered me," said Brynn. "She didn't any of the other times. They *aren't* stuck eternally."

Oh. This was about last night's Hunt again. "Sometimes they are. I've been talking to ghosts a lot longer than you have, Brynn."

"How many corrupted ones have you met and talked to before destroying them forever?" she shot back.

I pressed my lips together and looked away.

"Maybe they couldn't have been redeemed," said Brynn, her voice softer. "My point is that we didn't even try. We didn't talk, we didn't investigate. We swept in like... like they were prey, and we *ended* them."

Nobody else said anything. I had to really listen to hear the others even breathing; it might have just been Brynn and I in the kitchen.

"Fine. Maybe you're right," I snapped, then winced at my own tone of voice. "But it's done. We destroyed them like monsters and, you know, I am—"

"Stop that," said Cat, his voice an unexpected rumble.

"Stop it, yeah," said Amber, almost at the same time. "Don't say that about yourself."

"I just don't know what the point of talking about it now is," I said, pacing in a frantic little circle. "This is it, this is our life, we accepted this; I don't know what she wants us to do."

"I want us to do it differently next time," Brynn said. "That's all. We're not predators. We're… executioners, but there should be, like, a trial and an investigation and stuff first. Or something. I'm not going to trust some hunk of metal left behind by a crazy violinist to tell us if a soul is irredeemable. If it's supposed to be like that, why should there be people involved at all? It's important that we're mortal, I know it is."

"That makes sense," admitted Yejun. I glanced at him and he gave me a familiar half-smile.

I remembered what Gold Horse had said about mortality. I was only half-mortal myself, stuck between two worlds. Balanced? It didn't really feel like it. I looked at everybody else bound to the Wild Hunt. They all had their own seesaws they tried to manage. Brynn had been the most human of all of us before our binding, and it was she who carried the horses.

Investigating future ghosts would mean I'd screwed up last night: screwed up and destroyed souls, because I wanted the inconvenience of their curse to stop messing up my attempt at a normal life. My stomach twisted in a knot that exploded out of me in a sob, and I turned away, hanging onto the counter like I'd fall without it.

Yejun was beside me in a flash, his hand on my shoulder. I shrugged him away and hunched over. A moment later, Jen's hand touched my arm instead. "I'm sorry," I whispered. It wasn't an apology to her.

She understood. "We'll investigate in the future," she said. It was both a decision, and an attempt at comfort.

I nodded. It didn't really help the twisting of grief and self-hatred, but it was the only thing that might. Eventually.

Brynn came up on my other side. "We'll do better. It'll be okay. We're still learning, right?" She seemed so young to me suddenly. She was so far from the world I'd lived in my whole life, and she could worry about it with an outsider's eyes without being hurt by what she'd done. Innocence.

I reached over and hugged her, then hugged Jen, too. Then I turned around to where Yejun leaned against the table, watching me.

I took a deep breath. "Okay. Brynn is right. Next time we get called, we do everything we can to sort it out without destroying the ghost first. I'm on board."

"All right," said Yejun.

"Fine with me," said Amber, and Cat nodded.

And that was that. We were the Wild Hunt, we were executioners, but we would investigate first. There'd be something like a trial. I had no idea how that would work, but we'd figure it out. And that *did* help, a little. I wasn't a ghost. Change was a lot easier for me, for us. Time to take advantage of that.

My phone buzzed, interrupting my thoughts. Mundane reminders. I glanced at the clock. The calls of a mortal life. Balance.

"I'm going to be late for school. Uh, Yejun? Walk me to the bus stop?"

He shrugged. "Sure."

A few minutes later I'd washed my face and grabbed my book bag, and we were on the roadside.

"So," I said. "Those horses."

"Yeah," he said. "I never wanted to rush you, anyhow."

"I'd still like to see the movie. As friends, yeah?"

"Sure," he said. "Shall I invite Amber? Or Brynn? Ooh, or both. That'd build up my reputation in this little town real fast." He smiled at me.

I smiled back, relief and pleasure washing through me. He wasn't upset. He wasn't even hurt. But he still seemed to care. We could be friends, nothing *just* about it. It was wonderful.

"How about Cat?" I suggested, and we argued about it all the way to the bus stop.

William dropped down on the rise to where one of his brothers lay on his belly in the lush, green grass, looking through some binoculars at the field of fading flowers below. "How is it, Harold?"

Harold looked through the glasses for a moment longer before pulling them away and rolling down the hill just enough to sit up. "Not good, boss." The other changeling twisted his spine, stretching the kinks out, because even immortal bodies could cramp when they held one position too long. "Take a look for yourself."

William did so. A hazy figure moved in the field of flowers, outside a small cottage made of crumbling brick, or a giant tree stump, or maybe a weathered giant's skull. The figure was as hard to make out as the cottage: a small, dragonfly-winged girl, a silver-skinned creature of gears and steam, a column of white flame. But the location was what mattered. William was in the right place, so he knew he was looking at Yeracha the Sprite.

The sprite was hanging laundry out to dry and it wasn't going well. Clothespins snapped at her fingers. The wind gusted, tangling the laundry around her head. A bird flew through a carefully hung sheet and dragged it off. William could tell from the sprite's jerky motions that she was getting more and more angry. She said something with the tonal quality of a curse and stomped a delicate, bare foot. The entire field of flowers shivered.

William put the glasses down and rubbed his eyes. Staring at the sprite was painful; Harold had been specially modified to endure it. "How long has this been going on?"

"She was picking berries earlier," Harold said glumly. The sound of spritely cursing rose again from below. "She kept getting pricked by thorns, and half her berries were rotten. She almost started crying once. I wanted to go down and comfort her."

"Don't be a fool, Harold." William took a closer look at his subordinate, noting his reddened eyes and ears. "Should I swap you out? You deserve a vacation."

"I'll be getting one soon enough. I'm not going to stick around once Miss Yeracha loses her temper, believe that."

"All right. You'd know best when that's going to happen. I'm going to report in. Stay in touch and run before she trembles." William rose to his feet and went back down the slope, walking until he was beyond the range of the cursing.

Then he closed his eyes and opened himself to his master, calling for him silently.

Instantly, Tarn, Duke of Underlight, was in his head. *What have you learned, my William?*

It is as you suspected, my Lord. The sprite is getting cranky, and the mortal world will notice.

For a moment there was silence. Then William felt the soft brush of Tarn's sigh. *I wish we could soothe her, stop this from happening.*

William scowled, glancing over his shoulder at Harold's silhouette. *Underlight will be much stronger after Yeracha has her tantrum. And she is too powerful to approach, even via Harold. You must stop making him soft, my Lord. It will only hurt us all.*

Tarn's laugh tickled William's spine. *My stern William. Very well. You must go to the mortal land where Yeracha's stomping will be heard the loudest, and warn their ruler when and where.*

William didn't say anything in response, and Tarn's voice became coaxing. *It would benefit us all if they learned we aren't always an enemy. You can see that.*

Yes, said William slowly. *But that foolishness at the Thanksgiving holiday, between Honeychord and Winterwhen. Their stupid game. The mortals do not allow any of us near their white palace now. How should I deliver this message? Wouldn't it be easier to simply announce the information publicly?*

Easier but not better. Trust me as I trust you, my William, and find a way to whisper the message in his ear.

William blew out his breath and bowed. *Yes, my lord. May I return home first?*

With a fond mental flick against William's hair, Tarn said, *Time is short. Come home after, to a well-deserved reward.* Then his presence vanished.

William pulled his mouth to one side, annoyed. The ground vibrated behind him, and Harold called, "Better get moving, boss. I'd guess less than a day left."

"It will be sufficient." William strode down the hillside to the road, bending the landscape around him as he did. As it was, the road would take him back to the ruins of Underlight, but his destination was a different part of the mortal world, and he didn't have time to enjoy the sights. So he'd have to push the flexible fabric of the Faerie worldscape so that he rejoined the road at a more useful place.

Bending the landscape was dangerous, but he had strong motivation. That would help. The predators of the uncharted lands were drawn to distracted dreamers and casual explorers, leaving the secrets of the Faerie land to the obsessed and the soldiers. Even so, there were dangers still.

The ground and the sky, the night and the road: all were

more than just elements of the landscape. They were specialized creatures in their own right, nailed to the Backworld to create the foundations of Faerie. And, like any creature of Faerie, they were prone to making mischief when they had an excuse.

The terrain changed under him, the hills becoming gentler and the grass changing. The distant road became a shimmering haze of faraway water. After a moment of walking, William heard the sound of the village where he'd been a child, hundreds of years ago and a world away. He didn't go to see, even when he heard his father's raised voice, calling for him as he'd crept among the sheep. He'd given all that up willingly when Tarn asked; he'd outlasted all his people by half a millennium, and he did not regret it.

The sound of the village faded, but the hills stayed the same. The road stayed no more than a faraway glint between slopes. William concentrated, placing his feet deliberately as he walked, hunching his shoulders as if he walked into a cold wind. After a moment, groaning came from beyond the hill.

His regular pace skipped and faltered. It was the sound of dying men and he wondered—

Yes. He heard the silver bells and the distant murmur of Tarn's voice. It was an inspired lure: all he had to do was go over the hill and he could watch Tarn save him and his men by transforming them into his servants. He'd like to see the procedure from the outside. He remembered the odd tenderness on his lord's face as he cradled William in his arms. It was a peculiar intensity that the Duke rarely displayed: when he and a mortal mingled their essences in an intimacy that mere sexual relations could never match. That expression had earned Tarn William's limitless loyalty.

Oh yes, he was tempted to go and see it again.

But if William did that, he'd be giving control over to the land and its tricksy dreams. It might take him days, or the aid of his master, to find his way free. Either way, Tarn would be disappointed and that possibility was the antidote to any temptation.

He picked up his pace again, pressing his mind against the land. Finally it sighed, the grass flickering across a green rainbow, and the road appeared between two hills. As soon as William stepped on the road, he relaxed his focus. The rules that regulated the road were far more restrictive, but as long as he followed them it would take him where he needed to go.

This gave him the luxury to turn his attention to other matters. He needed to change his clothes and grooming before going into the mortal world. As it was, he looked like exactly what he was: a wild-haired changeling soldier of a faerie Duke. Sometimes the greater faeries referred to his kind as goblins, although one and all they'd been human once and mostly still bore the basic look. But the differences stood out; he'd have no chance of speaking with anybody close to the mortal leader if he didn't adopt their look.

There was a way station near the soft spot where he intended to depart the road: one of the safe structures maintained by the road itself. It would be stocked with basic supplies, which probably included a mirror or paintings. With either of those, he would be able to approximate some acceptable mortal garb.

In this case, it turned out to have something even better.

A greater faerie loitered within, smoking a long cigarette and laying back on a plush leather couch. When William stepped inside, they sat up, flicking ash hair away from their face. "Ooh, have you come to bring some fun to my dreary day?"

William paused on the threshold, inspecting the faerie. They wore one long sleeve and one short, and a buttery bodice that billowed at the top and clung at the waist, over trousers that shimmered like metallic zebra skin. "Your Magnificence. Are you serving here?"

The faerie pouted. "Penance. I'd much rather be doing something else, believe me, but first I have to pay my dues. Who are you, little goblin?"

William bowed and introduced himself properly. The faerie noble didn't return the favor, nor did William expect them to. Instead William just categorized them as Their Magnificence, from the Duchy of Arcwine, and hoped they were feeling benevolent. Otherwise, Tarn might have a mess to clean up later.

"Off to the mortal world, I imagine," said Their Magnificence, giving William a keen, knowing look. "Well, I can make you over however you wish, but in return you must create a memory for me."

"What sort?" William put his gear on the floor and stretched, quite used to the faerie noble's expression. It was the look of one artisan assessing the craftsmanship of another. But William knew he was good work.

"Oh, I'm not particular. Go find something you wish you had but never will, and experience it for me. Then come back and I'll pluck it straight from your pattern, a gift from you to me." Their Magnificence beamed.

"Not particular at all," said William wryly. But it was a reasonable payment compared to what the faerie could have demanded. When a waykeeper was in residence, they were required to serve, but they had the power to state their own price: time, trinkets, a service in return. William had paid in blood before, and not his own. A memory would be easy.

He thought about the kind of memory, then amended the thought to, *mostly easy*. More importantly, he didn't have time to haggle. "Agreed."

"Exquisite," cooed Their Magnificence and stretched their fingers. "Where shall you be playing? The beach? The stage? Will you be in front of a camera? I can make you look as stunning on camera as you are right here, despite the *wretched* quality of the lighting there."

"No appearing on cameras," said William firmly. "I need

to look respectable. Trustworthy." He hesitated then added, "Inconspicuous."

Their Magnificence frowned. "In that body? What *is* your lord about, I wonder? No, no, don't tell me. I'd only find myself in more trouble." They whisked a thin crystalline tube out of thin air and spun it between their fingers. "Well, as it happens, I know exactly what to do. There were a great number of *that* sort interfering in my last jaunt. I shan't give you a gun, though. Nasty things."

"Probably for the best." William watched the spinning rod warily. Their Magnificence was looking anywhere but him as the rod danced over their fingers. It made William remember long ago: a different lordling, a mortal one, and a trap sprung. He didn't let himself tense up, but he held onto his memory of what had come after, of Tarn holding him, like it was a talisman of protection.

Suddenly the wand snapped forward, pointing at William. "Hey, presto." Sparkling light flared around him. The magic crept over him, starting with his fingertips, mingling with Tarn's magic in a way that was strange but not unpleasant. It spread up his arms and across his face, and down his chest and thighs, culminating at his toes.

As the light faded away, Their Magnificence flopped back on the couch, putting their arm over their eyes. "Done. Now please leave before I'm forced to gaze upon what I've done to you."

William took a moment to inspect himself. His very useful claws had been trimmed down and his boots were now stiff, tough shoes. He wore black slacks and a tie around his neck. And his hair was smoothed down.

"There's a pair of sunglasses in your pocket," added Their Magnificence, as if describing a tragedy. "Go, go. It's not going to last. I could hardly get my will behind it."

William glanced at his gear on the ground: the spear, the belt with the knife, the helmet. Then he turned and left it behind.

Gear was replaceable and, in this case, time was not.

Returning to the road, he reached the soft spot in the Veil after a short hike. Going through was just a matter of tuning himself to the right shift and then stepping forward.

But it didn't work out quite that easily. The Veil wasn't as soft was it should have been. When he should have felt the fabric between worlds parting around him, he instead felt a sense of vertigo. Something spun him like he was playing a children's game, and when the mists cleared away, he wasn't where he expected to be: within sight of the great white monuments of elder statesmen.

Instead he was in a narrow alley that opened onto an anonymous city street. There were two lanes of vehicle traffic, small shops lining the sidewalk, and a distinct air of poverty. He emerged from the alley, shook the unfamiliar clothing into something resembling comfort and strode down the street, looking for some hint as to where he was. Hopefully he hadn't been spun too far off course, or he'd have to resort to something dramatic.

He hadn't expected interference before he even arrived in the mortal world. It meant that the earthly powers had found a way to influence the Veil—a way that didn't rely on any faeries. As far as he knew, the faeries were the only *public* manifestation of the supernatural—so who was the white palace working with to protect itself?

Something caught his eye: a store crammed between a pawn shop and a payday loan service. CHARMS OF PROTECTION said the window lettering, and KEEP YOURSELF SAFE FROM THE STRANGERS. The shop had crystals and leather-bound diaries and tarot cards in the window, but they were scattered around like set dressing. Printed on a card was a very credible Geometric diagram, illustrating the circle of binding that actual mortal practitioners of magic used to construct what they, yes, called charms.

Despite his hurry, he went inside. It was set up as a bookstore, but the few shelves were sparsely populated. There *was* quite a display of small crystal pendants on a large rack near the counter, with more expensive necklaces under the glass.

The man behind the counter had wild salt-and-pepper hair and a friendly smile. But he was dressed in a suit as tailored as William's, which meant William's first thought was: *one of Their Magnificence's 'ordinary men with guns?'*

"What can I do for you today?" said the man, and the way his eyes went over William's clothes reinforced William's first impression. This was a man prepared for William to say anything. And the magic he'd hung about his person made it clear he was just as prepared for William to *do* anything.

"Why the pendants?" asked William. They were ordinary pieces of costume jewelry: cheap polished rocks in steel settings.

"Ah, those would be the charms," said the shopkeeper. "We have to bind them to you, of course. A brief ritual."

William narrowed his eyes. "No. Why the pendants *really*?"

The shopkeeper narrowed his eyes right back, this time clearly looking past William's clothes. "Ah." His entire posture changed. Instead of radiating 'friendly, helpful shopkeeper,' he became wary, territorial. Then he made a conscious effort to relax, pulling a pipe from behind the counter and fidgeting with it. "Well, they're props. Clients don't believe we've done anything unless they get something to take home. We thought about a nice embossed certificate of Now Resistant To You Bastards, but the pendants seem to go over best."

"Who's we?" asked William, letting the You Bastards slide. Most of his fellows were, after all. By one definition or another.

"Oh, a loose organization of like-minded individuals," said the shopkeeper-wizard. "Just a few of us who didn't feel like waiting around for the folks on Capitol Hill to organize an *official* way of protecting our citizens from folks like you."

William was pretty sure the shopkeeper had his hands on the magical equivalent of a shotgun behind the counter. If this had been playtime, he would have amused himself with a little provocation. But his master would not approve, not on this mission of goodwill.

"Well done," he said, instead. "And is your 'loose association' also responsible for the misdirection around that region of the city?"

The shopkeeper's look became thoughtful. "I just run the shop." He finished working on his pipe. "I don't have anything to sell to your kind, so you might as well run along."

William hesitated, curious just how far the shopkeeper's connections went. Perhaps it would be better to warn him—and his organization—of Yeracha's impending tantrum. Surely Tarn would value increased goodwill with a group of mortal wizards— William was sure they had *some* connection to the government— more than William wasting time trying to get to the Commander in Chief.

But there was no voice in his head instructing him one way or another. He would have to decide on his own.

William thought about it a moment more as the shopkeeper became increasingly uncomfortable. *No,* he decided. This person wouldn't understand Tarn's motivations. He turned and went to the door, then said, "What you do here... it is a good thing."

The shopkeeper blinked. "*You* think so? Hah, I don't believe you."

William spread his fingers. "The ones who don't wish to play ought to have at least a little protection. We aren't *monsters.*" He gave a little smile. "That's another set of individuals entirely."

When he left the store, he heard the man come around the counter to watch his departure. Perhaps he'd planted a seed for

Tarn's future plans. He could be proud of that.

But time ticked away, and he had no more to spend on side projects. He went to the end of the narrow street and turned down a larger one. He still didn't quite know where he was, but the streets were full of drivers who did. Some of them wanted paying, and some of them were private citizens, and oh so *few* of them carried protective charms.

He started out with a bus, waving a glamoured leaf at the bus driver as he stepped on. He wasn't quite sure what the driver saw instead of the leaf, but William intended it to be something official that would negate the need for a fare. And it worked to get him on the bus—but he drew attention as he moved down the crowded vehicle. All the seats were taken. He found a place apart from the other standees and gazed out the window until he realized people were staring at him.

One little boy with a purple smear around his mouth said, "Do you have a gun, mister?"

William thought about what he'd promised Their Magnificence and didn't answer. And as soon as the bus rolled into a transit center, he left. His glamoured leaf would serve him just as well with a taxi, even if some of them seemed to have the kind of magical protection sold by the shop. That was the advantage of glamouring an object: it wasn't enchanting a person, it was tricking the world.

He found one waiting, driven by a woman with her hair cut short; the license hanging from the roof read 'Joanne Harrison.' She gave him a wary look as he climbed inside but when he told her where he wanted to go, she relaxed and pulled out into traffic.

William leaned back and looked out the window. The driver had a talk radio station on. The voices were arguing about what had happened when the Faerie Court called Moonspindle had pulled a meteor down into the heart of China. They were wrong, as mortals usually were. And they didn't seem to understand that Moonspindle was a sovereign entity, just as China was. After that, they went on to talk about Bonefete and what they were doing in Russia. It was amazing. They could actually use the right names but still assume they were both arms of a single tentacular beast.

William shook his head and said, "Is this all they talk about?"

The driver glanced in her rearview mirror and frowned faintly as she met his gaze. Then she shrugged. "It's big news. I haven't gotten bored yet. Have you?"

"Bored isn't the word I'd use, exactly. Surprised, maybe. Once upon a time, we had other things to worry about. Wars. Human monsters." He glanced out at the clouded sky. "The weather."

"But this changes so much," argued the driver. "What they can do, what they *might* do."

"Not as much as you think," murmured William. "Life does go on."

Joanne didn't seem to hear him. "I mean, this group, Bonefete. What if they decide to help Russia take over Ukraine?"

"Does Russia *need* Bonefete's help against this other country? What did you call it?" William asked.

She gave him a puzzled look. "Ukraine. Well... what if Bonefete helped Ukraine instead?"

William thought about Bonefete, beholden to Air and Winter, and traditionally aligned against Underlight. "Perhaps that might keep them busy for a time. Although I imagine they're unlikely to *help* anybody."

"Well, yes. There's that, too." When William didn't respond, the driver fell silent, listening to her radio station again.

William leaned back against the seat, modeling approaches to his target. If the glamoured leaf worked as well on the target's bodyguards as it did on random citizens of the capital, it wouldn't be nearly as challenging as he anticipated. All he needed was a few minutes, and then it didn't matter what happened to him. They could capture him or slay his body, and Tarn would still gather him home again.

Though if he came back to Faerie without procuring a payment for Their Magnificence, it could cause some annoyance to his Lord. Best to deal with that first. It wouldn't take long. He opened his eyes to ask the driver to adjust their destination and stopped as her gaze met his in the mirror. The car jolted before her gaze flicked away and the ride smoothed out again.

Frowning, William moved until he could see himself in the mirror. The magic pasted on him by Their Magnificence was already fading: his hair had returned to its normal spikes, and the smooth blandness of his features had subtly shifted back toward Tarn's personal handiwork. At least the suit remained pristine, although that didn't do much to offset his annoyance. He'd *probably* still pass for mortal. To anybody who wasn't looking closely. But it'd be that much harder for the glamoured leaf to act as his pass card now.

In a determinedly breezy voice, the taxi driver said, "Have you come for the hearings? They won't let you in, you know."

"The hearings?" William slouched back again, putting one foot up on the back of the seat in front of him and watching out the window for some sign the driver had changed her heading without being asked.

"Oh, come on." The breezy tone vanished. "The Congressional hearings about the faeries. About your kind."

"Oh," said William. Tarn had mentioned those once, but William hadn't been too interested. He didn't put much faith in the decision-making capabilities of a group of over a hundred people. In his experience, even a group of three people could overcomplicate things. "Are they even worth trying to attend? I expect they'll be pretty dull. A nice way for a bunch of rich lordlings to look busy and not much else."

The driver shook her head in disbelief or wonderment. "Not lords. Well, not really. You really aren't from around here, are you?"

"You've spotted it. Well done. Is there a children's playground somewhere in the vicinity where you could drop me off?"

She looked troubled. "I can find one. What are you going to do there?"

"You are extremely nosy for a driver," William pointed out.

"I have to be careful," she said impatiently. "And I don't want you to hurt anybody. If I think you're going to, I have an obligation to call—somebody," she finished with a flush that William noted and filed away.

"I'm not going to hurt anybody. I'm going to pay a bill for services rather badly rendered, but rendered all the same. And then I'm going to hail another cab, perhaps with a less nosy driver, and continue on my way to the Capitol."

"I told you, they won't let you in! My brother said you're far too dangerous to be allowed near Congress. Like, you have weapons that can't be taken away."

William smiled. "Well, that's true, at least. But I don't want to speak to your prosy Congress. I don't care about them. I care about the chain of command, and I must speak to the top man."

Joanne glanced over to one side, then turned her vehicle, focusing for a few moments on her driving. Then she pulled over to the side of the street and turned off her meter. "Here's your playground. I'll wait until you're done." She got out of the cab and leaned on it, crossing her arms.

William reached out for his lord, wishing for his advice or at least his encouragement, but all he felt was a touch of amusement and a mental shove before Tarn took his attention away. Blowing out his breath in exasperation, William emerged from the car and inspected the playground. Three boys, two girls, and a child of indeterminate gender raced around a wooden structure that combined slide and swings. Two adults loitered on the far side of the structure, studying their phones and making desultory small talk.

William eyed the adults and decided they wouldn't interfere. Sometimes those phones seemed to provide all the distraction glamour could, without the risk of attracting the wrong kind of attention. He took a deep breath and loosened the tie Their Magnificence had put him in, then took off the coat and laid it across the cab's hood, beside Joanne.

Then he reached down inside himself, deep down and far back again, to when he'd been a mortal. It was a point between the two memories that the landscape of Faerie had tempted him with, a point crushed under centuries of immortality and cynicism. Slowly, he peeled away the layers of boredom and irritation and servitude, back to when he'd dreamt of a different future.

Then he spun a tiny thread of glamour around himself, just enough to offset any caution a sensible child might have around him.

Once, he'd dreamt of playing with his own children. Once, before he'd been betrayed, trapped, killed, and reborn. He hadn't even had a bride, but he'd always wanted to raise his own sons and daughters with the same affection his father had given him. If nothing else, there were always orphans in those days. Always children who needed loving parents.

Things hadn't changed that much between now and then, after all. The curiosity of the children brought them to him, and he showed them how to spin pink clouds into elephants with their fingertips, showed them how to make leaves into paper birds that really flew. He learned their names and ages and told them his own, and threw the youngest into the air and smiled as she giggled.

Then, as the caretakers started to notice—without even a pause for curiosity, going straight to concerned—he backed off and returned to the taxi driver as she leaned against the car. Her phone was out too, but she never seemed to look at it.

He put on his jacket again. As the approaching caretakers saw his companion, they hesitated. Joanne waved, and they turned away to scold their children instead.

"Your presence makes me less frightening to them? Odd," said William.

"It's a dark world," said the driver, shrugging. "You told them your name was William."

"Yes," he said. "Hush a moment." He took another deep breath and pushed the memory of playing with the children deep down inside, burying it with spikes and duty and a different kind of love. And then more spikes, because it *was* a dark world, and he'd chosen his light long ago. When he was done, he felt more like himself again. But he'd still be glad when Their Magnificence could take the burden he'd created from him.

The driver remained silent, watching him the whole time. He raised his eyebrows at her and said, "Will you take me to the next place I want to go now? Or did you decide you needed to call—somebody?"

"Are you going to hurt anybody?"

He wondered why she'd bother asking that, why she'd expect an honest answer. "The entire point of this little exercise is to stop people from getting hurt."

She studied him, just as she'd been studying him all this time. Then she said, "Get in."

Once they pulled into traffic again, she said, "You can't just stroll in to talk to him, you know."

"I would be aghast if I could," said William, trying to inject as much boredom into his voice as he could. He didn't want to talk about this. He wanted to get there, deliver his message, and go home again.

Joanne shook her head. "If I did call somebody, he might be able to help."

"Look. I don't need your help. All I need you to do is drive."

"Fine," she snapped and stayed quiet until the white mansion was in sight. When she pulled the vehicle to a curb, she said, "I don't suppose you have any ability to pay me, do you?"

He waved his glamoured leaf in her direction, more out of habit than hope, and she narrowed her eyes. "That's not real."

"No," he agreed. "It doesn't work very well on people who know something's going on." He glanced in the mirror, frowned, ran a hand through his hair, and then shrugged and opened the door. "Thank you for the ride."

She grimaced, and he guessed that she was thinking about following him around some more. He hopped out and slammed the door, walking away before she could make up her mind. Most mortals were easily distracted, but some could be so very persistent. It made them interesting to Tarn and sometimes worthy of respect from William. But he was glad she didn't follow him. He'd already spent too much time talking to mortals instead of delivering his message.

He looked up at the huge, white house, shook his head at what was considered grand and elegant these days, and set out to find a way to the Commander in Chief.

AN HOUR LATER, he was starting to feel frustrated. The magical leaf most definitely didn't work on the guardians of the white mansion, who had extremely good magical protection and *always* believed something was going on.

It would, he felt, serve the humans right if he failed in his mission and the sprite Yeracha's tantrum caused unchecked havoc. Not only did they have mortal guards in place—so *many* mortal guards—but they had supernatural traps, too, and not traps set by any faerie. No, they had an angel working with them, and that was unfair and wrong. The angels weren't supposed to get involved like that anymore.

He leaned on a tree in the park next to the house and wiped blood from a cut over his eye. The last trap had been hard to avoid: the shadow of a bird, on the shadow of a power line, both of them ripped loose from any mooring or sense of sanity as they lashed around him, opening cuts with edges nobody but him could see. When reddened, lidless eyes opened along the shadow line, William backed off. He knew better than to go up against that kind of madness alone.

Was it an angel protecting the Commander in Chief? Or something worse? The nature of the traps suggested something worse, but there were still the unmistakable traces of angel magic. It was a sort of sparkle, a shine of purity and self-righteousness and implacable focus—but it glittered over a twisted knot of torment that suggested either an angel on the edge or the most unholy of alliances.

"William?" said a man striding up to him, startling him out of his contemplation of the problem. He whirled around, his stance changing instinctively to a combative one. Which reminded him that he didn't have his spear, because he was in the mortal world, and he wasn't going to be fighting anybody.

The man raised his hands, laughing nervously. "No threat." He wore black slacks and a white button-down shirt, and his beard looked like he couldn't decide if he needed a shave or not. Not a soldier, and not one of the bodyguards either. But William didn't relax, because the man had called him by name. It meant he was an agent of *somebody*.

"I can see you're definitely William," said the man, still laughing. "Look, man, can I buy you a cup of coffee or something? I'd love to talk to you."

"Who are you?" William took a step backward: not a retreat but a repositioning.

The man scratched his beard. "John Brady. Hey, are you trying to get in like that crew at Thanksgiving?"

William ran his hand through his spiky hair. "They were morons." And then he couldn't stop himself from adding, "And so was everybody else involved. They just wanted to help celebrate your feast. They had no intention of hurting anybody. And neither do I."

"I was there," said John Brady, apologetically. "It looked like they were playing some kind of sport on the White House Lawn. With good china and turkeys. It's the sort of thing that makes the Secret Service pretty nervous, especially when it comes from aliens like yourself."

William scowled. "If any folk are the aliens, you are."

John Brady shrugged. "And yet that's your legal description and what the hearings are all about." He looked William up and down. "I admit, it's a pretty useless description."

Meeting the man's eyes, William realized that he wasn't anybody's agent after all. Gloomily, he said, "You're that driver's 'somebody.'"

"Joanne's my sister, and yes, she called me." He hesitated, then added, "I'm a journalist. And I'd really like to buy you a cup of coffee."

William looked past the mortal at the White House. "I'm better than those clowns at the feast," he muttered. "I could get in. But not while leaving a positive impression."

"You do seem smarter than them," agreed John Brady. "Why exactly are you trying to get in?"

"I need a cup of tea," said William slowly.

"Excellent." John grinned. "This way."

He guided William to a little cafe, trying to ask him questions the whole walk. William couldn't be bothered to chat. He had to come up with another plan. But his choices depended on first getting a cup of tea.

The cafe thought a bag in a cup of hot water counted as tea, which was depressing. After he and John Brady sat down outside the cafe, William tore the bag open and let the leaves swirl in the hot water to steep directly. Then he fixed his gaze on his host, staring him into uncomfortable shifting.

"What is it you want, John Brady? Not to make small talk, not to turn me over to your soldiers. Why did your Joanne think you were the one to call about an 'alien' like me?"

"I'm a journalist. I want to talk to you and write about what you tell me." He watched William stirring his tea with interest. "Why did you tear open the bag?"

"Because I need to check the time," said William, purely to amuse himself at the mortal's confusion. He waited until the tea turned deep brown, then added several heaping spoons of sugar, and took a long drink of the brew. Then he scooped out some of the soggy leaves and spread them on the napkin. Casting his thoughts outward, he reached for Harold.

It wasn't the same as reaching out for Tarn. He had no interest in touching Harold's mind; he just wanted Harold's opinion. It was hard for them to exchange anything as concrete as words, and feelings were useless in an operation as time-sensitive as this one. So the tea leaves came in handy. Once he'd attracted Harold's attention and held himself aligned, he peered into the scattered black bits on the white napkin, and an image emerged from the pattern: the hill, the sprite. Harold's hand, signing something.

William slumped in his chair.

"Yeah, I have trouble getting the time from tea leaves, too," said the journalist, with an unbelievably straight face.

"I found out the time."

John Brady narrowed his eyes. "Oh? What time is it?"

"An hourglass that is rapidly emptying." William didn't have time for any of his more elaborate plans. He eyed the reporter, then swallowed hard. "What would you do, mortal, if you had to get a message to the Commander in Chief?"

"Ah, well. What I'd do isn't what everybody could do," said John Brady, in such a comfortable way that William wanted to box his ears. "I have connections. But they're not the kind of connections to be casually exploited. I'd have to have a very good reason to use them." He raised his eyebrows at William invitingly.

William hesitated, then shook his head. "If I tell you and you do the wrong thing with the information, it could be very bad. And it would certainly disappoint my lord."

"I see you have connections too," said John Brady happily. "Maybe we can make some kind of deal. Something where you do something for me, and in return I do something for you."

Tiredly, William said, "I haven't the power to do things for mortals. I could put in a word with my lord if you wish, but it probably won't do anything you couldn't get on your own."

"You've got the power to talk to me. You're doing it right now."

"Ah, have we made an exchange, then? Very good."

"I want a lot of talk, man. And I want to write it down and share it with the world. I want to know where you came from and what you do with yourself when you're not carrying messages to world leaders. I want to know who picked out your clothes and about that leaf you tried to pay Joanne with and about the kids—"

"Not about the kids," said William, and he was pleased his

voice didn't crack. "Some of the other topics, perhaps. But first my message has to be delivered."

"How do I know you're not going to run out on me after?"

William blew out his breath in exasperation. "How do I know you're going to deliver my message? Perhaps you're a liar too."

John Brady gave him a cocky, confident smile. "I guess you're just going to have to trust me."

William ground his teeth together and tried to remember that only a handful of years ago, this mortal had also been a child. It took so much more than a handful of years to really grow up.

The pattern in the tea leaves taunted him. Tarn's expectations tormented him. His lord had wanted him to deliver the message personally—but his lord wanted the message to be delivered. He wanted mortals to be saved.

His lord trusted him.

"Fine," William snapped, and relayed the message.

A FEW DAYS LATER, William stomped his way through the Veil between worlds until he came to his lord's court. The sweet smell of jasmine and patchouli and pomegranates rose around him, and the silk hangings obscuring the fragile walls of the court's heart shimmered delicately. Much of Underlight was still shattered from his lord's previous attempts to meddle with human fate, but this place remained as long as Tarn did.

The faerie Duke lounged on his throne, reading a newspaper. He didn't seem to notice William's return but started reading aloud.

"The 7.2 earthquake that rocked the Pacific Northwest Tuesday evening was preceded by an unusual—and unexpected—early warning system. With a little less than an hour's notice, the government was able to issue a widely distributed warning which allowed doctors to delay surgical procedures, traffic to be halted on dangerous spans, and residents to depart at-risk buildings. In addition, local fire departments and the National Guard were already mobilized to take action to assist those who didn't get (or disregarded) the message. Current estimates suggest 73% fewer injuries as a result, and some believe the early warning system also prevented property damage.

"What was this system? Not a technological system at all, but a warning carried by one of the Strangers, a faerie of the Underlight, a group associated with the earth and tides. Despite the suspicions about these visitors—and the debates over their fate in Congress, where they have not been allowed to speak for themselves—this particular Stranger delivered his warning, saving hundreds of lives. Afterward, we managed to get an interview with this brave hero, in which he tells us some of what it's like to serve a Faerie Duke."

The paper rustled as Tarn turned the page. "Ah, and here's a splendid picture of you with the President, William. They describe you as stoic. How little they know."

William hesitated on the threshold, trying to gauge his lord's mood. Then Tarn looked over the paper at him and smiled. "Welcome home, William," he said and William relaxed, back in the place he belonged.

Branwyn Lennox: Red hair, dyed green. Green eyes. Taller than me. Human. Smells of iron, loam, and cloves. Wears jeans or vintage. She's fierce and a little bit scary. I don't think she likes it when people say no to her but she never gets visibly upset. Can smell her annoyance though.

Penelope Karzan: Sleek dark brown hair, matching eyes. Taller than me. Human? Smells of pears, pepper, and cypress. And… something else that I don't know how to describe. Killer outfits with expensive labels. She's easy to talk to but a little bit distant. Mysterious but not scary.

Marley Claviger: Wavy brown hair, bright blue eyes. Taller than me but not by very much. Nephil. Smells of amber, strawberries, rain, and oak. I don't think she pays attention to her clothes very much. She is very quiet and the opposite of scary. Usually.

Zachariah Thorne: Black hair, ice-blue eyes. Way taller than me. Elder Nephil. Smells of autumn leaves, laurel, linen, and steel doors. Conservative dresser, but he always looks great. Kind of scary, especially when it comes to his kids.

Corbin Adair: Black hair, dark eyes, kinda blue? Grey flecks. Way taller than me. Nephil, grown-up but not old. Smells of sandalwood, musk, aluminum, and secrets. He goes for rugged clothes, jeans and stuff, because he doesn't like shopping much. He is my friend and I'm not scared of him at all.

Tia Zelaya: Dark brown hair, hazel eyes. Taller than me but not by very much. Demon. Smells of fire, sunshine and peaches.

And wrath, sometimes. Everything she wears is tailored. Mostly business suits. She is pretty scary but also my friend? I think? Sometimes she has red wings and glowing marks on her skin.

Severin AKA the Whispering Dark: Dark hair, eyes the color of Don't Look. Taller than me when we first met. Then he got shot and came back even taller. Something to prove? Monster. Smells like blue smoke, burnt sugar, blood, and hate. Black skeletal wings, vortex. Really, really scary.

Tarn, Duke of Underlight: Black hair, pied eyes (green, brown). Too tall. Faerie. Smells like pomegranates, ocean, and laughter. Whimsical clothes. Seems to like being out in public. Don't really know him. Maybe scary?

Ettoriel: This guy. Blond hair, blue eyes except sometimes they're gold. I bet he just can't resist that. Avoid guys with gold eyes. Tall enough to be annoying. Angel. Smells like sunrise, platinum, irises and a child-thief. Don't care what he wears because hopefully I'm never seeing him again. Scary in an abstract way.

Absolven: Golden hair, blue eyes. Avoid guys with actual golden hair too. Especially if they have griffin shadows. Too tall. Nephil. Smells like eagles, horn, sand, and ancient dust. Scary in a fun way but I hope we never meet again. Probably won't.

Kari: Auburn hair, electric blue eyes. Shorter than me! (Because she's a kid.) Nephil. Smells like raspberries, sugar, chalk, and explosions. Their uncle dresses them cute. Not exactly scary.

Lissa: Auburn hair, electric blue eyes. Shorter than me! (Because she's Kari's twin.) Nephil. Smells like blackberries, caramel, dancing slippers, and explosions. Keeps her clothes neater than Kari. All little kids are unnerving right?

Howl Lennox: Blond hair, teal eyes, it's stupid, he's not even magic. Taller than me. Did I mention totally non-magical human? Smells like aluminum, black ink, and loam. I think somebody else buys his clothes. Branwyn's younger brother, don't really know him but he seems kind of intense. Not at all scary

Hunter: Dear old Dad. Dirty blond hair, yellow eyes. Definitely too tall. Monster. Smells like blood, musk, pain, and broken glass. Don't care what he wears. Done here.

Brynn Lennox: Light brown hair, brown eyes. Shorter than me, but it might not last. Started out human. Smells of loam, glass, horses, and bravery. Cute clothes; I'd raid her closet any day. She is an annoying tagalong and my friend. A little bit scary because she's unpredictable. ♥

Amber Montague: Blond hair, hazel eyes. Taller than me. Of course. Started out human, took a detour through monster spawn. Smells of blood, celestial musk, talcum powder and, lately, anise. She dresses like a teen magazine cover girl. Super annoying, not at all scary. My friend. ♥

Yejun Park: Black hair, black eyes. Just the right amount taller than me. Started out human. Smells of tea, cedar, basil and copper. Wears super-casual clothes but I like it. He can be annoying and also really scary but he is my friend anyhow. Maybe more? Working on friends for now though.

Jennifer Cole: Greying black hair, crystal blue eyes. Taller than me. Smells of myrrh, willows and lilies. Started out human, took a detour through dead. Business casual dress Nice, patient. My friend. A little bit scary when her patience runs out.

Cat Jones: I just made that last name up just now. Blond hair, blue eyes, not a hint of gold thank you. Taller than me. Smells of glue, black ink, horses, and steel. Dresses in layers all the time. My friend. Gentle mostly but a little bit scary all the same

Alastor: Light brown hair, brown eyes. Taller than me. Demon. Smells of fire, ice and bones. Wears rumpled suits in weird colors. Scary enough. I don't like him.

Fiddler: Black hair, silver eyes. Too tall. NO IDEA WHAT HE IS. Smells of WTF and stone. Wears a long coat. Should be scary but he's not. Has a black stone violin.

Mr. Black: Bald, blue eyes. Taller than me. Elder Nephil. Smells of scabs, steel, balsamic vinegar and laughter. Always in a tailored suit. Head of Senyaza security in LA, Corbin's maternal grandfather. I could never tell if he liked me or thought I was a tool. Kind of scary.

Elizabeth Black-Adair: Brown hair, brown eyes. Exactly my height! Nephil. Smells of steel, silk, and embers. Wears gardenia perfume and nice jeans. Corbin's mother. I kind of liked her the two times we've met. Still a little scary.

Aedrian Adair: Black hair, Corbin's eyes. Taller than me. Nephil. Smells of myrhh, dust, embers, and musk. Wears off the rack suits. I did not like him. He was very quiet and I was always afraid he was going to lash out. Scary enough. Corbin's father.

Antonio Catalano: Black hair, brown eyes. Taller than me. Nephil. Smells of vanilla, lions, scales and thunder. Wears the same suit everyday. Door guard at Senyaza. Scary enough that I'd rather find another way in than try to get past him.

Madeline Claviger: Brown hair, hazel eyes. Taller than me. Human. Smells of patchouli, ginger, and honey. Reluctantly a nice dresser. I really, really liked her when she invited us over for dinner. Marley's mother and a little bit scarier than Marley.

Simon Mitsukuni: Bleachy brown hair, light brown eyes. Taller than me. Nephil. Monster-hunter. Smells like milk soap, Scotch, oranges, and lightning. No sense of style at all. Not scary even a little bit. I kind of want to adopt him.

Grendel Jones: Brown messy hair, twilight eyes. Nobody is actually as tall as he is, it's ridiculous. Nephil, monster hunter. Dresses tough. So so hairy. Smells of blood, musk, walnuts, nettles and malt. Nicer than he looks. We used to play tag. Pretty sure he's not the original Grendel. Kind of scary.

Ice Jones: White-blond hair, chrome eyes. Taller than me.

Nephil, monster-hunter. Smells like snow, spruce, vanilla, and coffee. Not particularly nice but he taught me things without hurting me, especially about tag. Not very scary.

Mack Jones: Shaven head, brown eyes. Too tall. Nephil, monster-hunter. Smells like highways, leather, marble and falcons. Dresses tough. He is really, really good at tag. Kind of scary.

Finn McCool: White-blond hair, green eyes. Really too tall. Elder Nephil, monster-hunter. Smells like clean water, green grass, spearmint and surf. I've only met him once. He was pretty calm and seemed cool, but somehow… really scary.

AFTERWORD

That's it! Thank you for reading along. This volume came from a project to reach beyond my limits and stop being so afraid of the short story. I think it worked!

As USUAL, reviews are very welcome. In this case, even if you don't read all the stories, I'll still be happy to see your thoughts and other readers will find your opinions of use. And if you're not yet on my mailing list and would like to be, you'll be able to sign up at www.dreamfarmer.net.

THE NEXT SENYAZA book takes place a year after Matchbox Girls. If you'd like to see an early chapter from Branwyn's perspective, read on.

B ranwyn tapped her foot as she stared at the tablet screen, waiting for her youngest sister to get her act together. She'd decided to fill out the paperwork for Meredith's new music school at her own studio instead of at her family's house, because her family's house was endlessly noisy and distracting. It had been a good idea. But she'd failed to get all the bits together in advance. It turned out filling out paperwork for a school was a lot more complicated than Branwyn had realized. Or at least *this* school. She hoped fervently it was the only school she'd be filling out paperwork for in the next decade.

Meredith fumbled through a file folder, babbling a mix of cheerful apologies and enthusiasm. Their mother, Holly, hovered in the background. "You can just bring it by and I'll get it done, sweetheart."

"You've got enough to do, Mom. I said I'd send Meri to this place, so I'm going to do the paperwork," said Branwyn, digging deep into the patience reserves. She was so, so glad Tristan, one of her middle brothers, could fill out his own paperwork for the drama seminar she was sending him to.

"It's just so generous of you," said her mother anxiously. "Are you sure you don't want to save the money for a rainy day instead?"

Branwyn laughed, looking around her studio and the detritus

of a dozen very profitable commissions. "I have a *waiting list*, Mom. I'll be busy for years."

"Yes, but it's for all these... magic people," said her mother fretfully. "How reliable can that be?"

"Found it!" said Meredith, pulling a sheet of paper out of the folder.

"It'll be fine, Mom. I'm ready, Meri," Branwyn lifted her pen.

"I just don't want you to end up in trouble like Jaime did," explained Holly.

"Mom, go away," said Meredith impatiently. "She's going to send me to *Gleason Academy of Music*. Dad already signed the form. Why are you trying to talk her out of it?"

Holly just shook her head and moved out of the line of sight of the camera.

"Quick, while she's temporarily defeated," said Branwyn, and Meredith read off the information Branwyn needed. She noted it down neatly, then slid the final form into the envelope. "There we go, brat. I'll send it off today and you'll get a letter in a couple weeks. And now I have to go, because I'm already late for lunch." She ended the call mid-gush without a twinge of guilt. Meredith's enthusiasm could eat up hours.

"That kid does go on," said a familiar voice fondly behind her. Branwyn picked up her backpack and turned to see Rhianna, the oldest of her younger sisters, leaning on the open door of the studio.

"Hey, Rhianna," Branwyn said, standing up and looking over the younger woman curiously. She'd cut her red hair recently— exactly the same hair that Branwyn would have if she didn't keep hers dyed green— and had smoothed the curls out so that it framed her face in a sleek bob. "Mom didn't mention you were in town."

"I haven't told her yet." Rhianna moved into the studio and

looked around. "You've changed the place." It was true. What had once been Branwyn's art studio was almost a storage space now, with boxes of supplies stacked as high as Branwyn could reach. In one corner a partially open door had been painted on the wall, and the darkness beyond had a depth to it that hinted at its true nature: a passage to the Backworld where Branwyn did much of her real work. Rhianna only gave the door a glance before her gaze fell on the large inscribed metal hammer laying on the table beside Branwyn's tablet. There was a black gem embedded in the head. "Nice war hammer."

Despite the fact that Branwyn was standing, Rhianna then seated herself in the nice chair, the one Branwyn normally offered to potential clients. She spun the chair, lifting her feet up out of her shoes to make it go faster.

"Ah, you're not even pretending this is a casual trip. What's going on?" Branwyn let her backpack slide down to the ground again, but she didn't sit down. Rhianna worked for the federal government, in the kind of job she couldn't admit to having, and since the previous October, when the faeries had emerged back into the human world, she'd only been home for the briefest of weekend trips.

"What makes you think something's going on?" asked Rhianna absently, watching her feet as she flexed them in and out.

Branwyn stopped the spinning chair. "Your hair looks nice. Different, but nice. How do you chew on it when you're studying, though?"

Rhianna gave her a small smile. "I haven't figured that out yet."

Branwyn waited for a moment but Rhianna didn't say anything else. "You haven't come for a commission, have you? I mean, I've been a little surprised I haven't heard anything from your crowd but it's all good. I've got a three page waiting list of private customers."

"In a way, that's why I'm here," said Rhianna and sighed.

It was the sigh that did it. It was too much. "You're softening me up," said Branwyn flatly. "Either spit it out or come back later, because I'm late for lunch."

Rhianna gave her a subdued smile and Branwyn felt a twinge of alarm. Either Rhianna had gotten even better as an actress, or something really was bothering her. Rhianna wouldn't hesitate to use her own trauma to manipulate somebody else, but she was usually delighted to admit it when Branwyn caught her.

"All right. Do you remember the key you gave me last October?"

"The key to this very studio that I impulsively gave you and then regretted later because I'd locked myself out? Yes, I remember." Branwyn had used her artificing magic on the key before giving it to Rhianna, waking up the inert metal into something with a Geometric node and the beginnings of an intrinsic nature of its own. "Did it become something useful?"

Rhianna took a deep breath. "Yes. It did. It was incorporated into a device that allows a supernatural entity to fully manifest in our world." Her eyes widened innocently. "They can't normally, you know. There's a field in place that inhibits them. But the device erases the field for the wielder."

"It's called the Hush," said Branwyn slowly, staring hard at Rhianna, trying to see through all her projected body language. "It was incorporated.... And who did the incorporation, Rhianna?"

Rhianna shrugged. "A lot of us contributed something, but it was overseen by our Senior Adviser."

"Your Senior Adviser," Branwyn said. "I want to know more about your Senior Adviser. Is he the one who put those empty charms on you?"

"My protections? Oh yes." Branwyn gave her a sunny smile. "He's a supernatural entity too, but he's not like the faeries. He wants to *protect* people."

Branwyn remembered Penny saying something very similar a year ago. It was back when Penny had been entangled with an angel who wanted to destroy two little girls as a way of 'protecting people'. She sank back down into her desk chair, feeling sick.

"What's wrong?" asked Rhianna, moving closer, her smile fading.

"You're not in love with this guy or anything, are you?"

Rhianna drew back in surprise. "You're kidding, right? Oh my God, Branwyn. He's like my boss's boss's boss. And a lot more freaky than the faeries, to be totally honest. We're glad to have his help but he's an adviser, not some kind of celestial playboy."

Branwyn went limp with relief. After a minute, she pulled herself together. "Senior Adviser sounds more *governmental* than you usually admit to. What's up with that?"

Rhianna looked self-conscious. "It seemed like the right corporate term for him would have been 'angel investor.' Nobody was really comfortable with that."

Branwyn laughed despite herself and stretched her legs out. "All right. Your Adviser is a supernatural entity who took what I gave you and made a device that would let him fully manifest on Earth."

"Yep! It's even better than what you and Jaime did for the faeries."

Shooting a dirty look at her sister, Branwyn said, "I used the faeries to save Penny; I didn't give them anything in the end." Which was a little bit of a lie, but in the context it was true enough. "And they used Jaime to get around their door; he didn't do anything for them on purpose."

Sweetly, Rhianna said, "And now here they are, running all over the world causing trouble. Don't you watch the news?"

"I do, but I hardly need to. I have an up close, personal

understanding of how dangerous they—and other supernaturals—can be, Rhianna! Penny almost died to one of the ones who *wasn't* a faerie, and I—" Branwyn stopped herself. She tried not to think too much about her own brushes with a fate worse than death at the hands of monsters. "But never mind that. You're not worried about your supernatural guy *at all?*"

"Nope. I wasn't before, because we've got nothing else to help us out against the faeries and I've seen the unpublicized reports on what they've been up to the last year. And I'm definitely not worried about him now. I've got something much better to be worried about now."

Branwyn wondered what the secret reports said. She'd heard bad things about some of the stuff happening in the rest of the world. In the USA, the most popular face of the faeries was the Nightwell movie production studio that had formed in Hollywood. They were friendly and sociable with the media, and very happy to put on demonstrations of magic. According to interviews they were positively thrilled about the idea of entertaining the masses with special effects-laden films. Their announced list of projects was... ambitious.

But pretty faeries in Hollywood aside, there'd been some awful clashes between some of the faeries and humans. A lot of the faeries who'd emerged from their Backworld prison weren't particularly trying to integrate themselves. Many, many humans refused to welcome those who wanted to try. And the faeries had enormous power when they chose to exercise it: over the weather and nature, over the minds of the unprotected, and over illusions.

On the other hand, humans had numbers and, while less well known, their own magic. It was a problem to be solved and Branwyn was secretly glad that her sister was part of an organization with the resources, information and willingness to try. But...

"What are you worried about now?"

Her sister reached for a strand of hair that was too short to chew on. "I'm worried about how the device has been stolen."

Slowly, Branwyn leaned her chin onto her palm, letting the silence drag out as she thought of who she didn't want to have stolen the device. Then she took a deep breath. "All right. And the million dollar question: why are you here telling me? Do you expect me to make you another one? Because—"

Rhianna laced her fingers together. "Well… you've been doing a lot of work with Senyaza. We've got the records. You're tight with them right now. Do you know about their history with my organization?"

Branwyn narrowed her eyes. *The records.* She'd given up almost all of her privacy almost a year earlier, in a dangerous deal with the faerie Queen of Stone. It had been a serious wrench. But she didn't think Rhianna had been talking to the Queen of Stone about her work schedule. No, Rhianna had *records,* because she worked for an organization that had zero respect for anybody's privacy.

And it didn't bother Rhianna at all. How had Branwyn's sister's ideals ended up so far from her own? It was mind-boggling.

Her irritation spilled out. "Given that your organization doesn't even have a name, how could I possibly know about any mutual history?"

Rhianna flashed a smile. "You don't like Acme Integrated Solutions?" Branwyn just gave her a steely look and she added, "The President calls us the Office of the Unexpected. OX."

Her throat tight with conflicting emotions, Branwyn asked, "Rhianna, have you *met the President?*"

Pursing her lips, Rhianna said, "Met? No. Been in the same room as while he talked to my boss's boss? Yes. Anyhow, OX has been monitoring the exploitation of supernatural resources—magic—for a long time. A lot longer than the faeries have been running around. We used to be just a little office in a basement.

But we've gotten quite a bit of a budget boost lately."

"Yes, I can imagine."

"So… Senyaza is the biggest collection of magic users around. OX has never been exactly happy about that. But as long as magic was on the down low and they didn't use it to influence the economy or anything, all we had to do was monitor them and the other magical weirdos. And Senyaza was so good at managing out of control magic that when it did happen we could just sort of help out with paperwork after. It's not like we had the resources to do anything else."

"How long has your Senior Adviser been on the scene?" Branwyn interrupted.

"Oh, a while. Years. Though he didn't always have a formal position. For the longest time it was just my boss and my boss's boss as the human staff, stuck in a basement below Acme Integrated Solutions. *Anyhow*, a couple of weeks after our talented stepfather's song unleashed the faeries, OX contacted Senyaza to find out if they had a remedy planned. We spent a couple months talking about how to send the faeries back where they came from, but apparently there were problems on Senyaza's end?" Rhianna gave Branwyn an inquisitive look.

"I wasn't involved in any of this. All I know is that you were home for a weekend in February, and I made Mr. Black a belt that lets him talk to Titan One."

Rhianna shrugged. "February was a quiet month, comparatively. Anyhow… March was the Congressional hearings, and we had to manage those so the faeries didn't influence them—"

"Yes, it would be just *awful* if Congressional hearings for deciding what to do about a group of people were actually influenced by those people."

Rhianna gave her a scowl and went on. "Meanwhile Senyaza started—" then hesitated and backtracked. "Actually, wait, really,

Branwyn? Really? You really think it was wrong of us to not allow entities with both the ability to influence minds *and* the ability to manipulate natural forces into the Capitol? They don't let in people with bombs either, even if they're discussing what to do about terrorists. At least the faeries were allowed to present video statements."

Branwyn ground her teeth. "I'm sorry. Go on."

With a severe look, Rhianna went on. "Senyaza started planning a big company meeting, and we started making our own plans. With a lot more fingers in the pie, because yay, Congress. In May Senyaza had their meeting. They invited most of their contractors and OX was invited to observe. All very nice and polite."

There'd been an invitation, Branwyn vaguely recalled. She'd been in the middle of something, and she hadn't been able to imagine why anybody thought she'd want to go to a Senyaza company meeting. She'd assumed it would involve boring financial figures and maybe a few product demos.

"So, um, yeah, it started out nice and polite. But the new initiative OX has been given didn't really go over well in the pre-meeting briefing and tensions kind of… flared during the meeting and there was a pretty vocal disagreement and that's why we think Senyaza has stolen the device." The words tumbled out of Rhianna in a flood.

Branwyn, experienced with Rhianna trying to obfuscate something, zeroed right in. "New initiative?"

"It's not really relevant to the topic at hand," Rhianna said airily. "What I'm really hoping for is that you can use your connections to Senyaza to find out if they took the device."

"Clearly I'm going to be angry when I find out. I'm already angry now. Let's get it out of the way so I won't have to change gears later," Branwyn urged. "It will be more efficient for everybody." When Rhianna still hesitated, she added, "Otherwise I'll find out from Senyaza. Wouldn't it be better to find out from my own sister?"

Rhianna stood up and deliberately moved so the chair was directly between Branwyn and herself. "They—the government—*we* want to license magic users. I mean, we license drivers. So we need existing magic users to register. Including the faeries and the nephilim." She squeezed her eyes shut as if afraid of a conflagration.

"Including faeries and nephilim, who can't *not* be magic?"

Rhianna nodded.

Branwyn put her hands behind her back. "Right."

Rhianna opened one eye and then the other. "You aren't mad?"

"I'm furious," Branwyn assured her. "I'm going to tell Grandma that you're working for cryptofascists. You'd better go visit the kids while you can because once I talk to her you're going to be disowned and barred from the house."

"*Branwyn!*" Rhianna protested. "Don't be a jerk. These people are dangerous. We have to find some way of managing the situation and this lets us find out who's willing to work with us. It lets us identify those who are willing to *try* to avoid being dangerous. It's barely more than an extra field on a census form. And the faeries, at least, *are* undocumented. And once the licensing system is in place, we can provide training, we can provide verification, they can sell their services to ordinary people who have some recourse against scams—"

"Were you *surprised* when Senyaza didn't like this idea?" Branwyn demanded.

Rhianna looked at her sidelong. "No."

Nodding, Branwyn said, "That's your guilty conscience at work. You know it's wrong to declare an entire group of people illegal just for existing."

"We're not doing that," said Rhianna sullenly. She turned around and went over to look at Branwyn's hammer, avoiding Branwyn's gaze.

"I have no idea how you expect to compel the faeries or Senyaza to register—God, no wonder you think Senyaza stole the device, no wonder you built it. It's your enforcement stick. What did Senyaza actually *say* at the meeting?"

Rhianna gave her a wide-eyed look that reminded Branwyn of a child about to confide an impressive discovery. "Um… they told my boss that they were more powerful than the federal government. In not very nice language."

Branwyn laughed despite herself and guessed, "Your boss said, 'How do you expect to stop us?' and somebody there said, 'Fuck you, that's how.'"

"Pretty much," Rhianna agreed. "So will you help us?"

Branwyn groaned and pushed her hands against her head. "Rhianna. Why should I? You pretty much know that there's no way I'm going to support some kind of Nonhuman Registration Act, even if you dip it into training/licensing/profit chocolate."

"Well," said Rhianna earnestly, "We're *pretty sure* Senyaza stole it, but we'd like to be *absolutely* sure. Because if Senyaza stole it, we're not worried they're going to *use* it. They'll just stick it in that Repository of theirs. But if somebody else stole it…. We may have a bigger problem. So if you could confirm Senyaza has it, it would be *so* nice."

Once again, Branwyn thought of who she hoped wasn't involved. There was one—and another—and another. So many. She didn't want *any* celestial able to manifest completely. Once even one could, *everything* was going to hell fast. She dropped her face into her hands, contemplating the horrifying possibilities ahead.

"I'll see what I can find out."